BLANCHE HERIOT;

OR,

THE CHERTSEY CURFEW.

A ROMANCE.

BY THE AUTHOR OF THE HEBREW MAIDEN; KATHLEEN; &c, &c.

LONDON:

PUBLISHED BY E. LLOYD, 12, SALISBURY-SQUARE, FLEET-STREET.

BLANCHE HERIOT;

OR,

THE CHERTSEY CURFEW.

FROM THE DRAMA,

BY ALBERT SMITH.

CHAPTER I.

THE HOSTELRIE.—THE QUARREL.—AN ARRIVAL.

THOSE of our readers who have visited the secluded village of Chertsey will probably agree with our general assertion, that it is one of the most dull and inactive places within our bustling sea-girt island. This remark, however, only applies to that place at the present day, for to those who have glanced over the pages of history, it may hardly be necessary to observe that, in by-gone days, when the abbey was peopled with its pious inmates, several important transactions connected with the history of our country took place within its immediate precincts. Among other occurrences, and, indeed, the only one to which we shall direct the reader's attention, is that which we are about to relate, as leading to the important results connected with our present narrative.

The precise period to which we allude, is that when the rival houses of York and Lancaster had kindled the torch of civil warfare, carrying destruction throughout the country, and devastating the land from one extremity to the other. In the locality which we have chosen for the scene of our story, the madness of party feud had manifested itself, and the rival partizans gave way to the heartburning and rage which usually attend commotions of this kind. Numerous persons usually resorted to an open space in the midst of the village at the close of each day, manifesting by their riotous conduct the particular views they had formed upon the all-engrossing subject.

To avert as much as possible the popular feeling thus exhibited, the Earl of Warwick—surnamed the "King-maker"—was obliged to have recourse to such means as appeared most likely to favour his own views. Emissaries were, therefore, sent down by him to pacify the discontented by the most artfully devised misrepresentations, and a profuse distribution of bribes was made for effecting their much-desired reconciliation with his own party.

One evening in the spring of the year 1471, several artizans and tradespeople were assembled in the public room of the Golden Cross, a hostelry so called from its vicinity to the beautiful structure which at that period graced the place of which we are speaking. Various groups were formed in different parts of the room, and, as usual, the conversation turned upon the sanguinary contest then raging between the Yorkists and the Lancastrians. This exciting subject naturally gave rise to angry words amongst the rival advocates of the two parties— menaces were uttered—swords were drawn, and bloodshed would doubtless have quickly ensued had not the host interposed himself between the excited partizans, and, by prayers and entreaties, prevailed upon them to suspend their fury till a more fitting time and place presented themselves. A sudden pause ensued, and the terrified host, following up his temporary advantage, most earnestly entreated them not to inflict an injury upon him by making his house the scene of their violence and riotous conduct.

"Peace, good neighbours, peace, I prithee," he exclaimed, as soon as the clamour had subsided. "This is no place to discuss whether a Yorkist or a Lancastrian shall be our king, and should our good prior hear of this riotous conduct, it is likely that I and my wife may be turned from our home to seek our fortune in some other town where these party feuds are less known."

"Ay," cried the termagant wife of the host, who at this moment presented herself before them, flourishing a brace of pistols in her hands; "hence, to your homes, roysterers and madmen that ye are, for it were better for yourselves to keep the peace than thus to disturb the quiet of our house."

"Avaunt, woman!" exclaimed Hugh Laneret, who from the first had been foremost in the fray; "avaunt, I say, or expect no mercy to thy weaker sex from men whose blood has been heated to madness. I am for King Edward the Fourth, and those who dare gainsay his title to the crown had better look to their own safety."

"And I am for King Henry the Sixth," cried Dickon the tanner; "and am ready to do him service against any traitor that would uphold the cause of his enemies."

"Shame on ye both," interposed the hostess, "for thus seeking to mar the quiet of our house with these mad broils. But ye have been warned, and now look to yourselves, I say, for, woman as I am, the first that again breaks the peace shall have a bullet through his heart."

"Nay, good dame," said Dickon, "reproach not us, who have only ventured to espouse the part of our lawful sovereign, but rather let thy wrath light upon those scurvy knaves who would take up arms against good King Henry. Trust me, dame, we, who are liege men, and true to the cause of our monarch, would not injure thee or thine."

"Humph!" muttered Hugh Laneret, "hear how scurvily the knave speaks of men that are better than himself."

"Ay, ay," shouted a voice from one of a party at the further end of the room;

"speak freely, Master Laneret, and fear not, for we are here who will not stand idly by and see thee put down by yonder boasting knaves. Say thy say, man, and fear not the consequences."

"He will do well to take the caution I have given him," cried the hostess, again flourishing her pistols with an air of determination. "I have warned him, and will not fail to keep my word, should he seek to renew the quarrel that has just been quelled."

Whilst she was uttering these words Hugh Laneret eyed her with a sullen glance, and removed himself a few paces to consult with his party, at the other end of the room. As he did this, the hostess lowered the points of her weapons, and thus proceeded—

"Shame on ye all, I again say, for I care not to which party ye belong, who would thus disturb the quiet of our house with these vexatious brawls and jealousies. Ye know well enough that in an instant my good man and myself may be rendered houseless wanderers, and that a word from the prior would drive us from hence in sorrow and utter ruin."

"Ay, neighbours, and there is no saying where our misfortunes would end," cried the alarmed host, venturing at length to follow in the wake of his termagant spouse, "for should the reverend prior think proper to eject us from our house, he may at the same time procure for us a more disagreeable asylum in one of the numerous dungeons beneath the abbey. May Heaven and the blessed Virgin protect us!"

"Amen, with all my heart," responded the hostess, at the same time crossing herself.

Whilst this was passing between the host and his better half, Dickon and Hugh Laneret, as the leaders of their parties, were eagerly consulting with their adherents as to what would be the better course to pursue. All now appeared calm, and not a sound was heard except the low whispers which passed among the company as they were conversing in different parts of the room. At this juncture the solemn tolling of a bell was heard, and the host, starting as from a reverie, exclaimed—

"Gentlemen, hear ye not the curfew sounding from the abbey belfry? 'Tis now time that you take your departure, and let me conjure you to go in peace, lest worse come of the fray that has broken out among you."

"Peace, thou babbling fool," cried Hugh Laneret, "and speak not where your interference is not required. Dickon and I know and hate each other; this night has evidenced the breach between us, and if he has half the courage he boasts, he will now draw his sword and prove whether he is more skilful with the weapon than myself."

As he said this he made a furious rush towards his antagonist, and would have slain him, had not Dickon at the moment started on one side, and thus avoided the treacherous assault. Upon this an exclamation of rage burst forth on both sides; every dagger was, in an instant, snatched from its scabbard, and the rival parties were advancing furiously towards each other, when they were arrested in the midst of their impetuous wrath by the voice of Dickon.

"Hold," he exclaimed; "hold, I charge ye, and deluge not this peaceful hearth with blood for the cowardly attack made upon me by yonder treacherous villain. This is no place to settle the differences that are between us, and doubt not, time and opportunity will be found more fitting than the present."

With a malicious sneer of derision, Laneret was about to taunt his adversary with deserting his party on the first appearance of danger, when the quick trampling of a horse near the door, withdrew for a moment the attention of every one from the feud in which they were engaged.

"The saints be praised," ejaculated the host, "'tis doubtless the headborough and his assistants." Then turning towards his quarrelsome guests, he continued, "now, good neighbours, let me entreat of you to stay the mad affray that has broken out among you. Go to your homes, and forget, if you can, that there has ever been the cause for this fearful outburst of passion. Come, come, be persuaded for once by a simple tapster, and— —"

"Here the knight of the spigot was interrupted in the midst of his harangue by the loud and commanding voice of the new comer, exclaiming from without—

"What, ho! sirrah tapster! hostler, knave, are all in the house asleep, and the curfew only just ringing?"

"Go, prating idiot," cried Hugh Laneret to the host; "dost thou not hear thyself called, or art thou so in love with peace and speechmaking, that thou would'st leave thy customers to look after their own cattle? By St. Paul, thou art a marvellous proper host, truly."

Casting an imploring look upon both parties, as if humbly imploring a cessation of hostilities during his absence, the host slowly withdrew to wait upon the newly arrived visitor, who he found at the door, abusing in no very measured terms a lazy fellow, who was loitering about the place, and who he had mistaken for one of the people belonging to the house.

"I'll tell you what it is, master," exclaimed Guy Addlepate, the person to whom the impatient speech had been addressed; "if you want favours done, you must learn to keep a civil tongue in your head, or you may chance to stand groom yourself for once in your life."

"Humph, you are not the hostler then?"

"No, I'm Guy Addlepate."

"Then, for once in my life, Guy Addlepate, I prithee bestir thyself," exclaimed the stranger. "My horse and I have journeyed far since morning, and since he is tired, and I not in the best of humours, you will do well to provoke me no further with this slothfulness."

"Saving your honourable worship's presence," said the host, who at this moment presented himself, "Guy will be more ready to do your bidding for a kind word than for all this anger. Or if it pleases you to walk into my house, I will myself look to your steed."

"Varlet," cried the other with impatience, and at the same time throwing the bridle angrily into the hands of mine host; "it is well for thee there is no decent hostelrie near, or thou would'st surely have lost a customer this night by thy most unseemly negligence."

"I crave your pardon, gentle sir," replied the other, as he assisted the stranger to dismount; "I was but endeavouring to pacify some angry neighbours who have assembled in my house. Will it please your knightship to take up your abode with us this evening?"

"Why, ay," returned Neville Audeley, for such was the name of the visitor; "and see that I have a snug dormitory, and my gelding a warm stable."

"That," answered the host, "I can promise thee without doing much violence to my conscience."

"And hast thou a room where I can sit and sup alone?"

"Why no," returned the host, "there is not one at present; but if you can put up with the inconvenience of sitting in the public room for a brief space, the company which I have now in the house will be gone, and then you may have the place all to yourself."

"Well then, be it so," replied Neville, after a pause; "travellers may not always be choosers in such cases as these, so lead the way, friend, without further parley."

The host now gave the horse to the care of Guy Addlepate, and leading the way into the house, the guest was in a few moments ushered into the room which had just before been the scene of so much confusion. Silently taking a seat apart from the other guests, the stranger cast aside his travelling cloak, in which, till now, he had been closely wrapped, and throwing himself back in his seat, appeared studiously to avoid any communication with those around him. This appeared to create some surprise and curiosity amongst the company, which he heeded not in the least, nor did he seem to observe the host, who stood bowing and smirking before him, as if waiting for further commands.

At length, however, he roused himself from the thoughts which had occupied his mind, and beckoning to the landlord, he desired his company to assist in emptying a bottle of canary, a request which the other most willingly complied with, and seating himself opposite his guest, a conversation arose between them upon general matters. The host now began to grow communicative, and as he answered all queries with perfect freedom, the stranger ventured to inquire if he knew aught of one Blanche Heriot, who lived not long since at Redwynde Manor House, in that neigbourhood.

"Ay, marry do I. ' replied the host, "and few there are, I believe, who know her not, for she is loved by all, gentle and simple, that live about the place."

The quick eye of Neville Audeley soon discovered that his question had created some interest amongst his auditors, and he was about to change the conversation to another subject, when Hugh Laneret, starting from his seat, exclaimed—

"Your voice, sir, assures me that you and I have not met now for the first time. We are rivals for the hand of Blanche Heriot, and, being such, we cannot now be otherwise than sworn foes."

"Hugh Leneret," returned the young man, "it matters little to me in what light we meet together. I am perfectly willing that we should be enemies, yet surely this is no place to pick a quarrel upon such a subject."

"And what have you or I to do with time or place?" demanded the other, haughtily. "Let it suffice that I hate you, and will let no opportunity pass that may serve to rid me of a rival."

"Hah! would you threaten me?"

"I will do more than utter vain threats," replied Laneret.

"Humph! perhaps you will slay me unawares?"

"There will be no need for that," answered the other, "your life will ere long be at my disposal, and be assured I shall not hesitate to make use of my advantage."

"Come, come, Laneret," exclaimed Dickon, "a stranger has come among us, and we will not see him treated thus scurvily. We have nothing to do with your quarrel, and by St. Paul he shall not be insulted, even if I stand up alone in his defence."

"You will have enough to do to take care of yourself," muttered Laneret. Remember there is a score to be settled between you and me; we have been interrupted to-night, but many hours shall not pass away without either you or I claiming the mastery."

"I ask no one to interfere between us," exclaimed Neville Audeley, "nor shall Hugh Laneret have it in his power to brand me with the name of coward whenever he may think proper to offer me a fair challenge."

"We shall not meet in single combat," answered Laneret, "but in the field of battle, where you and I shall be found fighting in the opposite ranks. I am for Edward the Fourth, the rightful sovereign of these dominions, and you advocate the cause of Henry who at present usurps the throne of England."

"The throne is is by right," exclaimed Neville Audeley, "and all who dare gainsay it, I denounce as traitors, and will do my utmost to bring them to the punishment they merit."

"Nay, gentles, let us hear no more of this, or there will be a renewal of the quarrel that has just been quelled," cried the alarmed host. "What have any of us to do with the Yorkists or Lancastrians, since in a short time there will be blood enough spilt in the affray, and the sword will decide which party shall prove victorious. So prithee let all now depart in peace, or we shall have the head-borough and his men here, and Heaven only knows what the consequence will be should they find my house filled with disorderly company after the great curfew bell has tolled."

"You understand me, Neville Audeley," said Laneret, without heeding a word that had been uttered by the host. "We are rivals, and therefore enemies."

"That I knew long ere we last parted," answered the other, "and it has never been my wish to claim friendship with one who would so far outrage the name of manhood as to force his attentions upon a helpless female, who has with sufficient candour declared her aversion to him. Blanche Heroit knows you for what you are, and never will become the bride of him she loathes."

"And if she loathes me," cried Laneret, " who have I to thank for it except yourself? But let her scorn me as she will, Blanche Heriot shall become my prize, even though I wade through blood for the attainment of my object."

"If it be my blood you seek," exclaimed the other, " you shall not find me unwilling to risk it in defence of her who has honoured me with her regard. The maiden's choice has been free and unfettered, and since it has fallen upon me, I should indeed have been unworthy of her favour, were I to yield her up at the bidding of Hugh Laneret, whose evil practices have branded him with the name of villain amongst all honourable men."

"Villain in your teeth, Neville Audeley !" cried the other, drawing his sword, passionately. " I would have spared you for the present, that my revenge might hereafter be greater ; but you have pronounced your death doom, and thus will I revenge the insult you have cast upon me !"

Scarcely had he uttered these words, than he rushed furiously upon Neville, and would have carried his threat into execution, had not his antagonist skilfully avoided the thrust, and thus given himself time to throw himself into an attitude of defence. The countenance of Hugh Laneret now betrayed the fearful rage that had taken possession of his heart, and the combat grew so fierce that those who were spectators of the scene were unable to part them. At length, however, Hugh Laneret slipped, and fell to the ground, and the other, wound up to a pitch of fury that he could not controul, was about to pass his sword through the body of his prostrate foe, when the door was burst open, and the headborough, followed by a number of his assisstants, rushed into the room, and arrested the weapon as it was about to complete its fatal work.

"What means this outrage," exclaimed the head borough, gazing alternately upon the two combatants. " Is the king's peace to be broken thus by a couple of brawlers, who think proper to quarrel over their cups ?—and thou must needs settle it by drawing your swords upon each other." .

"Our quarrel is not quite so sudden a one as you seem to imagine," answered Hugh Laneret, sullenly. "He is my hated foe, and shall yet repent that he has been the cause of the fury he has given rise to."

"That remains to be proved," exclaimed Neville, "when next our swords are fairly measured against each other. Within the last few minutes you have been at my mercy, and it may happen at our next meeting fortune will not be less propitious to me. My arm was staid by these intruders, or you would not have been living to have given utterance to the threat."

"When next we are opposed to each other in mortal strife," replied Laneret, " I pray Heaven there may be no meddling fools to interfere between us. You now know me for your enemy, Neville Audeley, and I warn you to beware of one who will neither ask nor give mercy."

"I will ask none, even were your sword at my throat," returned the other, haughtily. "As foes we shall, doubtless, meet again ere long; and, should chance prove adverse to me, I can at least die satisfied with the thought that I perish to save Blanche Heriot from the evil machination of a black-souled villain."

"Come, come, let us have no more of this," interposed the headborough, pompously. "Remember, I'm armed with the authority of the law, and, if either of you rebel against my commands, I have aid enough at hand to compel your obedience. So, now let the house be cleared, or you will endanger the worthy host and hostess by keeping the house open after the great abbey-bell has given warning that it is time for all honest people to be in their beds."

"The stranger sleeps here to-night," observed the host to the man of authority, "but, for the rest, you may clear my house of them with as much despatch as you please. They have almost turned my brain with their quarrels already, and, should they begin another affray, our good Father Abbot will not fail to turn my poor dame and me from house and home. So, leave us, Master Hugh Laneret, and my earnest prayer is, that you will not again honour me with your patronage."

"Why, that will depend upon circumstances," answered the person he had last addressed; "for wherever Neville Audeley is, I shall not be far off. He has made me his enemy, and let him look to the consequences."

With these words he turned sullenly away, and left the house, which, proving so far satisfactory to the constable, he next addressed himself to those who remained, exhorting them, in a set speech, to make the best of their way home, and not to interfere in affairs that concerned them not.

"You have nothing to do with either Yorkists or Lancastrians," he continued, "for that is a matter that must be settled by wiser heads than our own. If great folks choose to quarrel about who shall be king, it is no business of ours, and we should therefore be quiet till we see which side is likely to gain the day. Then it will be time enough for us to throw our caps into the air, and shout for the winning party, since we might happen to take the weaker side, and get ourselves into trouble before we are aware of it. For my own part, I shall continue to serve the king that now sits upon the throne; but should he be obliged to give it up to his rival, I can change as easily as a weathercock, and thus save my head, when many a busy fool will be brought to the scaffold, to answer for their treason."

This counsel was listened to in silence at the commencement; but, as the headborough proceeded, his audience gradually stole away from the house, and by the time he had brought his speech to a conclusion, he found there was no one left but the host, his wife, and Neville Audeley. This somewhat disconcerted him; but a draught of ale restored him to tolerable good temper, and he left the house, wondering how so excellent a speech could have been so coldly received.

———

CHAPTER II.

THE GUEST.—THE NIGHT ATTACK.—THE RESCUE.

FOR some time after the departure of the guests and the headborough, Neville Audeley sat gloomily meditating upon the scene that had just taken place, and endeavouring to obtain through it a glimpse into futurity. The ferocity displayed towards him by Hugh Laneret, augured, indeed, much trouble and difficulty to himself, but he saw only the danger to which Blanche would be exposed in consequence of the resolution with which his rival intended to woo her, and his thoughts were, therefore, turned towards such means as would be most likely to aid her from the persecutions of a man against whom she entertained no feelings save those of scorn and detestation.

Whilst he was thus meditating, Master Froth, the host of the Golden Cross, was busily occupied with his wife in clearing away the drinking utensils, with which the tables were crowded; and having completed this to his satisfaction, he drew a chair near to that which was occupied by his guest, and having in vain sought to attract his attention towards himself, he, at length, gave a loud hem to clear his throat, and then hazarded an inquiry whether his guest would like to retire to bed at once, or take any further refreshment before he went.

"I would be alone," answered Neville, rousing himself; and then, after a moment's reflection, he added: "but I had strangely forgotten myself where I am, good host, and so, on condition that you bear me company for a short time you may repeat my quantum of canary, over which we may discuss sundry matters, in which I feel deeply interested."

This order was quickly obeyed by Master Froth, and having placed the wine upon the table, he poured out a cup for his guest, and another for himself, which, having quaffed with much apparent zest, he said—

"I warrant me now, you are a stranger in these parts, or at the very least that you have not visited it lately."

"Your guess is a tolerable shrewd one," answered Neville, with an inclination to smile that he could scarcely suppress, "for never till this day have I set foot in your good town of Chertsey."

"Humph! and yet it seems you claim acquaintance with pretty Mistress Blanche Heriot, of the old manor house, down yonder?"

"I knew her when she lived with her father some few miles from hence," answered Neville.

"And you are aware, of course," continued the host, "that her father being dead, she is now under the guardianship of Sir Philip Warrenne?"

"I am."

"And are you sure he will consent to the young lady receiving you as a lover?"

"Your question is a singular one to ask of a stranger," exclaimed Neville, "but as I am not disinclined to make you my father confessor, I will, at once, inform you that Blanche Heriot and I are cousins."

"And, therefore, not the less likely to be a lover," returned the host, laughing heartily at his own conceit.

"That, at any rate," answered Neville Audeley, gravely, "is a matter that I shall not at present explain. Blanche, you say, is under the guardianship of Sir Philip Warrenne, and I have yet to learn whether he is likely to forbid my visits to his house."

"Why, that I can hardly undertake to say," replied Master Froth, "for there are various reports about him, and some people say that he is morose, and certain it is there are few persons suffered to enter his house."

"Then Hugh Laneret, I suppose, is among the number of the excluded?"

"Hugh Laneret is not a man to be easily thwarted, when once he has made up his mind to a thing," replied the tapster. "He may or may not have been forbidden the house; but that he often finds his way into the presence of Mistress Blanche, I believe there is very little doubt."

"Curses light upon the villain!" exclaimed Neville, vehemently; and then suddenly correcting himself, he continued, "are you aware whether his visits are encouraged by her you have mentioned?"

"Not being in the lady's confidence I am unable to answer your question," replied Froth, "but as her father was a warm friend of the Lancastrian party, I should hardly think it likely she could give her love to a man who is one of the staunchest adherents to the opposite party. Besides, Sir Philip Warrenne is on the same side that her father was, and I know he would sooner see the devil himself than allow a Yorkist to enter his house."

"Yet you say Hugh Laneret finds admission there?"

"Ay, but he does it by stealth."

"In that case I would have him beware how he again ventures into the presence of Blanche Heriot," exclaimed Neville. "We are foes, and bitter ones, too, and either his blood or mine shall be shed if he dare repeat his insolent intrusion."

"I prithee take care how you get into another quarrel with Master Hugh Laneret," said the host, "for he bears but a strange character in these parts, and fails not to practise the foulest means when he is determined to carry his object. You will do well, therefore, to act with caution, and not tempt him to violence till you are well assured of getting the best of him."

"You heard his threats just now, sir," interposed the dame, who until now had been a silent listener to the conversation, "and when once Hugh Laneret makes up his mind to do a thing, he never hesitates even to commit a crime should he think it necessary."

"It may be as you have said, my good dame," answered Neville Audeley, "yet in this instance he may have one to deal with who will be able to defend himself. I have seen him before to-night, and have reason to know that the reports circulated against him are not exaggerated. I trust, however, that my own courage is not inferior to his, and should he give me fair play, I have no fear of the consequences to myself."

"But he will not give you fair play," cried Master Froth. "And besides, young sir, you know not the temper of Sir Philip Warrenne, and should this quarrel of yours have a fatal end, it might be the means of causing your separation from the lady you seem so desirous of making your wife."

"That is indeed a hint worthy of my consideration," answered Neville. "And yet, the villany of this man, may, after all, force me to an act fatal to my own fondly-cherished hopes."

At this moment the door was hastily thrown open, and Guy Addlepate, rushing in, secured the bolts and locks, and having made all fast, announced the startling intelligence that a great crowd was approaching, with the intention, as he verily believed, of making an attack upon the house.

"Alas! alas!" cried the hostess, wringing her hands in despair, " and has it come to this, that we are to be driven forth like wild beasts, to wander friendless through the world? Yet the villains shall suffer for it if they come, for we are not without arms, and we will defend ourselves even though we perish for it afterwards."

"Peace wife," exclaimed her husband, "and let us first know whether the errand that brings them here is one that need occasion us any alarm. This may be merely a frolic, and it would only get us into trouble if any lives should be lost through over-haste."

"At all events," added Neville Audeley, "I dare say the extent of their mischief is directed against myself, and should that prove to be the fact, I shall quietly submit myself to their superior numbers, rather than bring either of you into trouble."

"Master talked just now about it's being nothing but a frolic," observed Guy Addlepate; "but for my own part, I've a notion it's likely to turn out a serious one."

"And why so?" demanded the host.

"Because people don't often come out by torchlight in great numbers, unless they mean something," replied Guy. "Now there seems to be, between two or three hundred of these frolicksome blades, and if they haven't got mischief in their heads, why never take my word in future, that's all."

"The poor, simple, knave is in the right," cried dame Froth, whimpering with terror. "The villains want to rob us, and they take advantage of these disturbed times, to come in a body and ruin us poor, hard-working folks. But I've told you what I'll do, and as sure as they enter this house, I'll have no mercy upon the first of them that comes in my way."

The dame had scarcely done speaking, when the latch was forcibly raised from without; and from the jarring of the door, it was evident that some of the mob were trying to force their way into the house. This seemed to abate the courage of the hostess in no inconsiderable degree, and her spouse seeing the necessity of exerting himself, advanced, and in as bold a tone as he could, demanded who was at the door at that unreasonable hour.

"Those that are determined to obtain admittance," was the reply from without.

"Not if I can help it," answered Froth. "I have done nothing in contempt of the law, and will let no one in till a reasonable hour in the morning."

"You had better not refuse us," exclaimed another voice on the other side.

"By whose authority do you come?" asked the host.

"By our own, to be sure."

"And for what purpose?"

"To arrest one Neville Audeley, who is suspected of foul plots against the state."

"The person you seek," exclaimed Froth, "is my guest, and you must have something better than suspicion before you drag him from this roof."

"Why, then, we must force an entrance," exclaimed a voice, which appeared to be that of Hugh Laneret; "and if you drive us to that extremity, you will have little mercy to expect from us."

"Hear me, ruffians that ye are," exclaimed Neville, for the first time interposing; "if it is me you seek, I am ready to surrender myself on condition that no violence is offered either to the host or his wife."

"With your good leave, sir," cried the dame, "I'll take care to keep them where they cannot offer any of us violence." Then speaking loudly to those who were without, she added—"It would be well for ye, villains that ye are, to disperse quietly without attempting to force your way into the house. We are armed remember, and he who first enters the place will meet the death of a dog."

"We'll run the risk of that at any rate," was the reply, "for we are in pursuit of a traitor, and are not to be frightened from our purpose by the threats of a woman."

Whilst he was yet speaking, a violent battering was heard at the window shutters, and from the frequency and force with which the blows were repeated, it was quite plain that the siege could not hold out much longer. Seeing this, Neville Audeley made towards the door, for the purpose of thowing it open to his enemies, but the host and his better half placed themselves before him, and earnestly entreated that in compassion to themselves, he would desist from his purpose.

"Let us keep the vile rabble at bay as long as we can," exclaimed Froth, "and it may give time for the arrival of assistance. Surely all in the neighbourhood cannot be against us; and if that should be the case, a party of friends may yet come to rescue us from the violence of these fierce men."

"And if the worst should befal us," added the dame, "they have had fair of warning what they have to expect."

"Let there be no bloodshed on my account;" said Neville, "I alone, it seems, am the object of these men's fury, and when I have surrendered myself into their hands, I shall at least have the satisfaction of knowing that you are relieved from all further danger."

"See, master," cried Guy Addlepate, with terror, "the shutter begins to give way, and we are lost."

At this exclamation they directed their gaze towards the spot alluded to, and the truth of the rustic's words were at once apparent. A large aperture had indeed been made, through which the light of numerous torches glared upon them; and as the entire shutter gave way to the force of the assailants, a loud shout of triumph was heard from the infuriated mob. In another instant the window itself was burst in, and when this was done, a number of persons were seen scrambling for admittance, each apparently anxious to be the first to seize upon the object of their search. The desperation of the dame was now wound up to the highest pitch; and ere Neville could interpose to prevent her design, one of the pistols was discharged towards the beleaguered spot, though without doing the mischief that was intended. This circumstance, however, served to increase the rage of the assailants, for loud murmurs of vengeance were heard; and the place being immediately afterwards filled with the rabble, both the host and his dame were secured, whilst Neville himself was seized in the firm grasp of Hugh Laneret.

"So, at last, sirrah, you are our prisoner," exclaimed the latter-named personage. "We have had some trouble, and as it seems, no little danger in effecting your capture; but you are safe enough now in our hands, and it will be no easy matter to escape from them."

"And upon what grounds has this act of violence been offered against me?" demanded Neville, haughtily; "and yet, I need scarcely have asked the question, since I am well assured I owe it all to the malevolence of a heartless villain."

"Ay, rail at me as much as you please, for I can endure all with patience, since my purpose has been fulfilled," answered Hugh Laneret. "You are fairly trapped, good Master Neville Audeley, and my friendly offices shall not be wanting to bring you to a fate that will for ever r d me of a hated rival."

"I doubt not your malice," returned the young man. "but innocence is not thus to be trampled upon; and be assured the time will, ere long, arrive when you will feel all the bitterness of disappointment at beholding your base schemes frustrated. Yet, why do I parley thus with one I despise for a villain? Lead me where you please, and you have my promise that I will make no attempt to escape."

"But I shall make no promise of the kind," exclaimed the host, who had in vain tried to shake off the grasp of the fellow that held him. "I maintain that I have been wrongfully treated, and those who have dared break into my house like thieves and vagabonds as they are, must look to the consequences."

"Master Hugh Laneret," cried the dame, menacingly, "I warn you, look to yourself. You shall come with force and malice against those who have done no wrong, and I am only grieved that the bullet I sent among you did no mischief."

"Peace, old woman, and excite not my rage by these useless outpourings of disappointed anger," exclaimed Laneret. "Keep a quiet tongue, dame, and I pledge my word that no arm shall happen to you or your husband, since my object has been achieved by the capture of our intended prize."

"I am not to be silenced so easily as you believe," answered the hostess. "I have suffered wrong from you, Hugh Laneret, and mark my words, I'll be revenged for it. You will die the death of a dog, or I am no true phrophetess."

"Silence the jezabel with a poniard, some of you," vociferated a voice from the further end of the room. "Kill the foul witch, I say, and let's hear no more of her frantic ravings."

"In mercy, good friends, I beseech you spare her!" exclaimed the alarmed tapster. "She knows not what she says in her anger, and——"

"Peace, thou prating idiot," cried another voice, "or we may be tempted to do more than the business that brought us here."

"Ay, ay," shouted a comrade, "let us not do things by halves, but set fire to the house, and burn it to the ground. 'Tis chiefly built of wood, and will make a cheerful blaze to light us on our way back."

The suggestion thus thrown out was instantly caught up by the mob; tables, chairs, and other smaller articles of furniture were hastily piled up in the midst of the room; and when a heap had been made nearly reaching to the ceiling, one of the ruffians advanced with a lighted torch, and was in the act of setting fire to it, when Neville, unable any longer to restrain his indignation, burst from the grasp that held him, and, snatching the brand from the fellow's hands, struck him with tremendous violence to the ground. This was a signal for a general attack upon Audeley,—swords were instantly drawn, and Hugh Laneret was in the act of plunging his weapon into the heart of his foe, when his arm was struck up, and a stranger threw himself between the villain and his intended victim. All this occurred with so much suddenness, that every one stood aghast with astonishment, and the stranger taking advantage of the momentary pause, exclaimed reproachfully—

"Shame on you all, for cowards that ye are! What! does it need so many upon one, that twenty swords must be drawn for the destruction of a single enemy?"

"Herrick Evenden," muttered Laneret, "your presence here was neither looked for, nor required. We came to arrest a suspected rebel, and, if we have offered him the violence you witnessed, he has himself to thank for it, since he was the first to begin it."

"I was," replied Neville Audeley, "but the act was forced upon me. I saw your cowardly ruffians about to commit the house of these poor people to the flames, and would have perished in their defence rather than live to see the con-summation of so foul an outrage."

"And now," demanded Herrick of Hugh Laneret, "what answer have you to make to an explanation such as you have just heard ?"

"None to you, Herrick Evenden," returned the other sullenly. "I own no superiority in you, and will explain my conduct to no one but those who have a right to demand one."

"You brave it out well, sir," exclaimed Herrick, "and yet methinks your present advantage is not quite so great as you imagine. This young man has been wrongfully seized upon, and I, who am here to see justice done, demand his instant liberation."

"And by what right do you assume this authority to control my actions ?"

"By the right which every man possesses to see fairness done between his fel-low creatures," answered Herrick Evenden.

"You know the prisoner, then ?"

"I know him slightly," answered the other. "He is Neville Audeley, a faith-ful adherent of our reigning sovereign, King Henry the Sixth, and therefore most unlikely to be the traitor you would fain prove him. It is true he advocates a cause opposite to your own ; but it follows not that he is to be thus hurled into the snares of his enemies."

"I pray you, generous sir, let him have his own way," said Neville. "The triumph he at present boasts will be but a short one, for my innocence can be easily proved, and the shame of this cowardly act will fall upon him who merits it. I know, too, the cause that had led to all this violence ; he has dared aspire to the hand of Blanche Heriot, and seeks my destruction, because he imagines I am the only obstacle in his way."

"Blanche Heriot will never be a bride of his," exclaimed Herrick, "for she abhors vice, and would not link herself with one who has long since abandoned all pretensions to honour."

"Your tongue takes too much licence, young man," muttered Laneret. "Thus far, my patience has been kept within its bounds, but how much longer I may be able to restrain my anger will depend upon the prudence you may henceforth observe. You can now leave us, sir, for the prisoner remains with me, and shall not quit my sight till he is safely harboured between four good stone walls."

"I shall not take my leave whilst my task is only half performed," answered Herrick, boldly. "I am here to save this person from your malice, and you will do well to take your own departure in peace, ere I am compelled to show you that I have the means to enforce my demands."

"Hah !—come you hither to swagger and threaten ?"

"I came for no such purpose," replied Herrick Evenden ; "but to preserve one, who will perhaps henceforth allow me to call him my friend. Audeley is faithful to his lawful sovereign, and it would be hard indeed if King Henry should hesitate to give him his countenance and protection."

"In one word," said the host, growing wondrous bold, now that his own dan-ger began to diminish; "in one word, Master Hugh Laneret, do you mean to clear my house of your presence, or must we take other means of getting rid of yourself and the racally crew you have brought with you?"

"Were you worth my notice," replied Laneret, "I would answer you with the point of my rapier. You shall, however, live to repent this insolence, as well as those who have abetted you in it. I have assistance with me more than sufficient to enforce my commands ; and you, and all who are of your party, shall be dragged from hence to a place where you may be kept in safety."

"Your boasting will prove of little avail," exclaimed Herrick Evenden ; "for you may be assured I came not on this errand without first of all assuring myself of its perfect success. Behold, here are those present who will prevent any further exercise of your tyrany."

As he spoke, the headborough, accompanied by a strong party of stout English bowmen, entered the house, and ranged themselves so as to protect Herrick and his friends from those of the opposite party. The countenance of Laneret betrayed the feeling of rage which this unexpected circumstance had produced; but he quickly assumed a more composed demeanour, and said, with a sneer——

"For once, Herrick Evenden, it must be confessed you have outwitted me. I am foiled even at the moment when I thought my triumph was certain. You will however, from this time regard me as your mortal enemy; and look to it well, sirrah, or the advantage you have this night gained will be but of brief duration.'

As he uttered these words he frowned portentously upon those to whom they were uttered, and strode haughtily from the place. Those who had accompanied him, quickly followed the example he had set; and in a few minutes afterwards, Master Froth and his dame had the satisfaction of seeing their house cleared of the lawless rabble that had just before threatened it with destruction.

Herrick Evenden would now have prevailed on Neville to accept the hospitality of his father's house, but the young man refused the offer which had been thus kindly made, alleging that his presence might be necessary to allay the fears of his host and hostess. Herrick therefore pressed the subject no further, and took his departure, after exacting a promise from his young friend that he would visit him at the earliest opportunity.

CHAPTER III.

THE HEROINE.—THE RIVAL.—THE LOVER.

WE must now shift the scene to Redwynde Manor House, the residence of Sir Phillip Warrenne, and the present home of his fair ward, Blanche Heriot. It was on the morning after the events narrated in the last chapter, that our heroine heard of the outrage that had taken place at the Golden Cross, and with the anxiety natural under such circumstances, she eagerly inquired of her attendant, the name of those who had been principally engaged in the cowardly transaction. It so happened, however, that Kate Poynet, though curious and inquisitive to a degree, had been unable to obtain any very full particulars, and the only information she could give was that a stanger, who had taken up his lodging there for the night, had been attacked by Hugh Laneret and the rabble, and that he had been saved from the outrage by the intervention of Herrick Evenden and a party of the king's royal archers.

"'Twas a noble act and well worthy of commendation," replied Blanche; "yet methinks, Kate, it would have been no difficult task to have learnt the name of him who so narrowly escaped the violence of Hugh Laneret."

"Heaven and our blessed lady know that I lost nothing for want of inquiry," answered Kate; "but no one knows anything about him, and all I could gather about him was, that he is a stranger, and that business or his own pleasure brings him this way for no other purpose than to visit the Manor House of Redwynde."

"Indeed!" exclaimed Blanche; "then the mystery will soon be cleared up."

"That's just what I've been thinking myself," answered Kate, "and so eager have I been to satisfy my curiosity, that for the last two hours I've been watching the arrival from the highest window in the house. But he has overslept himself I suppose, for not a soul has entered the gates except Antony Amblewit, and I would almost as soon see the devil himself as that simpleton."

"Yet Tony, if I mistake not," observed the young lady, "has a sneaking kindness for some one I could name."

"Why, to confess the truth, the poor fellow does pester me with his addresses," answered Kate.

"And you have never told him that he had nothing to hope from your favour?"

"I should have been foolish to do that," replied Kate, "for unfortunately he happens to be the only man that ever thinks it worth his while to pay me any attention. So I keep him as fowlers do a bird in a trap—merely as a lure for others."

"Methinks, girl," exclaimed her mistress, "that is the very way to frighten others from venturing to make an offer."

"It's very well for you, my young lady, to think so," replied Kate, "because you have a lover to your liking. Master Neville Audeley is something like a man for a husband, though sometimes I think it rather strange that you have heard nothing of him since he went away."

"And yet 'tis scarcely to be wondered at," sighed Blanche. "for his journey ended not till he had reached the further extremity of England, and in these wild times of blood and warfare, there is little opportunity for him to communicate with distant friends."

"Or he may chance to have fallen into the hands of the Yorkish party," observed Kate. "They are said to muster very strong in the north, and should they have made a prisoner of him, I fear you will have to look elsewhere for a husband."

"Now Heaven in its mercy forbid that your prognostication should prove true !" cried Blanche, turning deadly pale at the bare thought of such a mischance. "I have myself feared lest any danger should have befallen him, but have thus far sustained myself with the hope that my terrors were groundless."

"Then let not anything I have said cause you any alarm," exclaimed Kate. "I am a sad thoughtless girl in speaking my mind, but now I come to reflect upon it, I think if Master Neville Audeley had been in danger, your guardian would surely have heard of it. So, take no heed, my dear young lady, of anything I have said, but look forward to the best, and I dare say your cousin will return when he's least expected."

"But Sir Philip Warrenne maintains a strict silence whenever I mention the subject to him," returned our heroine. "He will neither give me his opinion nor advice, and that sometimes makes me think he knows of that which he dares not utter."

"Ay," exclaimed the attendant, "but Sir Philip, you know, is a man of very few words, and so I take very little heed of his silence in this respect. Besides, he was always partial to your cousin."

"Ay, that was when he was a child," replied Blanche; "but Neville has now grown up to manhood, and I know not whether he will like him so well when he knows him to be the declared lover of his ward."

"He must be blind, indeed, if he has not made a shrewd guess at that before now."

"It may be as you have said, girl," returned Blanche; "and yet it would be strange, too, that guessing such a thing, he has never once mentioned it to me."

"Now, to my thinking, it's all the better that it should be so," replied Kate; "for it shows he can't have any great objection to the match. But Heaven help me ! you lovers have so many crinkum crankums in your head that you can never see matters in a proper light. But I must run away and leave you now, madam, for I have set Tony to watch for the coming of this stranger, and if I should hear or see anything of him, I'll run back and give you the earliest information."

With this she bustled out of the room, leaving Blanche to reflect at leisure upon the events of the last night, and to form her own conclusions as to who could be the person whose liberty had nearly been sacrificed to the violence of Hugh Laneret. At one time she had made up her mind, that it could be no other than her long-expected cousin; but then, on the other hand, she could not believe Neville would be so near without sending an intimation of his arrival. The more she thought the matter over, the further she seemed from arriving at the truth, and abandoning all speculation as useless, she rose from her seat to go in search of her guardian, when a hasty and heavy footstep was heard near the door of the apartment, and the next moment, to her terror and consternation, Hugh Laneret presented himself before her. A frown of anger passed over her brow as she recognised the person of her detested suitor, and making towards the door, she endeavoured to effect her escape from his presence, when he seized her hand to detain her.

"Nay, fair Blanche," he exclaimed, "we must not part thus, for the object of my visit here was to see you, and hear your final determination. It would be useless to repeat the vows of love that I have so often uttered before; if is sufficient that you know my purpose, and I now come to ask you if your heart is yet softened towards me?"

"There was little need for the trouble you have taken, Hugh Laneret," she replied, coldly. "My answer has already been given, and you might have spared me a visit that you know was not desired on my part. You have heard my determination, and I now desire to be at liberty to retire from your presence."

"Still haughty—still bent upon driving me to extremities!" muttered Laneret.

"Your threats, sir, will not change my resolution," answered Blanche, with firmness and dignity. "You ask my hand, which I refuse, and surely I may be permitted to exercise my judgment freely in a matter wherein my own future happiness is so nearly concerned."

"But I know the cause of all this coldness towards me," exclaimed Hugh Laneret. "I am despised and driven away from your presence to make way for one who it is in my power to crush. Neville Audeley is your favoured lover, and I now warn you that his life depends upon the answer you this day give me."

"Your threats will not move me from my purpose," replied Blanche, "for I now know you for the villain I have ever suspected, and no consideration of danger to myself shall prevail upon me to give encouragement to your visits. Begone sir; and, by hiding yourself from my view, manifest at least some sorrow for the conduct you have thought proper to follow."

"Your frowns, pretty Blance Herriot, will not deter me from the course I have marked out for myself," he answered, insolently. "I did not expect all at once to prevail on you to forget your old love; but it is possible I may tell you that which will cause you to reflect. In short, your favoured swain, Neville Audeley, is not far from this place; and it depends upon myself whether you ever see him again."

"Ah!—would you murder him?"

"Why, murder is an ugly word to make use of," exclaimed Hugh Laneret; "but I may be compelled to take such measures as will remove him from my path."

"Villain," she replied; "and you think by this means to terrify me into compliance?"

"You may please yourself about that, proud girl," he said; "for having been thus far plain with you, I now leave it to yourself to decide how the matter is to be arranged. I have told you Neville Audeley is not far off; yet for all that you may never see him again."

"I understand it all now but too well," cried Blanche, after a brief period had been given to consideration. "An attack was made last night upon the hostelrie, because a stranger had arrived there to seek shelter and repose for a few hours. That stranger was Neville Audeley, and the motive that led you to attempt the violence, was hatred for a man who had never injured you."

"He has injured me past all reparation," answered Hugh Laneret, "since but for him there would have been no obstacle in the way of our union. But he has made me his enemy, and nothing but his resigning all further pretension to your hand can save him from the wrath he has kindled in my heart."

"You believe then, that he is to be intimidated, and that I am to be won by this violence?"

"I know not how that may be," answered Hugh; "but desperate men adopt the wildest schemes to carry out their purposes, and since you have branded me with the name of villain, I may yet prove myself to be one, should you drive me to extremities."

"You have been answered, sir," she exclaimed, "and surely that should be sufficient to put an end to this unseemly visit. Go, Hugh Laneret, quit my presence for ever, and repent, if you can, the cowardice that prompted you to threaten a helpless female."

"Then you would sacrifice the life of Neville Audeley rather than become the bride of one whose love has driven him to these desperate lengths?"

"Neville Audeley," she replied, "is well able to protect himself in fair combat against he who has declared his enmity towards him. In secret you may, perhaps, work your villany; but remember, should any harm befal him, there is one tongue that will denounce you as the perpetrator of the crime."

"Blanche, you are mad to urge me thus!"

"It may be so," she replied, "for my brain burns with anger that you have already kindled. But I would be alone. Hugh Laneret, again I bid you depart, or my cries shall bring those to my aid who will not fail to punish this insolent in-trusion."

"I will not go," he exclaimed, "till you have promised to become mine."

He grasped her tightly by the arm as he uttered these words, and overcome with pain and terror, she screamed loudly for assistance. Still, however, he relaxed not his hold, until Sir Philip Warrenne rushed into the room and tore her from his arms.

"What means this violence, Hugh Laneret?" demanded the knight, fiercely. "Is the privacy of my house to be so little respected that you enter it unbidden to insult a helpless girl?"

"I have offered her no insult," replied Hugh.

"Believe him not," cried Blanche Heriot. "He would have compelled me by threats to become his; and, when I refused, vowed the destruction of Neville Audeley."

"Dare you deny this maiden's words?" demanded Sir Philip Warrenne.

"I deny nothing," answered the other; "Blanche has herself heard what I had to say, and she knows best how to allay the anger I have expressed against my rival."

"Neville Audeley has the reputation of being a good swordsman," exclaimed Sir Philip, "and you will, perhaps, do well to keep beyond the length of his weapon. But enough of this. Blanche has candidly avowed her preference for another, and I, therefore, pray you to depart in peace."

"And what if I refuse your bidding, Sir Knight?"

"You will then rouse my anger beyond control," answered Sir Philip War-renne; "and though age hath somewhat weakened my arm, I believe there is yet strength enough left in it to chastise the insolence of a villain whose purposes are but too well known."

"For the love of Heaven quarrel not with this rash and headstrong man!" cried Blanche, throwing her arms round the neck of her guardian. "He seeks a quarrel with you, sir; and should swords be drawn, he will never sheathe his till he has plunged it in the heart of his adversary."

"You give me credit for more powers than I thought I possessed," answered Hugh Laneret. "However, you may take my word for it, that I bear no ill-will towards your guardian, and if he thinks proper to let this matter take its own course, he will find me rather inclined to be a friend than a foe."

"I will accept no friendship from the man I have just branded with the name of villain," replied Sir Philip. "In your heart I know you to be my enemy, and never will I place myself in the power of one whose treachery I am but too well assured of."

"Yet you may be in my power sooner than you expect," muttered Hugh Laneret.

"What mean you, sirrah?"

"Simply," answered the other, "that there is a fair chance of the English throne changing possession ere long. Edward is now on his way to this country with a strong body of foreign troops; and as the people in the north are enthusi-astic in his favour, there is every certainty of his obtaining the crown for which he is ready to do battle. Nay, victory is certain; and then you, and all others who have joined the Yorkist party, will be held as traitors, and suffer for it accordingly."

"You make sure then," exclaimed Sir Philip Warrenne, "that the unjust cause will prove triumphant?"

"It is the righteous cause," answered Laneret, "and, therefore, must succeed."

"But you forget," replied the knight, "that Henry the Sixth, who I have the honour to serve, has thousands of brave subjects ready to rally round the throne of their lawful sovereign. The Earl of Warwick is already at the head of a large army; and should a battle take place the victory is most likely to be ours. In that event, Hugh Laneret will do well to look to himself, for, as a traitor to his lawful king, he will have neither mercy nor compassion to expect from the monarch against whom he draws his sword."

"And will it, indeed, come to this?" cried Blanche, despondingly. "Must the curse of civil war fall upon our land, and deluge the country with the blood of its children? 'Tis fearful to think that fathers will be opposed to their sons, brothers to their brothers, and all this to satisfy the ambition of a man who seeks to possess himself of a throne that belongs not to him by right!"

"You are mistaken, fair Blanche," answered Laneret; "for Edward claims it as his inheritance, and there are thousands who, thinking as he does, are ready to venture life and limb in his behalf. But we will quit this subject, upon which we are not likely to agree; and, since we must now part, Blanche, let it be upon better terms than we met. Weigh in your own mind the advantages a union with me will give you, and by accepting my offer, procure security for yourself and Sir Philip Warrenne."

"Let her not give a thought to me," exclaimed the knight, "for I am old and can willingly throw away the few remaining years of my life rather than see her become the wife of such as thou. My best days have been spent in the defence of my country's rights, and dishonoured would be my name were I to suffer this sacrifice for any paltry consideration of my own. You have now heard us, Hugh Laneret, and it is my command that you never enter my presence again, unless it be as a penitent for your past transgressions."

"I see you are still obstinately bent on your own destruction," returned the other, "and it would, therefore, be in vain to argue any further upon the subject. But you have both been warned; and remember, whatever happens after this, will be your own doing. I would willingly have spared Neville Audeley from the ruin that must fall upon him; but since Blanche decrees it otherwise, she alone must be answerable for the consequences."

He strode haughtily from the room as he spoke, and the dark frown that was upon his brow bespoke but too plainly the vindictive feelings that were engendered in his heart. Blanche was terrified lest he should take instant means to revenge himself; and all the persuasive eloquence of her guardian failed to remove the fearful apprehensions that racked her soul.

"There is less to be alarmed at, child, than you seem to think," he said; "for Hugh Laneret is not yet without hopes of making you his own, and it is hardly likely he will commit an act which must secure for him your lasting hatred. Neville will, therefore, be safe from him for some time to come; and even should it be otherwise than I suspect, he has both courage and skill sufficient to oppose against his arrogant rival."

"But it is treachery we have most to fear," answered Blanche, with a sigh. "We know Hugh Laneret to be destitute of every principle of honour. All the actions of his life prove it, and my fear is that he will concert means to destroy Neville when the blow is least of all anticipated!"

"Why that would be murder!" exclaimed the old knight; "and in such a case he would be certain to meet the punishment of his crime."

"At any other time than this it might be so," answered our heroine; "but at this wild, distracted period, all law is set at open defiance, and men may commit the most heinous offences without fear of being called to an account for it. The brawl last night at the tavern is a proof of my assertion, for, had such an outrage occurred at any other period than this, Hugh Laneret would have had little chance of coming here afterwards to threaten me into compliance with his imperious demands."

At this moment the door was thrown open, and Neville Audeley presenting himself, received in his arms the now joyous and happy maiden of his love. Sir Philip Warrenne also welcomed him with more hearty warmth than he had expected; and when the young man would have apologized for the abruptness of his intrusion, he interrupted him by saying—

"Nay, young man, I will hear nothing you have to say upon that subject, for as the chosen friend and lover of my dear Blanche, I am rejoiced to see you as a visitor beneath my roof. Make it your home, Neville; and if you take the honest advice of a friend, you will not leave it till a certain foe of yours is far enough away from hence."

"You allude, I suppose, to Hugh Laneret?"

"Why of course I do," answered Sir Philip, with all the freedom of an old friend. "You have no other enemies, I hope, that you need ask such a question?"

"None," replied Neville, "but he, I think, is not likely to pay a visit to this house, since he last night mingled in a disturbance which it is probable will oblige him to play at hide-and-seek for some time to come"

"Nay," sighed Blanche, "so far from that being the case, he had only just left the room when you entered it."

"Hah!" exclaimed Neville, "would that we had met then."

"It is better as it is," answered our heroine; "for his blood has been heated by disappointment, and a meeting between you under such circumstances, would perhaps have been fatal to yourself."

"The girl is right enough there, Neville," interposed Sir Philip. "He was in a furious passion at being rejected by her; and had he chanced to meet his more successful rival, there is no telling what fearful tragedy might have been committed beneath my roof."

"Yet, as a soldier, Sir Philip," exclaimed Neville, "you surely would not have me avoid a meeting with this man? Last night proved the hatred he bears me, and, but for the number by whom he was surrounded, I had either called him to a severe account or thrown away my life in the attempt."

"Oh, beware of him, I pray you, dear Neville," cried Blanche, earnestly. "He is no common foe such as men may guard against, but treachery is in all his acts, and never will he rest content whilst you live to triumph over the disappointment he endures. Even now he threatened you with his fiercest wrath; and much I fear some dread calamity, should an unfortunate chance throw you in each other's way."

"Nay," he replied, "you pay but a poor compliment to my prowess, if you believe it inferior to his own."

"Your prowess I doubt not," answered Blanche, "but what is that when opposed to the treacherous arts of a villain? He will attack you unawares, and thus make sure of the vengeance he burns to accomplish."

"He will have but little chance of that, dear Blanche," returned Neville Audeley, "for, since my errand must be told, I came but to take farewell of you, previous to joining the army under the command of the great Earl of Warwick."

"Alas!" she sighed, "and are we, then, to part so soon?—But, no you shall not leave us, Neville; there is peril in the coming strife, and should you fall, what misery and despair will be my portion."

"Duty, and the justice of my sovereign's cause, both demand the poor aid it is in my power to give," answered Neville. "You will not, therefore, seek to turn me from the path of honour, since, should I hesitate to pursue it, shame, and the scorn of the world, will henceforth follow me through life."

"He is right, girl," exclaimed Sir Philip; "so, if you really love him, you will not oppose the generous resolution he has formed. It is hard, I confess, to part with a lover when he is going to meet danger; but women must make such sacrifices when the good of their country demands it. So prithee leave off weeping, my pretty Blanche, and go with us to the Cedar Chamber, where we will talk over this matter more at large."

The heart of Blanche Heriot was too full for utterance; and led by Neville, she accompanied her guardian to the apartment he had spoken of. Till this period she had been comparatively happy, but the thought of her lover's danger brought tortures with it, and, for the first time in her life, she became the prey of the most agonizing grief.

CHAPTER IV.

A NEW ACQUAINTANCE.—THE ALCHYMIST.—THE PREDICTION.

WE will not attempt to describe the scene which took place during the interview, since it will be sufficient to observe that Blanche used all her pursuasive eloquence in vain in her attempts to prevail on her lover to abandon his intention of joining the army. In fact, Neville saw no way to retract with honour to himself, and now all his efforts were directed towards consoling the sorrowing maiden with an assurance that the danger was not so great as she apprehended, and that he should ere long return to her with honour for his reward, and the glorious consciousness that he had performed a sacred duty when his country demanded from him his best exertions in her behalf. Sir Philip Warrenne joined in this attempt to prevail over her fears, and eventually she became so far reconciled to the stern necessity as to resume some of her former composure; and at length when the period for their parting arrived, she took leave of him with an appearance of firmness, that she in fact possessed not.

On leaving Redwynd Manor House, which he did with a heavy heart, Neville Audeley walked onwards, without being conscious whither he directed his steps. Indeed, so absorbed was he in his own thoughts, that he heard not his name called three or four times, nor did he know anyone was following him, till a slight touch on the arm startled him from his reverie, and looking round, he saw Herrick Evenden, whose laughing countenance formed a striking contrast with the gloom and despondency that was settled upon his own.

"Why, what in the name of all that's miraculous," exclaimed Herrick, "ails you now? I have followed you from the house of your heart's idol, and yet your face wears such a melancholy aspect that one would suppose you had parted from her in anger."

"Had you said in sorrow," answered Neville, "you would have been far nearer to the mark."

"Humph!—a lover's quarrel, then, I suppose?"

"On the contrary," replied the other, in a more cheerful tone, "we both met and parted on the most gratifying terms."

"Then I'll warrant me," returned Herrick, "the old Cerebus of a guardian has taken it into his head that you shall be no husband of his fair ward."

"Wrong again," replied Neville Audeley; "for the old knight gave me a most cordial reception, and there is no barrier whatever to my union with Blanche— that is to say, after I return from the wars in which I am about to engage."

"Ah! now I see it all," exclaimed Herrick; "the lady was unwilling to part with you when danger was in the way. Hysterics are a very natural consequence of these lovers' partings, and the poor maiden, I dare say, give way to the full tide of her grief."

"You are jesting with me, I see," returned Neville; "but I can pardon the levity for the service you did me last night. You saved my life, and I was on the way to your house to thank you for your fortunate intervention."

"Psha!" ejaculated Herrick, "as if one man cannot do another a good service without all this fuss being made about it. What if I did save you from a stab of Master Hugh Laneret's sword? The act was nothing more than a duty, and so there's and end of it. So now tell me, my friend, why you have resolved to take part in this quarrel that has occurred among the great ones of our land?"

"From a sense of duty and loyalty," answered Neville. "The cause of King Henry is a just and holy one; and cheerfully will I lay done my life, if need be, to assist in destroying the faction that has been raised against him."

"You are for the Red Rose, then?"

"I am for King Henry the Sixth, whose badge you have just mentioned."

"Would that I could join you in it!" exclaimed Herrick, "for my heart is in the cause, and nothing would give me greater pleasure than to assist in giving those rebellious Yorkists a sound drubbing. But 'tis in vain for me to feel valorous, for my father happens to have a mortal antipathy to all fighting, and he has forbidden me to bear arms under pain of being disinherited."

"He has never been a soldier, then?"

"What, my father?" cried Herrick Evenden. "No, no, if England and its people were ten times more mad than they seem to be at the present moment, he would be content to let them fight it out among themselves, whilst he set himself down gravely to his studies."

"And what may his studies be?" asked Neville.

"Very abstruse ones, I assure you," answered the other. "He reades the stars to discover the fates of men and nations—searches for the philosopher's stone, which no one has yet been able to find—and is at the present moment engaged in discovering the means by which our baser metals may be converted into good gold and silver."

"In other words, he is an alchymist?"

"Ay, or a conjurer, if you will," replied Herrick; "you people in these parts, will have it that he has dealings with the devil; and yet, between ourselves, friend Neville, there are few more quiet or harmless men in the world than my poor, pains-taking, though much-mistaken, dad."

"And what thinks he of these idle reports?"

"I verily believe he never thinks of them at all," answered Herrick Evenden; "or if he does, it is merely to smile at the credulity of ignorance and superstition. But if you have nothing better to do with yourself, you shall accompany me home, and have an introduction to him."

"Which," observed Neville, "he is very likely to deem an impertinent intrusion."

"There you are mistaken," replied the other, "for he is ever affable and courteous to those whom I introduce to his notice. Perhaps he depends upon my prudence in forming new acquaintances; but be that as it may, he interferes but little with my pleasures, so that I laugh not at the studies in which he is engaged. In truth, he will be glad to see you, and it may happen that your visit will not be altogether an unprofitable one."

"What mean you?"

"Why, that the sage opinions of an old and experienced man may prove advantageous to a youth who has resolved upon plunging into strife without having given the subject a fair consideration. Nay, do not knit your brow thus, my friend Neville, for I speak the honest truth, and should be glad if anything my father may say should turn your thoughts in another direction."

"Are you jesting, Herrick Evenden?" asked the other, "or am I really to understand that you would have me sit down quietly when my country requires the services of every loyal son of the soil? Edward is on his way here at the head of a foreign host; and it is to save England from being overrun by these people, that we are preparing to give them battle on their arrival."

"Well, well," exclaimed Herrick, "I can, at any rate, give you credit for honest zeal in the cause you have so warmly at heart. But we now stand at the door of my father's house; enter it with me, and I can promise you will see no reason to repent having done so."

Neville offered no objection to this, and the door being shortly afterwards opened by the domestic, Anthony Amblewit, they both of them entered the house, and our hero soon found himself in a spacious apartment, furnished even luxuriantly for the period to which our story belongs. He looked in vain, however, for the master of the mansion; and Herrick, who had left him for a few moments, returning to the chamber, said—

"It is exactly as I expected—my father heard of your being here without surprise, and has bid me take you into his presence. In fact, Neville, between ourselves, I have half a notion that the stars, or something else, forwarded him of your arrival."

"And he would see me, you say?"

"He desired me to take you into his study without delay," answered Herrick. "But do not laugh at the strange things that will there meet your gaze, for the room is crammed with oddities such as few persons have had the good fortune to see huddled together in so small a compass."

"Nay, I will promise to be upon my best behaviour," exclaimed Neville Audeley, "for h's courtesy will demand from me at least that token of respect. So, lead the way, that we may keep him no longer waiting for us."

He now followed his conductor from the room, and was led up a winding, narrow, stone staircase, that evidently afforded access to the upper part of a spacious turret. Being somewhat dark, the way was rather difficult to find; but at length hey reached the top, and turning into a short passage, they paused for a moment while Herrick knocked at a small low door, before which they stood. A voice was then heard within, bidding them enter, and as Neville stepped into the sombre turret chamber, he was struck with the venerable yet majestic form that was seated before him. The old man slightly rose in acknowledgment of the young stranger's salutation, and then pointing to a seat on the opposite side of the table, he desired him to take his place there. A silence of some few seconds succeeded, and then Master Basil Evenden, addressing himself to his guest, said—

"Your visit here, young man, was not so unexpected on my part as you may imagine."

"Indeed!" exclaimed Neville, scarcely knowing what reply to make. "It was altogether unpremeditated as far as I am myself concerned, and it was not till within the last quarter of an hour that I had the least notion of entering your house."

"That," exclaimed Herrick, "I can answer for."

"You have both spoken truly, I dare say," answered the old man, "yet long study has made me conversant with the stars, and from certain indications, I knew of this stranger's speedy arrival here. Nay, more, he has thought of rushing headlong into the tide of war, though there are not wanting those who would fain prevail on him to relinquish his dangerous intentions; even beauty itself has failed to move his heart from its purpose."

"Thus far you are right," answered Neville, "and may I now be bold enough to inquire whether I shall survive the battle in which I shall soon be engaged?"

"You will."

"And will the side on which I fight prove victorious?"

"Seek not to know too much, young man," exclaimed Basil; "I have said your life will be spared, but it is doomed to much misery. Hope itself will be blighted for awhile; and the malice of your greatest foe will prove triumphant over his victim."

"This is in truth a gloomy prospect of the future," exclaimed Neville; "and yet it is to be hoped better fortune will smile on me afterwards to make amends for all the trouble I may have to undergo?"

"That will depend upon the faithful zeal of a friend," replied the old man. "Thy life will hang upon a thread, and should that friend lag on the errand upon which he will be sent, thy blood will be shed to satisfy the malice of him who has sworn himself thy foe."

"You hear the prediction," exclaimed Herrick to the young man, "and now let me prevail on you to take warning in time, so that fate may for once be cheated. Come, come, Neville, give up this scheme of yours; if men must fight let them do so without your assistance; marry the girl of your heart, and leave the rest to chance."

"Never!" cried the young man, resolutely. "My sword shall be drawn in the cause of justice, and when peace shall bid me sheathe it again, I will boldly cla'm the hand of Blanche Heriot, who would scorn to bestow herself upon one that was unworthy of her."

"Ay, 'tis the hot, mad blood of youth that prompts thee to this course," interposed Basil Evenden. "Thou wouldst seek honour, even though it should be found in a bloody grave."

"I would serve my country," answered Neville, proudly; "and no consideration of danger shall deter me from what I conceive to be the first duty of every one. England is in danger of falling under the rule of a tyrant and usurper; my lawful sovereign looks to his faithful subjects for assistance, and those who do not obey the call are undeserving the world's respect."

"There, father," exclaimed Herrick; "you hear that, and yet it is through your commands that I am sitting idle at home, whilst all besides are up and stirring, either on one side or the other."

"What would you, boy?" demanded Basil.

"What!" cried his son; "why, buckle on a sword to be sure, and follow our friend here to the wars."

"Wouldst thou have me curse thee?"

"No, by Heaven, anything but that."

"Then stay with me," returned Basil, "and thus show your ready obedience to the will of your father. You are my only stay and prop in life, boy—the only memorial of her who I loved beyond all things else in the world. Whilst she lived, Herrick, I mingled with the busy throng of men, and few were happier than Basil Evenden. But she perished in giving birth to thee, and from that moment I became an altered man. To relieve the weary hours of seclusion, I turned over the pages of mystic lore, until I became a firm believer in those arts which till then I had laughed at with derision. The study may have been an unprofitable one, Herrick, but it has withdrawn my mind from melancholy thoughts, and thus cheated me of many an hour of sadness. Still you have been the object of my care, and I believe my son cannot cast upon me the reproach of having neglected him even for the severer studies in which I was engaged."

"You have spoken truly, father," replied Herrick.

"Then why," demanded the old man, "wouldst thou now leave me to go and cast away thy life in a quarrel with which thou hast nought to do?"

"Because," answered Herrick, "to remain at home in idleness at such a time as this, will be called cowardice."

"Let men call it what they will, for there is no reason why thou shouldst heed them. Plead thy father's commands—say that hadst thou left my house upon such an errand, it would have brought down upon thy head the curses of an incensed parent; tell them that filial duty is the first law of nature, and then let them call thee coward if they dare."

"They will call me one for all that," exclaimed the young man, gloomily.

"Nay," interrupted Neville Audeley, "do not insense your father by urging this subject any further. I can bear witness that it was your ardent desire to aid in supporting the cause of your king, and I can also bear testimony that the only reason for your not doing so was your wish to obey the positive commands of your father."

"But the world is hard of belief," observed Herrick, "and where you find one person to accept the excuse, ten thousand will be found to sneer at me for a pitiable coward, that durst not face the enemies of his country."

"Herrick, no more of this, I command you," exclaimed the old man; "you have heard me, and it now remains for you to decide between duty and your own inclination. But, perhaps, a father's love grows troublesome to you, and if such is indeed the case, leave me on the instant ; and shouldst thou ever return hither it will be to learn that thy desertion slew him who gave thee life."

"I will urge this subject no further," answered Herrick, "for I can endure anything rather than the reproaches of one whose kindness has extended from my birth even to the present moment. I am not ungrateful for your favours, my father, and will prove my worthiness of them by yielding up my own wishes to your commands."

"Why that's well said, boy," exclaimed Basil Evenden, "and once more I can smile upon thee as I have been ever wont to do. The stranger, too, that thou didst bring with thee, hath done well in urging thee to yield thy wishes to mine, and he has earned for himself the thanks and blessings of an old man."

"But I dare say he would rather have been spared the scene he has witnessed," said Herrick, "for he scarcely expected to hear a lecture when I invited him into the house. But, perhaps, it is as well as it is, for he is not much past the years of discretion yet, and it may prove a lesson to him that will be worth remembering hereafter."

"Yet it seems I shall scarcely need it," returned Neville, "for you have just now heard that I am to be sorely tried by afflictions, and adversity is a school that brings most of us to our senses. I will now, however, take my leave, for I have already made my visit here longer than I intended."

He then bade farewell to the alchymist, and descending the stairs of the turret, preceded by Herrick, returned to the room into which he had been ushered upon first entering the house.

"You now see," exclaimed Herrick, "how impossible it is to move my father from this determination of his. He has taken it into his head that I shall not buckle on my belt, and so I suppose I must sit myself down contentedly, like a sighing maiden, to wait the results that more fortunate men than myself are to assist in bringing about."

"But," answered Neville, "you will have the consolation of knowing that your having yielded this point has given happiness to your father, and prevented a breach between you that might never have been healed."

"Upon my life, Neville," exclaimed the other, " I am much obliged to you for any little piece of consolation you can give me. Egad, there's nothing like having a friend, for in one's sadness he's always sure to find some way or other to bring in a little bit of comfort."

"At any rate, I'm glad to find you are so inclined to jest upon the matter," returned Neville.

"And I," answered the other, "am equally well pleased to see that my father's ominous prognostications have not had any very serious effect upon *your* spirits. Of a verity, I thought he spoke out pretty plainly ; and should one half of the misfortunes he spoke of come true, you will have enough trouble to your share to last for a whole lifetime."

"At all events I shall not meet my troubles half way," replied Neville, smiling at the recollection of what had been predicted. "I may chance to be on the losing side, which Heaven forbid for our monarch's sake ; but if the victory does turn against us, it is more likely that I shall be found among the slain, than that I shall live to suffer the misfortunes alluded to."

"And in that case," observed Herrick, "your rival will find no difficulty in forcing Blanche Heriot to become his bride."

"Ay," answered Neville, "that is the barb which, most of all, festers in my heart. But, though our acquaintance has been a brief one, Herrick Evenden, I have sufficient confidence in your honour to believe that you will become her champion against the artifices of a villain."

"Ay, that will I," exclaimed the other, warmly, "for, though I am somewhat given to mirth and folly, yet there are points upon which I can prove steady ; and when a woman's in the way, by Jove, I can freely risk life and limb to shield her from the snares of villany."

"And you will become the defender of Blanche Heriot, should she unhappily need one ?"

"Ay, truly will I," replied Herrick. "To be sure I am not yet much used to handling a sword, but only give me a good cause to draw it in, and I'll warrant you I can do some service with it. Besides, I have no great liking for this Hugh Laneret, and I don't know that anything would please me better than to have just one bout with him. They say he's too much of a bully to be a brave man, and, in that case, I might have as much chance with him as any one else."

"Yet have a care that you make him not your enemy till the time comes when your friendship for me may be called into action," said Neville. "I know him to be treacherous, and should he suspect your intentions, he would not fail to put any base design that he might form against you into execution."

"I am quite aware of the sort of customer I have to deal with," replied Herrick Evenden, "and it shall be no fault of mine if he gains an advantage that common prudence might prevent. I shall not fail also to keep a close look out upon Redwynde Manor House; and should I find that he is lurking about the place, it will be pretty certain that it will not be long before my services must be put into requisition."

"There is not much to be apprehended on that account," answered the other, "for in a day or two he will leave this place to join the forces that are collecting in the north, to favour the landing of Edward and his troops somewhere on the eastern coast of England. But should any evil fate befal me, and he survive the battle, it will then be your time to look after him. But I must now bid you farewell, and to-morrow, when we meet again, I will speak further with you upon the subject."

The friends now separated; and upon being left to pursue his own reflections, Neville Audeley could scarcely suppress a superstitious feeling as he thought of the prognostications uttered by the venerable alchymist.

CHAPTER V.

FAMILY JARS.—THE VISITOR.—THE MESSAGE.

On reaching the inn where he had slept on the preceding night, Neville was met by the host, who, with an air of profound mystery, informed him that a stranger had been inquiring for him; and, after waiting some time for his return, had gone out to seek for him, taking the direction that led towards Redwynde Manor House. At first Audeley was inclined to attach some consequence to this circumstance, but upon reflection he thought the person, whoever he was, had been sent to watch his motions by Hugh Laneret; and feeling tolerably well assured that such was the fact, he determined to see the person, and either by threats or the offer of a bribe to obtain a confession from him. The host, who had been watching his countenance for some few minutes, at length said—

"I tried, sir, to fish the stranger, and obtain a clue from him as to what business he wanted to see you about; but Lord bless you! I might as well have held my tongue, for he wouldn't answer me a word for a long time, and, at length, he called me an inquisitive old fool, and bade me go and mind my own business."

"Which was the very answer you might have expected," replied Neville; "for if his business with me is of any importance, it was hardly to be supposed he would divulge it to a stranger."

"Humph!" muttered Fioth; "then this is all the good I get for taking an interest in your affairs."

"The truth is, good Master Host," exclaimed the other, "that people very seldom succeed in worming out a secret that they have no business with. This man's errand may be of very little importance, but I will wait here till he comes; and immediately upon his return, you can show him into this room."

"Very good, sir," replied the host; "but do you know, I have a strange sort of suspicion, that the fellow has been sent here by Master Hugh Laneret."

"Well, and what if he has?" demanded the young man, in a tone of impatience.

"Oh, nothing, certainly, to me," answered Froth, "only I was thinking that to you it might happen to be of some importance. Laneret don't bear a very good character in these parts; but, I suppose you needn't be told that, since last night afforded a pretty fair opinion of what he'll do when he makes up his mind for mischief."

"And what makes you think this man is an emissary of his?"

"I can scarcely tell you why I fancy so," answered Froth, "but strange thoughts do pass in our heads sometimes, and from the first I had a notion that he didn't come here to seek you for any good purpose."

"And yet," exclaimed Neville Audely, "you have not yet given any one reason why I should suspect this man as you do. He may be the bearer of a message from some other person on matters of importance."

"But if his message had been a friendly one," replied the host, "he wouldn't have been so surly when I tried to pump him in the most civil manner. His being so angry about it, convinced me at once that he could be here for no good purpose; and so I caution your honourable worship to beware of him."

"Ay, now we arrive at something like the truth," exclaimed Neville. "You are offended at the fellows bluntness of manners towards yourself, and at once set him down as a knave. I, however, must have better evidence before I fall in with your opinion; and should I find out that he is engaged in any plot against me, it will be well for him if he escapes from my presence with whole bones."

"And it's my notion that a sound thrashing will be no more than he deserves," returned the host; "for if there's anything in the world that I dislike more than another, it's a man that won't give a civil answer to a civil question."

"Still harping upon the old subject, Master Froth."

"Upon my life, sir, I can't help it," cried the host; "one's dignity is touched when people answer insolently; and to tell you the truth, I believe I should have given the scurvy knave a sound thrashing myself, only that my own dame came into the room at the moment, and I knew that discretion would be the better part of valour."

"And so she saved this fellow from your wrath?"

"Nay, I am no vain boaster," replied Froth, "and I don't say for certain that I should have inflicted chastisement upon him; but I might have done so, perhaps, for I was in a desperate passion, I can assure you."

"Which passion, by-the-by," observed Neville, "suddenly evaporated as your better-half entered the room. I fear me, Master Froth, you are a little too much under the dominion of the petticoats."

"Who, I under petticoat-government?" exclaimed Froth, angrily. "No, no, sir, my wife knows her place better than to presume so far, and she knows what would be the consequence of trying to domineer over me."

At that moment the shrill voice of the hostess was heard calling upon the name of her husband; and from certain harsh epithets that she applied to him, it was pretty plain that a sound rating was in store for him, as soon as he ventured into her presence. The poor host turned as white as the froth on one of his own ale jugs; his knees smote each other, and from the violent trembling that followed, it was very evident that all his valour had disappeared at the first sound of his wife's voice. Neville Audeley could not forbear smiling as he observed this marvellous change; and slapping the host on his shoulders to rouse him, he exclaimed—

"Master Froth; Master Froth; hear you not your dame's clapper at work? Go to her, man, and assert the pre-eminence that belongs to you by right."

"N—o—t for the world!" stammered the poor host, in terrible dismay. "She's awful in her passions, good Master Audeley, and to meet her now would be as much as my life's worth."

"Then she'll follow you to this room."

"If she does, do you be my friend," exclaimed Froth. "Tell her you wanted me here on business, and that I can't be spared for some time to come. Perhaps her rage may be softened in a little while, and.then I can coax her into good-humour again."

"Master Froth," said the other, "I thought you told me just now that the grey mare was not the better horse?"

"And I told you truly," answered the tapster; "but the fact is, when she gets into these passions, I'm sometimes obliged to let her have her way. The law, it's true, allows a man to chastise his wife with a stick, provided the said stick is no bigger than his thumb, but I never could make up my mind to hurt the poor creature; and so I always suffer her to get the upper-hand, when I find her a little out of temper."

"And she takes care to keep the upper-hand, I see."

"Why, it must be confessed she does," replied the hen-pecked husband; "but then she says she's the best manager of household affairs, and so I let her have way. Anything for a quiet life, you know."

At this moment the hostess, her face inflamed with rage, and her eyes almost starting from their sockets, bounced into the room.

"Why, thou knave! thou useless log! thou chattering idle fool!" she exclaimed furiously; "here have I been calling thee till my throat is hoarse, and here I find thee chattering and wasting thy time when there are customers waiting at the door to be served with thy best liquor. Out upon thee, for an oaf, I say, for thou art the very curse and bane of my life!"

And as she concluded this harangue, she dealt the unhappy wight such a sound box on the ears, that he fairly staggered to the further part of the room. Nor did even this seem to pacify her rage in the least, for she was about to administer a second dose of the same bitter medicine, when Neville, stepping between them, effectually screened the husband from any further infliction of punishment from his better-half.

"Peace, good dame, I pray you," he said, "or if you must give way to this unseemly violence, let me come in for a share of it as well as this poor man. I am the most to blame in this matter, since he remained here to answer questions that I put to him; and, therefore, he is not so much to blame as you imagine."

"Ah, sir," cried the dame, trying to shed a few tears, "you know not what a handful I have with that lazy, good-for-nothing husband of mine. He's a uselesss piece of encumbrance in the house; and a sad day it was for me when I took to myself a husband that does nothing but talk and chatter whilst I do all the hard work."

"And, it seems to me, all the talking into the bargain," said Neville, who could not help speaking a bit of his mind, even though it was at the risk of bringing upon himself a storm of invectives. The dame, however, had grown cooler by this time, and she replied, with a simper :—

"Why, the truth is, young gentleman. it's only fair that I should have all the talking if I do all the drudgery of the house. Besides, one can't help being out of temper sometimes, and Froth, I'm sure. can't but acknowledge that in general I'm the sweetest-tempered woman in all the world."

"Always," answered the host, "*except* when you get into a passion."

"And that never happens but when you deserve it."

"I believe, good wife, you are right," exclaimed Froth, who began to be afraid of a second explosion. "No doubt you keep me in very good order, and so let us be friends again, or we shall frighten this worthy gentleman away from our house."

"Pray," inquired Neville, "what has become of the customers that you said were waiting to be served?"

"Gone," replied the dame; "they grew tired of waiting, and have taken their departure to spend their money somewhere else."

"Which might have been avoided, had you taken the trouble to serve them instead of calling out so lustily for your husband."

"I've no patience with the idle fellow," cried the dame. "and won't encourage his laziness, he may depend on it. And what's more, I don't care how soon certain persons turn their backs upon the house if they don't like the way I manage my own concerns."

Neville Audely now saw that it was his turn to come in for a share of the dame's ill-nature, and was preparing himself for the storm, when the opening of the door fortunately caused an interruption, and Guy Addlepate, popping in his head, exclaimed—

"Here's some one that says he wants to see the gentleman that's stopping here."

"Ah! the person that's been inquiring for you, Mr. Neville Audeley," said the host. "Will it please you to see him, sir?"

"Certainly," replied the young man; "I have been waiting here for that purpose. Let him come to me in this room, and do you and your wife leave us to ourselves."

"Just as you please about that, sir," exclaimed Froth; "but wouldn't it be as well to have some one near in case the stranger should mean anything wrong?"

"I have no reason to apprehend danger," answered Neville. "The business he comes upon is no doubt of a private nature, and there must be no one present to overhear it. See that no one approaches the door whilst this stranger is with me, for should you, or any of your people, be caught listening, I will so pull his ears that he shall never have a desire to pry into other people's affairs again. You understand me, and I hope the caution will be sufficient."

"I never was given to curiosity in my life," exclaimed Froth; "and I am sure, after what you have said, my wife will have no inclination to make use of the key-hole."

"Away, and do my bidding," cried Neville, impatiently; "send the stranger to me, and let no one enter the room unless summoned by me."

Dame Froth dropped her best courtesy, and her husband made a most respectful bow; and quitting the room together, they left Neville Audeley to reflect in solitude upon the situation in which he found himself.. There was a mystery in this visit that all his ingenuity could not fathom, and though he did not apprehend any danger from it, yet he resolved to be upon his guard, and defend himself to the last extremity in case treachery should be intended. He was still occupied in pondering upon this subject, when the door was opened, and a stranger, closely muffled in a cloak, presented himself, and having secured the fastening to prevent intrusion, advanced towards our hero, and in a whisper, demanded if he was Neville Audeley.

"I am," was the reply; "and now perhaps you will do me the courtesy to tell me your name in return?"

"My name is of no concern, since you know it not," was the reply. "I am the bearer of a message, if it is your pleasure to hear it."

"From whom come you?—a friend or a foe?"

"A friend."

"How am I to know that?"

"By this token," replied the stranger, throwing open his cloak, and presenting Neville with a red rose.

"Hah!" exclaimed the young man, eagerly snatching it; "'tis the symbol of a party whose cause I espouse. You come from the Lancastrian camp?"

"I do."

"By whose orders?"

"By those of the brave Earl of Warwick," answered the stranger. "There will soon be warm work for the enemy, and your presence is required at the camp."

"Immediately?"

"Without loss of time," replied the man; "it is expected that Edward has by this time landed on the eastern coast of England, and it is the intention of the Earl of Warwick to intercept the enemy on their march towards London."

"And where," asked Neville, "has the Earl of Warwick pitched his camp?"

"In the neighbourhood of Tewkesbury."

"And there I am to join the Lancastrian army?"

"You are," replied the stranger. "You will set out from hence without a moment's delay, and I am to be your guide, for the roads are bad, and it will be difficult to traverse them in the night time."

"Would it not be better," asked Neville Audeley, "to defer our departure till the morning?"

"The earl's commands were, that not a moment should be lost," answered the other. "All the friends of King Henry are required to muster immediately, for everything depends upon the promptitude with which measures are taken for defeating the objects of the enemy."

"And how am I to know," asked Neville, "that you come from the party you have named?"

"The red rose I have just delivered into your hands was sent as a token that you would understand."

"But that," exclaimed the other, "may be a trick to deceive me. Did the earl send no letter by which I may know that no imposition is practised?"

"The Earl of Warwick would have had more to do than he could get through with," answered the stranger. "He has sent messengers in every direction to bring together his friends; and as there was no time to write letters to all of them, he sent a red rose to each, well knowing they would understand the meaning."

"Yet there may be treachery lurking beneath the symbol," observed Neville. "The rose may have been sent to entrap me into the hands of the enemy."

"I am sorry, young sir," answered the man, "that I have no means of convincing you that your suspicions are unfounded. You may, however, rely upon my word, for as a stranger to you, I can have no motives such as those you give me credit for."

"But you may have been employed by others."

"Had that been the case, I should not have come on this errand unarmed," replied the other; and throwing aside his cloak, he continued—"you see I have no weapons; and, therefore, should I prove treacherous, I should be entirely at your mercy."

"Well," exclaimed Neville, after some little hesitation, "I will trust myself to your guidance, but it must be on condition that you postpone our departure till the morning."

"Nay," returned the stranger, "that would be more than my life is worth. My orders were to return immediately, even if I went back without you; and therefore, if it is your will to cause any delay, I must to the Earl of Warwick, and tell him there is one friend to the cause less than he had counted on."

"Then it must be even as you have said," exclaimed Neville; "though it must still be confessed I begin this journey at night with reluctance. You will remain here for a short time to rest, and meanwhile I will go and take my leave of some friends from whom I would not part thus abruptly."

"If it is to see your lady-love," returned the stranger, with a penetrating glance, "I should say the interview would be better omitted. Women have terrible notions of war, and a few tears might have the effect of turning you from your purpose."

"She whom I would see," answered Neville, "holds my honour too sacred to utter aught that would hazard it."

"That may be true, but you would not like to part with her in sorrow."

"And therefore you would have me leave this place without letting her know of my sudden resolution?"

"There you mistake me altogether," replied the stranger. "Here are pens, ink, and paper in the room, I see, and a few lines would answer all the purpose of an interview without danger."

"Methinks," exclaimed Neville, "this unseemly haste of yours is suspicious."

"Nay, if you think so," answered the other, "I will return with a message from you to the earl, and he will thereby judge that you are no longer willing to lend your aid in a cause that requires the assistance of every one who would help to maintain King Henry on his throne."

"Hah! do you threaten me?"

"So far from it," answered the other, coldly, "that I would fain persuade you to adopt the only course that you can pursue with honour to yourself. I have told you that this business will suffer from delay, and having said thus much, it will now remain with yourself to determine whether I shall depart alone, or in your company. Besides, a note to your friends will be quite sufficient; and if farther apology be necessary, you can make it on your return to this place."

Neville Audeley felt sorely perplexed, for still he was not without his suspicion that treachery lurked under the message he had thus received. On the other hand, however, he was unwilling to refuse credit to the man's story, lest by so doing he should bring upon himself the dishonour of having deserted the cause of his king at the very moment when his services were most required. Under all the circumstances, therefore, he determined to accompany the stranger; and sitting down to the table, he wrote a hurried note to Blanche, informing her of the cause that had led to his sudden departure, and describing the route he was about to take. This he did in case of treachery, as in that event inquiries could be set on foot concerning him, which would at least satisfy his friends as to his fate.

Having sealed this epistle, he summoned Guy Addlepate to his presence, and slipping a piece of money into his hand, he said—

"You will convey this immediately to Mistress Blanche Heriot; and should she ask any questions concerning me, you will say that I have gone on pressing business of the king's, and shall return here as soon as my duty will permit."

"Hadn't you better have said all that in your letter, sir?" returned Guy, scratching his ear. "You must know I've but a short memory when love messages are concerned, and perhaps the young lady would not be best pleased if I was to forget anything you have told me."

"I have mentioned something to the same effect in the note you are to be the bearer of," answered Neville, "but she will doubtless make further inquiries of you, and I desire that she may be thoroughly satisfied as to the occasion of my abrupt departure. You will also look well at the countenance of this stranger, and should aught happen to me, you will be able to identify the person in whose company I leave this place."

"I could identify him from among a thousand," returned Guy, after having a good stare at the man.

"Your suspicions against me are unfounded," exclaimed the stranger, addressing himself to Neville. "I have come hither at no little risk to myself since a man can now scarcely tell a friend from a foe, and yet you persist in believing that I have some evil design either against your life or liberty."

"That," replied the other, "is because you have brought no proof by which I may know you came from friends."

"I gave you the red rose that I was desired to do."

"True, but red roses are by no means scarce at this time of the year," replied Neville, "and you may have plucked one on your way hither, for aught I can tell. However, I have said I will go with you, and will keep my word whatever may be the consequence. But beware of perfidy, for I am well armed, and will sell my life dearly if there be occasion for it."

"Know you," exclaimed the stranger, pointing towards Guy Addlepate, "that you are filling this fool's ears with things tha he would be sure to report where you have desired him to go on a message? Methinks, sir, you might have had more discretion than to do that which will excite alarm where none need be entertained."

"Leave us, sirrah," exclaimed Neville, impatiently, motioning Guy from the room. "You have received your instructions, and I desire that no delay takes place in carrying them into effect."

As the man took his departure, the stranger once more closed the door, and inquired of Neville whether he was now ready to depart.

"I shall be in a few minutes," replied the young man; "but surely there can be no need of the haste you appear so anxious to make."

"We have a long distance to go," answered the other, "and as we shall not be able to travel along the high-road for fear of interruption, it will be necessary to leave this place with as little delay as possible."

"How do you travel?"

"On horseback."

"Are you provided with a steed?"

"Oh, yes," replied the man; "I rode from the camp, but left my horse a little before I came to this town, lest any curiosity should be excited. These are difficult times, you know, sir; and should the Yorkist party learn that I belong to the other side, my life would not be worth an hour's purchase. So now, young sir, order your horse to be got in readiness, and, if luck attends us, we'll place half-a-dozen miles between ourselves and this town before we are an hour older."

Neville having made up his mind to run the risk of accompanying the stranger, now called to Master Froth, and telling him that sudden business of importance demanded his attendance elsewhere, he paid him his demands, and then desired that his horse might be immediately got in readiness for him.

"By St. Paul! but this is a sudden start at any rate," exclaimed the host. "I expected to have a good customer for a month to come, at the very least, and now it seems you are going to leave us at a moment's notice."

"You have heard my orders," answered Neville, impatiently, "and I have neither time nor inclination to enter into any further explanation. Hasten, sirrah, and do my bidding without further parley."

"You forget, sir," exclaimed the host, willing to make an excuse for delaying the departure of the guest—"you forget that Guy Addlepate has just been sent on an errand, and he's the only man about the place that we employ as ostler."

"Then for once do the office yourself, good host," said Neville, "for my business requires dispatch, and we have far to go ere our journey is at an end."

Master Froth, though rather reluctantly, left the room; and the stranger, once more addressing Neville, said—

"There will be no need to tell this prating fool the road we are going to take, for just now it is impossible to tell our friends from our enemies; and should he happen to take part with the other side, a word of his would be sufficient to cause a pursuit."

"I believe there is little to fear from him," answered the other, "for in the first place, poor Master Froth is too much of a simpleton to take any decisive part in these troubles; and, secondly, there is a degree of honesty about the man that I think is to be trusted."

"At any rate, it will be better not to afford him an opportunity," said the stranger, "for the hope of a reward might render him less honest than you seem to imagine. By-the-by, you threw out a hint just now to the fool that conveyed your note to the young lady, and if he should chance to mention it, there's no telling where the mischief may end."

"If your intentions are fair there is nothing to be afraid of," replied Neville. "What I said was done on purpose; and you now know that should treachery be afoot, there will be a fair chance of its being brought to light."

"You still suspect me, then?"

"I have seen no reason yet to do otherwise," replied the young man.

"Humph!—you will soon be convinced, then."

"I know it; and well for you it will be if my suspicions prove to be unfounded."

"Which they most assuredly will," returned the stranger. "It is a hard thing, too, that one man cannot do a good turn for another without being looked upon as an enemy in disguise."

"It is no fault of mine that I do so," exclaimed Neville; "for the mystery that attended your coming here, the very unsatisfactory answers I have received, and your anxiety to take your departure at night, all combine together to fill my mind with doubts. I have, however, a moderate share of courage and resolution, and should my worst fears prove correct, my arm shall do its utmost in my own defence. But the host returns to tell us my horse is ready. Lead the way, sir, and I will follow immediately."

Neville paused for an instant to see that his weapons were ready for immediate use; and having satisfied himself upon that point, he hastened to the door, and mounting his horse, set forward at a slow pace, accompanied by the stranger, who walked by his side. On reaching the outskirts of the town, the other paused at a small inn where his own steed was in readiness for him; and having leaped into his saddle, both he and Neville Audeley set forward at a brisk trot.

CHAPTER VI.

THE TRAVELLERS.—THE OLD HUT.—THE BETRAYAL.

THE night was dark and cheerless, but the two travellers proceeded for some few miles without altering their speed; but when at length they turned into a narrower and less-frequented road, they found their difficulties increase, and instead of the sharp pace they had hitherto kept up, they now found themselves obliged to proceed more slowly and cautiously, lest their horses should stumble and themselves be thrown into the mire.

"'Tis strange," said Neville, at last, "that you should have chosen this by-road, when the highway afforded so much better facilities for our journey."

"It is not strange," replied the other, "when you remember what I said before we started; I told you we must avoid meeting any one, and our only way to do so is to take the ways that are least frequented."

"And who, pray, have we to fear?"

"Thousands of persons," replied the stranger. "There are parties of our enemies constantly prowling about; and should we chance to fall in with any of them, we should be doomed to certain death. These are fearful times, and it behoves us to take every precaution we can against danger."

"But at the pace we are now going," said Neville, "we can scarcely expect to reach Tewkesbury under a three-days journey."

"We shall not always keep to such roads as these," answered the other. "Now and then we may venture upon the highway; and when we do so, we must make the best use we can of the opportunity."

"And you are now on your way to the camp of the Earl of Warwick?"

"I am."

"Know you what number of troops he musters?"

"I believe about thirty thousand."

Neville paused for a few minutes, and then inquired how many the enemy were expected to be able to bring into the field?

"About the same number, I believe," replied the other; "but accounts vary; some say they greatly exceed the Lancastrians, and others, that they fall very far short of them. The question, however, will very soon be set at rest, for the two armies will be drawn out against each other, and the issue will either establish one king upon his throne, or place another in his stead."

The road by this time began to present more difficulties than ever, and the conversation was necessarily broken off to enable the riders to pick their way with more certainty. Neville now regretted more than he had done at first, the ease with which he had been prevailed upon to undertake this difficult task in the dark; but it was too late to retrieve the error, and he proceeded onwards, his horse stumbling at almost every step, and himself occasionally giving way to the anger which had thus been provokingly brought forth. His companion, on the contrary, seemed to take the rough with the smooth with the most perfect composure, encouraging his companion to go on, and suggesting that, as matters had apparently come to the worst, there was every reason to hope they would soon mend. This might have been all very well if there had been any prospect of a favourable turn taking place; but the further they went, the more the difficulties increased, till at length the patience of Neville Audeley became fairly exhausted.

"Keep your patience, sir, I pray you," exclaimed the stranger, with the most provoking indifference. "The road is none of the best, I grant you; but we have contrived so far to keep from falling into bad company, and methinks that should be some consolation to you."

"A very sorry one," answered Neville, in a tone that indicated no very good humour. "My horse is worn out with the exertion he has been forced to go through, and I can foresee that it will be impossible to continue our journey much further without rest."

"And rest we'll have presently," replied the other; "for I foresaw that we should be obliged to stop somewhere, and accordingly made arrangements to put up for a little while at a cottage that stands by the road-side."

"How far is the place off that you speak of?" asked Neville Audeley.

"Oh, but a short distance," answered the other. "I ordered them to set up a light in the window, to serve as a guide for us; and see yonder where it burns. So now, sir, I give you joy, for our journey for this night is nearly at an end."

These words were uttered with a peculiar tone that once more roused the suspicions of the young man; and riding close to the side of his companion, he said, with all the firmness he could assume—

"There is something more in this, sirrah, than I can understand. You best know whether I have been betrayed or not; but should my suspicions be confirmed, your own life shall be sacrificed to my fury!"

"Really, sir," answered the other, "I marvel how you can suspect me of treachery. Have I not brought you thus far in safety; and if I had meant to have dealt unfairly by you, could it not have been done long before this?"

"You are the best judge of your own motives," exclaimed Neville; "but to say the least of it, your conduct gives ample grounds for suspicion. We have been companions together during thus much of the journey; but if you would convince me of your good faith, you will ride onwards, and leave me to pursue the remainder of my journey alone."

"Nay, you must be mad to propose such a thing," answered the stranger "The way is dangerous, I tell you, and surely there is more safety for two persons travelling together than for one."

"And what if I choose to risk the danger you talk so much about?"

"Why, then I should think you a wrong-headed youngster," answered the other; "and flattering myself that I possess more prudence than yourself, I should insist upon accompanying you even at the risk of incurring your displeasure."

"You grow insolent."

"At least I have honesty enough to speak my mind freely," replied the stranger, in the same careless tone that he had all along assumed. "You have taken it into your head that I mean you harm, but it is yet to be proved whether I do so or not."

"And if you do," exclaimed Neville Audeley, "you know the consequences."

"This is not the first time you have menaced me," returned the stranger; "and yet, supposing I meant to betray you, do you suppose I should have not taken means to prevent danger to myself?"

"That, perhaps, may be more easily said than done."

"Come—come, young man," exclaimed the other, "it is time you and I should understand one another better than this. Learn to think more favourable of me; for with all this vapouring of yours, there is no real ground of complaint yet. I grant you our road has not been the best that might have been picked out, and day might have been better for travelling than night; but we have been compelled to adopt both these alternatives, and, therefore, no blame rests upon me."

" I was a fool to come with you," cried Neville, " without better warrant that your purpose was a friendly one."

" Nay, don't begin to fall out with yourself," returned the other.   " What's done can't be undone, you know ; so the wisest thing you can do, will be to follow your destiny and trust to good fortune."

" All my good fortune seems to have abandoned me," answered the young man

SIR PHILIP WARRENNE FORBID HUGH LANERET THE MANOR-HOUSE.

with vexation. " I listened with too much credence to your words ; and if I have been deceived by them. I must release myself from the consequences in the best way I can.   At any rate, I will not submit to the loss of liberty, and will lose my life in battling against my foes rather than endure the mortification of knowing that my own folly has placed me at the mercy of others."

"It seems, sir, by your words," observed the stranger, "that you have private enemies."

"I have one that I know of," answered Neville; "and it may be, I have another who, at this moment, is no great distance from me."

"That, of course, is meaning me," returned his companion; "but who, I prithee, is the first mentioned?"

"One who I shall not name at present."

"You are in the right there," said the stranger, "for perhaps he is no more a foe to you than I am. But a truce to this;—we are now near the cottage I spoke of, and perhaps a little rest will serve to put you in a better humour."

"And our horses?"

"Will be taken good care of," replied the other; "I have made all necessary arrangements beforehand, and no doubt my orders have been strictly complied with."

They had now reached the door of a miserable-looking cottage, from whence not a sound issued to show that it was inhabited. The stranger gave a peculiar kind of whistle, upon which a bustle was heard within, and the door flying open as if by magic, a number of persons rushed out; and before Neville could offer any resistance, he was dragged violently from his horse, and the arms which he had about him were taken away. Still, however, he determined not to yield passively, and grappling with the first ruffian that came within his reach, he seemed for some few seconds to have the advantage; but a violent blow from a club laid him senseless.

How long he remained in this state he knew not; but on recovering himself, he found he had been conveyed to the interior of the house, and that an aged female, of forbidding aspect, had been occupied in restoring him to animation, whilst his captors, among whom was the stranger, were seated round the hearth drinking and carousing. At that moment a groan that he uttered startled them, and he heard one of the ruffians say—

"The youngster ain't dead yet, it seems; so, after all, we shall have the chance of seeing one of King Edward's enemies swinging on the church belfry."

"Ay, ay, Tom," responded the other; "I thought the gentle tap on the head I gave him wouldn't do the job. I only gave him a slight touch just to make him leave-go his hold upon your throat, and down he went upon the ground as if he had been shot."

"A gentle touch you call it," exclaimed the first speaker; "why it sounded like a bell; and all I can say is, Heaven preserve my sconce from such a slight rap as you call it."

"Why do I thus find myself a prisoner in the hands of men that I know not?" demanded Neville, as soon as he could gain the power of utterance. "By what right, I ask, do you deprive me of liberty."

"Why, you must ask Master Stephen Ratcliffe, if you want any questions answered," returned the man to whom he had addressed himself. "He claims the honour of being master over us; so of course we must not take the business out of his hands."

"And which among you is named Stephen Ratcliffe?" demanded Neville, gazing anxiously upon the faces that surrounded him.

"I am," exclaimed the stranger, who had so perfidiously led him into the snare.

"Villain!" cried Neville Audeley; "you have scarcely deceived me, for I all along suspected you to be the treacherous emissary of some secret foe."

"Come, come, fellow-traveller," returned Stephen, "let's have no hard names if you please. What I've done I'm to be paid for; and where is the man, I should like to know, who would refuse gold when it's to be earned in an honest way?"

"And who is it," asked Neville, "that has paid you to commit this foul act?"

"Why, I suppose there's no occasion to make a secret of it any longer," replied the other; "so I may as well tell you at once that I was employed by one Master Hugh Laneret, who, I dare say, you know well-enough."

"Too well," exclaimed the young man; "and he has done this base deed that he may rid himself of a rival who was more fortunate than he was in obtaining the love of a virtuous maiden."

"Ah! there was a girl in the case, I remember," answered the other. "They call her—let me see, what was it? oh, Blanche Heriot. A pretty name enough, my masters; but I suppose she'll soon change it to Laneret, which sounds almost as well."

A loud laugh followed this sally; the drinking cups were emptied and filled again; and it seemed that the revellers were about to change the subject of conversation, when Neville, unable to endure the suspense, inquired into whose hands he had fallen?

"Why, into very honest hands, I can assure you," replied Stephen Ratcliffe. "The truth is, we are the soldiers of King Edward, and——"

"Say, rather, of the rebel Edward," exclaimed Neville. "Yet you told me you were in the service King Henry, and had been dispatched on an errand to me by the Earl of Warwick."

"Why, to be sure I did," returned the other, "or you would never have fallen so nicely into the snare. Hugh Laneret found you were not to be got rid of by fair means, so he consulted me on the subject, and, as he offered a good round sum in gold, I undertook to relieve him from all further uneasiness on your account. His suit to Blanche Heriot will prosper now, and the foolish girl will soon be reconciled to the change, when she finds that her dear Neville is no more."

"Villain!" exclaimed the young man, "you may gibe me now, because I am rendered harmless by the numbers that surround you. But urge me not too far, or I may chastise your insolence, even though the next instant I perish under the daggers of your worthless associates."

"He calls us worthless," muttered one of the fellows. "Oh, that it would not anger our superiors were we to slay him."

"Nay, you must not do that, whatever provocation you may receive," answered Stephen Ratcliffe, with a caustic sneer. "Edward must need make an example of some that are in rebellion against him, and I see no reason why this youngster should not grace a gibbet as well as a better man."

"Very true," muttered his companions.

"Besides," he said, "it will be a satisfaction to Hugh Laneret, for he hates him as I do water, and will be well pleased to see him suffer an ignominious punishment."

"Let Hugh Laneret beware lest such a fate should fall to his own share," exclaimed Neville. "For my own part I can look forward to the future with calmness, well knowing that if I perish, there will be those left behind who will not suffer my death to be unavenged."

"A very comfortable consolation, truly," added Stephen Ratcliffe; "but suppose our side wins the battle—which seems likely—where will your friends be that are to do the service you talk about? Some will have fallen in the strife, and the rest will meet the fate that all traitors deserve."

"And if all traitors met their desert," answered Neville Audley, "your body would ere now have been blackening and festering on the gibbet."

"If you say that again," muttered Stephen, "I'll send my poniard through your heart!"

"Do so," exclaimed Neville, "for I am weary of the life that has been thus blighted. Nay, had I not been deprived of my weapons, my breathless corse had been the only prisoner you could boast of having."

"Why, that's just what I thought," answered Stephen, "and for that reason you were disarmed before any mischief was done. You shall hang, Neville Audeley, as surely as that I now tell you so."

"Come, Stephen Ratcliffe," cried the old woman we have before alluded to, "don't taunt the poor gentleman in this cruel way. He's your prisoner, and it's quite hard enough to know one must be hanged, without being told so."

'Peace, beldame, or you will chance to get a stab yourself," exclaimed the ruffian furiously. "He is an enemy to the noble prince we serve, and ought to be made to suffer for it."

"So he will if what you say is true."

"The less you say about this matter, the better it will be for you," interposed one of the men. "Master Stephen Ratcliffe is not a man to be thwarted in his pleasures, and if he pleases to torment the prisoner a little, it's nothing to you."

"Well argued, Luke Omerod," exclaimed Stephen, who, by this time, began to be the worse for what he had drunk. "That's putting the question in its right light; and all I have to say about it is, if the prisoner don't like it, he had better leave our company."

"I dare say he would, Master Stephen, if we would let him," replied the other. "But we know better than to do that, for, besides what you get from Hugh Laneret, we shall have a reward from our general for having made a prisoner of one of the Lancastrians. So, take another cup round, my friends, for the daylight will soon be upon us now, and we must be off to Cirencester with the earliest dawn, and there lodge the young gentleman till further orders are received."

"Well," exclaimed Stephen, raising his cup, "here's health and success to the noble King Edward the Fourth, and may he speedily be upon the throne that is now filled by an usurper. What say you to that, Master Neville Audeley? Will you drink the toast, man, and try whether it may save your miserable neck from the gallows?"

"I would rather perish by the slowest tortures that can be invented," answered Neville, indignantly, "than blacken my soul by wishing success to the man whom I regard as a rebel to my lawful sovereign."

"Ay, young man, you may spit your venom at him now," exclaimed Stephen Ratcliffe, "because the worst you can say or do can't make your fate worse. So we'll pardon the treason you have uttered, and drink his health without your assistance."

Every cup was then raised, and due honour having been done to the toast, Stephen desired the old woman to place more wine upon the table.

"There is no more," she replied.

"Thou liest, old hag!"

"I have told you the truth, Master Stephen," she said, "for the house contains not another drop of liquor."

"Then take the cup, since there's nothing more to put in it," he exclaimed, and throwing the vessel at her head with all his force, it dashed against the wall, and flew into a thousand pieces.

"Shame on you, Stephen Ratcliffe," exclaimed one of the men who sat near him; "would you harm the old woman because the liquor is all gone?"

"Ay, and I'll harm thee too, if thou preachest to me," he exclaimed, wrathfully; "what! am I to be called to account for every trifling act I commit?"

"It would have been no trifle had it happened to strike her," answered the other; "and it passed between half an inch of her head."

"And what, if it had struck her," answered the other; "would you have been the old hag's champion?"

"It's likely enough I might," returned the other; "and perhaps, bully Ratcliffe, you might not have got the best of it."

"We'll see that presently," exclaimed Stephen; and jumping from his seat, he seized his adversary with so sudden a grasp, that the other had not time to elude him. He, however, grappled with his antagonist, and passing both arms round his body, obtained an advantage which the other was unable to deprive him of. In this way they continued to struggle for a minute or two, when the other, raising the body of Stephen Ratcliffe in his arms, threw him with tremendous violence to the ground, but at the same time fell with him. The shock seemed for a moment to stupify them both; but after laying there for a short time, they both rose at the same instant, and Ratcliffe, drawing his dagger, was rushing forward to plunge it in the body of his antagonist, when Neville Audeley, hastily interposing himself between them, arrested his arm ere the fatal blow was struck.

"Ha!" exclaimed Stephen, "am I to be foiled—and by you too?"

"You may thank me for saving you from the crime of murder," answered the young man; "you have this day done me an injury, and I have returned it with a favour."

"And such a favour as I will return with interest," exclaimed Stephen; "for though he has been saved, you shall not so easily escape my vengeance."

"Nay, it's time this was put an end to," interposed Luke Ormerod, "for though we have made the young fellow a prisoner, we are not to kill him with our own hands. He shall be protected, Stephen, if I stand alone to do it."

"Well, I believe I've made a fool of myself," muttered Stephen Ratcliffe, who by this time had come a little to his senses. "But you must own I was provoked, for what right had any one to interfere, merely because I threw a cup at the old beldame's head? I didn't hurt her, and that's enough."

"The less that's said about it the better, or we shall only get to words again," exclaimed Luke Ormerod. "The affair has been settled comfortably; so now, as the daylight's coming on, let's to horse and away."

"With all my heart," said Stephen; "but whatever we do, let's take care of the prisoner. Remember, there's a heavy reward depending upon him, and if he attempt to escape, let a pistol bullet be sent through his head."

"You need be under no apprehension of that kind," replied Neville; "for in spite of what you have said, I cannot believe your superiors would commit a wanton cruelty upon a man whose only crime consists in entertaining a different opinion to their own. They may, perhaps, imprison me, but I feel assured my life will be perfectly safe in their hands."

"It will be a shame if they don't hang you after all the trouble I've had," exclaimed Stephen Ratcliffe. "However, we won't talk about that now, so follow me, comrades, and let it be your task, Luke, to see to the prisoner."

They left the house as he spoke; and the horses being ready at the door, the whole party was quickly mounted, and the word being given, they set forward at a smart pace towards the ancient town of Cirencester.

CHAPTER VII.

FEARFUL SURMISES.—THE OFFER OF FRIENDSHIP.—THE FOE.

WE must now leave Neville and return to Blanche Heriot, whose alarm was excited to the highest degree when she read the hasty note that had been sent by the hands of Guy Addlepate, who stood watching her as she read it, and wondering what it could contain to occasion so much agitation. At length, having perused it over and over again, she turned towards the messenger, and eagerly inquired what sort of person it was with whom Neville Audeley was about to take his departure.

"Why, really, Miss, I did not stop to take his portrait," answered Guy, scarcely knowing what to say; "and yet I did have a pretty good look at him too, for the young gentleman desired me to do so in case it might afterwards be necessary to 'dentify him, as he called it."

"It is plain, then, that he was not without suspicions that some foul plot had been formed against him," cried Blanche, with terror.

"That's just the notion I had about it myself," returned Guy, "for the chap didn't seem as if he liked me to look at him, and his face was so muffled up, that I think I should hardly be able to know him again."

"Did you hear what business he wanted to go upon?" demanded our heroine.

"No, they wouldn't say much before me," returned the other; "and yet, though folks sometimes call me a fool, I think I can see through a mill-stone as far as any of them. There was a red rose lying on the table, Miss, and——'

"A red rose?" cried Blanche, interrupting him; "and what augur you from that?"

"Ay, what indeed!" answered Guy Addlepate. "Why neither more nor less than that Master Neville Audeley has gone off to join the Earl of Warwick, who they say has got a large army under him to fight the enemy when they land."

"It must be so," said Blanche, inwardly; "and yet, had such been the case, he would surely have come to bid me farewell ere he took his departure."

"Perhaps he hadn't time," returned Guy, by whom the latter part of this speech had been overheard. "The stranger was in a desperate hurry to get him off, and all Master Neville could do was to write the note he sent me with."

"Alas! alas! I fear he has been betrayed!" cried our heroine, in accents of the deepest despair. "This is some scheme to entrap him; and he will be murdered by those who have been engaged in the cruel plot against him."

"Of whom are you speaking, my dear Blanche?" demanded Sir Philip Warrenne, who had entered the room unobserved during the utterance of these words, "your looks and accents are those of terror, yet I would fain hope your alarm has, in this instance, been unnecessarily excited."

"Would that you could convince me of it," she replied. "Neville Audeley has suddenly left the place in company with a stranger, and I fear some evil is intended towards him."

"Nay, you must not give way to careless alarm," answered Sir Philip, tenderly pressing her hand. "Neville is certainly master of his own actions, and I can see nothing very extraordinary in his having left the place, since, I dare say, business of importance has demanded his presence elsewhere."

"But he himself," answered Blanche, "was, I believe, not without suspicions that treachery was intended."

"Then why was he foolish enough to go with a stranger?" asked the knight. "No, no, Blanche, your woman's fears have, I see, prevailed, and you must needs believe your lover in some desperate dilemma. But who, I prithee, is the person he has gone with? Surely he must have known something of the man, or he never would have been mad enough to trust him."

"From what this person tells me," replied our heroine, "Neville knew nothing of him. A red rose was lying upon the table; and from that I infer he has been imposed on by a pretended message from the leaders of King Henry's party."

"And why may not such a message really have been sent?" demanded Sir Philip. "It is well known that a decisive blow will soon be struck for bringing this matter to an issue, and Neville may have been sent for to head his troops under the Earl of Warwick."

"Yet if that had been the case," returned Blanche, "what occasion was there for the stranger to observe so much secrecy?"

"Because it is dangerous for a man to express himself too openly," answered Sir Philip. "Besides, Neville Audeley must have been tolerably well assured of the man's fidelity, or he would not have gone away in his company. But I see you have a note in your hand, Blanche, which I suppose is from your lover."

"It is."

"And what says he in explanation of this affair?"

"Nothing that in any way serves to clear up the mystery," she replied. "He speaks of the stranger's arrival, and says it is necessary to depart with him immediately."

"Does he say what road they are going to journey?"

"Yes," she replied; "he speaks of Tewkesbury as being their place of destination."

"Oh, then I'll answer for it, there's nothing to be afraid of," exclaimed Sir

Philip; "for Tewkesbury is, I know, the rendezvous of Warwick's army, and in reaching that place he will be in the midst of friends."

"That is," sighed Blanche, "if he should ever be permitted to reach it."

"Which I very much doubt," interposed Guy Addlepate; whose presence had been almost forgotten.

"And what reason have you," demanded Sir Philip, "for coming to so sage an opinion?"

"Simply," answered the rustic, "because I didn't like the look of the man he went away with."

"An excellent reason," exclaimed the knight; "and pray did Master Neville Audeley seem to feel any scruples about following him?"

"To tell you the truth, Sir Philip, I don't think he half liked it," replied Guy. "He wanted to stop till the morning, but the stranger wouldn't have it; and so I was sent with a letter to the young lady with an apology for going away so suddenly."

"How comes it, sirrah," demanded Sir Philip, "that you know so much of what passed in what appears to have been a private conversation?"

"Why the truth is," answered Guy, "there was something so mysterious about the whole affair, that I thought to myself somebody ought to take an interest in the young gentleman's concerns, and though listeners seldom hear any good of themselves, I popped my hear to the key-hole, and overheard almost everything that passed."

"Humph! and what did you gather from it?"

"Nothing, so please your knightship."

"Idiot! then what good have you done?"

"Very little, I believe," replied the rustic, "but that was no fault of mine, you know, for I did my best, and if the strange gentleman wouldn't speak out his mind more plainly, I couldn't help it. It's certain, however, that something was said about the Earl of Warwick, and so I suppose they have set out to join the army."

"You merely imagine this?"

"That's all I can do," replied Guy; "seeing that neither of them thought proper to explain themselves before me."

"Well, after all, Blanche," said Sir Philip Warrenne, "I see no great reason for alarm. Neville, I dare say, was pretty well convinced before-hand that he had nothing to fear from treachery; and even if this man should be the villain you imagine, he will not, if single-handed, have any advantage over Audeley, who, I have heard, is brave and daring when beset with danger. He would surely be a match for this stranger if driven to extremity; and, in that case, I can see very little cause for alarm."

"I would fain think so myself," answered the maiden; "but the more I reflect upon it, the more danger there appears to be. If the man is treacherous, he will have taken care to be joined by his associates when least his villanous purposes are suspected."

"And thus it is," exclaimed Sir Philip, "that you torture yourself with imaginary dangers."

"Heaven grant they may only be imaginary ones," replied Blanche, with a sigh. "There seems, however, too much reason to suspect otherwise, though I have tried to believe my fears are groundless. It is possible, however, they may have taken the road to Tewkesbury, as the man said, and if there was only a certainty of it, I would yet make one effort to save Neville from destruction."

"Why, thou foolish, love-sick girl," exclaimed the knight, "what could thou do to save him from peril, even supposing he was threatened with any?"

"It should be tried, at all events," she cried resolutely.

"And you would get laughed at for your pains," replied Sir Philip. "Come, come, Blanche, get rid of this romantic notion, and take advice from one who is old enough to give it. Wait patiently, I say, for a few days, and if nothing satisfactory is heard of Neville Audeley, I will make a stir in the business."

"A few days hence may be too late," she replied, "and how bitterly should I then have to reproach myself for making no effort to rescue him from the hands of his enemies."

They were now interrupted by the arrival of Herrick Evenden, who, hurrying into the room without ceremony, exclaimed—

"Confound all bad roads, say I, for my horse is ruined for life, and I've had the mortification of coming back from a fruitless errand. They are gone, Sir Philip, and I believe the devil himself would not be able to overtake them, unless he had a better road to take than I have had."

"Of what are you speaking, Herrick?" asked the knight.

"Why, of Neville Audeley and that rascally stranger, to be sure," replied the young man. "I saw them leave the Golden Cross together, and being rather suspicious that something wrong was going on, I hurried home, saddled my horse with all speed, and followed in pursuit."

"And of course failed to overtake them?"

"I have failed most woefully," replied Herrick; "and have so strained my horse in one of the muddy lanes I went down, that being unable to get him any further, I was obliged to tie him to a tree and trudge back on foot. So, do you hear, Guy Addlepate, run with all the speed you can to a little beyond Mable's Cross, where you will find the poor beast in a miserable plight enough I can tell you. Bring him home, my good fellow, and this broad piece of silver shall be your guerdon."

Guy waited for no second bidding, and as he left the room Sir Philip inquired of the young man if he could throw any light upon the events of the last two or three hours.

"Very little, I'm afraid, Sir Philip,' replied Herrick. "You have heard, of course, that Neville has been foolish enough to place himself under the guidance of a perfect stranger, and I'm afraid he will discover his rashness when too late"

"I fear so too," sighed Blanche; "though my uncle would fain persuade me there is no cause for alarm."

"So I might have thought myself," replied Herrick; "but I saw that villain Hugh Laneret, lurking about the place; and then I was sure mischief was afloat."

"Hugh Laneret!" cried our heroine, in alarm—"then there is indeed too much reason to believe that the life of Neville is aimed at. I have suspectd from the beginning that was at the bottom of all this, and your words serve to confirm my worst fears."

"Nay, then I am sorry I said anything about it," returned Herrick; "but as I have unwittingly been the occasion of increasing your fears, I will, at least make amends by doing my best towards discovering the mystery that at present involves the fate of our young friend. Would that I kuew, for certain the direction they have taken, and this stranger, whoever he is, should find that he has brought an hornet's nest about his ears."

"I rather think it will not be so difficult as you imagine to trace their course," said Sir Philip Warrenne, "for the stranger mentioned Tewkesbury as being the place where he was going to, and there, no doubt, they may be found, if no time be lost in going in pursuit."

"There I cannot agree with you," replied the young man, "if the fellow said Tewkesbury was the place of their destination, we may be pretty certain that it was only intended as a blind. However, I will take an immediate opportunity to see Hugh Laneret, and will so mention the subject to him that I shall be able to ascertain whether he is really concerned in this affair or not."

"And thus involve yourself in a quarrel with one whose soul is bent on deeds of villany!" cried Blanche.

"Well," answered the other, "and if I do so, maiden, my hand is well enough able to take care of my head. This Hugh Laneret is a rascal, as I believe every body knows; but it follows not that he is to go on his evil ways according to the bent of his own humour. I, for one, at least, fear him not; and perhaps the time may not be very far distant when he will find one who heeds him not."

".Take care how you quarrel with him," exclaimed Sir Philip Warrenne; "for I should be loth to see your generous ardour involve you in the destruction that has befallen so many others. If he be concerned in this plot against Neville Audeley, he will have wit enough to conceal the fact from the world; and the end of it will be, that you get entangled in an affair that may terminate but with your own life."

"My life would be an unworthy one were I to be afraid of risking it to defeat the treachery of a scoundrel," answered Herrick, warmly.

"Besides, pretty Mistress Blanche, here, is grieving for the fate of her lover; and hang me if ever I could see a woman in trouble without doing my best to help her out of it; so come what may, I'll see Hugh Laneret, and ascertain whether he has had any share in this business."

"Your generosity leads you headlong in rashness," exclaimed Sir Philip. "For my own part I would, in my younger days, have risked my life in a cause similar to this; but I am now old enough to see that caution is the better part of valour; and therefore I entreat you to think well of this matter before you plunge into difficulties from which it will not be very easy to extricate yourself."

"And what will Blanche think of me," asked Herrick, "if I sit myself down quietly at such a juncture as this? Will she not think me a coward and unworthy to hold communion with my fellow men?"

"I shall ever think of your conduct with gratitude," she replied. "Sir Philip's advice, however, should be taken; and I therefore pray you to wait patiently till the morning, and I dare say some plan may be thought of that will lead to the discovery we have so much at heart. For my own part I have almost resolved upon a step that, though it may appear somewhat rash, will probably foil the base designs of those who have been plotting against the liberty, if not the life, of Neville Audeley."

"In the name of Heaven, what mean you?" demanded her guardian, with surprise.

"At present," she replied, "the secret must be kept deeply buried in my own heart. I may be called a rash and headstrong girl, but this is no common danger, and, banishing all womanly timidity, I will save Neville or perish myself."

"Girl! your words terrify me," said Sir Philip. "You surely would not venture to do aught that may serve to increase the fury of this wayward man?"

"If I do," she replied, "I will take care that the consequences of my own acts fall upon no one but myself. This is no time, however, to shrink from personal danger, for the life of Neville Audeley may be at stake, and it shall be my task either to save or perish with him."

"And what," asked Sir Philip, "can a young and timid girl like you expect to do against one of ferocious passions like Hugh Laneret? His evil deeds are known to everybody; and it would, therefore, be madness for you to attempt aught that may serve to increase his fury."

"I may be young, as you have said, sir," answered our heroine, firmly; "but timid I shall not prove to be when I have a task like this before me. Besides, Hugh Laneret already knows the contempt in which I hold him; and it will, therefore, be impossible for me to increase the anger my rejection of his addresses has given rise to."

"Nay," exclaimed Herrick Evenden, "let me add my entreaties to those of your guardian, that you will take no steps in this affair till it has been well weighed in your mind. I will myself undertake whatever risk it may be; and you have my sacred promise, Blanche, that I will use every means in my power to search out where Neville Audeley has been conveyed to."

"And in the meantime," sighed Blanche, "he may be sacrificed to the vengeance of the enemy."

"Of that I believe there is little fear," answered the young man. "Laneret may have formed a design against the liberty of his rival, but he will scarcely venture to commit an act of violence that he would hereafter be called upon to answer for with his own life."

"You would convince me, then," she said, "that Neville is not in imminent danger?"

"I think he is not," replied Herrick; "and can almost venture to promise that if you have patience, you will see him again."

Ere Blanche could reply to this, her attendant, Kate Poynet, entered the room with a flushed and disturbed countenance, that indicated no little purturbation."

"Oh, ma'am he's here!" she exclaimed, in terrified accents, "and seems so gloomy and sulky that I was glad to run away as fast as my legs would carry me."

"Of whom do you speak?" demanded Blanche, though her own fears had already anticipated the reply.

"Why, that ill-looking fellow, Hugh Laneret," answered the girl.

"By Heaven's he shall leave the house quicker than he came to it!" exclaimed, Herrick, drawing his sword and making towards the door. Sir Philip, however saw the danger he was about to bring upon himself, and taking his arm, he said—

"Your rashness, Herrick Evenden, though caused by a generous sympathy in our behalf, will bring ruin upon those it is your design to serve. Remember, boy, we are not yet certain that Hugh Laneret has had any share in this business, and this intemperance will give him an advantage that may prove fatal to us."

"Would you allow him then to enter your house, when there is such strong suspicions against him?"

"We must needs submit when there is no help for it," replied Sir Philip Warrenne. "He is here it seems, and if Blanche can endure his presence for a short time, he shall be admitted to an interview, during which we may hear something that will afford a link by which to connect the evidence we must endeavour to get up against him."

"Am I to tell him, then," said Kate, "that you will see him?"

"You are," answered Sir Philip; and Kate, though reluctantly enough, slowly left the room to deliver the message with which she was charged.

"I trust, my dear Blanche," continued her guardian, "that you will see the prudence of receiving Hugh Laneret with an appearance of courtesy. Your doing so will curb his violence, and we may gather something that will prove serviceable to him we would rescue. But hark! I hear his footstep! be firm, girl, and this may turn out better than you expect."

He had scarcely done speaking, when Hugh Laneret strode into the room with a haughty and insolent air. To Blanche and her guardian he bowed with constrained civility, but as his eye rested upon Herrick Evenden, a slight frown gathered upon his brow; and addressing himself to our heroine, he said—

"I had hoped, Blanche, that for once I might have been favoured with a private interview. It seems, however, that you are engaged with more agreeable company; and I will therefore take my leave till a more favourable opportunity presents itself."

"Those you see here are my friends," continued Blanche, coldly; "and if you remember the terms upon which we last parted, you can scarcely expect that I will again grant you a private interview. I will, however, give you the credit of some little kindness in the present instance, since I suppose you have come to offer your assistance towards discovering the mystery that hangs over the sudden disappearance of Neville Audeley."

"I will take no credit to myself but what I am conscious of deserving," returned Laneret, gloomily. "I feel too little interest in the person you have just named to make any exertion in his behalf; and even if I knew where he is, it is much to be questioned whether I should offer either advice or assistance towards discovering his retreat."

"Then, let me tell you, sir," interposed Sir Philip, "that your visit to my house might have been dispensed with. Neville Audeley is a friend whom I esteem; and those who regard him in any other light will be looked upon as enemies of my own."

"Yet I came," answered Hugh Laneret, "to offer you my services and friendship."

"Ay, upon certain conditions, I suppose?"

"Exactly so," returned the other. "Let Blanche receive me henceforward as her affianced husband, and it may be in my power to procure the liberation of him she is so deeply concerned for."

"Ah!" cried our heroine, eagerly; "then you confess to a knowledge of his present situation?"

"I confess nothing," answered Laneret.

"But you know where he is?"

"I do."

"Then, in Heaven's name," exclaimed Blanche, "I conjure you to tell me where we may find him."

"That," replied the other, "is asking a favour when you have expressed a determination not to grant one in return. You have yourself to blame, girl, for having made me his enemy, and should aught befall him the fault will be your own."

"Monster!" cried Blanche; "do you exult in thus possessing a fatal power over one who never harmed you?"

"He has harmed me," replied Laneret; "and your continued obstinacy confirms it."

"Methinks," exclaimed Herrick Evenden, "you might exhibit less bravado towards a female you profess to love."

"And you," retorted the other, "might have more courtesy than to interfere in an affair that concerns you not. I came here to speak to Blanche Heriot, and not to be insulted by a prating fool, whom I regard as being beneath my contempt."

"Hugh Laneret," exclaimed the youth, "if I draw not upon you now it is from deference to those in whose presence we both stand. You have chosen to insult me, and be assured, the time is not far distant when your life or mine shall be sacrificed in the quarrel that has originated with yourself."

"For Heaven's sake, let this matter cease without further anger on either side," interposed Sir Philip Warrenne. "Hugh Laneret, depart from us, I entreat, without seeking to widen the breach you have already made. Herrick Evenden is hot and impetuous; but it is my request that you will think no more of words that were uttered in sudden warmth."

"Since you intercede for him," said Laneret, with a sneer, "I will e'en forget his insolent bravado. You have my word for it that he is safe, unless he again wilfully tempts my anger."

"This insolence shall no longer be endured," exclaimed Herrick, making his way towards the door. "At the intercession of Sir Philip Warrenne, I would have looked over the past; but I now warn you to prepare yourself, for ere another hour passes away, I will demand satisfaction for your insults."

"Hugh Laneret," exclaimed Sir Philip, as the young man disappeared from the room; "I will for once trust to your honour. Yonder rash boy knows not what he utters, and I ask you to forget the impetuous words that have just escaped him."

"You need be under no apprehension on my account," answered Hugh Laneret, "for I hold him too much in contempt to notice an explosion of wrath that I despise. Besides, I leave this place immediately on taking my departure from your house, so that the young gentleman will have time to recover his coolness ere it is likely we shall meet again."

"And now, before you leave us," said Sir Philip, "let me know whether Neville Audeley is in danger?"

"I know but little of him," answered the other; "and that little would not be satisfactory to yourself."

"Ah!" cried Blanche; "his life is in peril, then?"

"That may depend upon circumstances," replied Hugh Laneret. "He is now a prisoner in the hands of the Yorkists; and he will be spared on condition that he joins the ranks of King Edward."

"Alas!" cried Blanche, "then he must perish; for I know he would rather endure the worst of tortures, than turn rebel to the cause in which his sword has been drawn."

"There is yet one other alternative," exclaimed Laneret; "let him give up all claim to your hand, Blanche Heriot, and my interest, which is quite sufficient for the purpose, shall be exerted in his behalf. Your looks tell me that you are still incredulous; but I warn you that the life of Neville depends upon yourself.

Reflect, then, upon my words; and, when next we meet, I trust you will receive me with more favour than you have now done."

He bowed coldly to her as he left the room, and Blanche could no longer restrain the tears which her situation called forth, though Sir Philip sought by every means in his power to convince her that the danger was less urgent than she imagined.

CHAPTER VIII.

A CONSULTATION.—THE PLAN DEVELOPED.—THE GUIDE.

AFTER a wearisome and restless night, Blanche rose on the following morning, still pondering on the miseries that villany had brought upon her. The certainty that Neville Audeley was in imminent danger from his enemies, was sufficient to rouse up all her energies in his behalf; and though labouring under all the disadvantages belonging to her sex, she resolved upon making a desperate effort to release him from the hands of those into whose power he had unhappily fallen. This, however, was not to be effected without the greatest hazard to herself, and her next plan was to think of some course by which she might reach Tewskesbury without her presence there being known to Hugh Laneret, whose utmost efforts would be exerted to frustrate her designs.

She was still occupied with these harassing reflections when Kate entered the room to inquire if she had any commands. The pale and anxious countenance of our heroine at once betrayed the troubles with which she was afflicted, and the attendant deeply grieved for the sorrows of her mistress at once guessed their origin, and inquired whether she could in any way afford either counsel or assistance.

"Alas!" sighed our heroine; "I fear, my good girl, you can do neither, for counsel would be thrown away upon one whose mind is already made up, and assistance cannot be afforded in the means I am about to take for the preservation of him whose danger has filled my heart with terror, that it is no longer in my power to control."

"And what scheme have you thought of," asked Kate, "that may save poor Master Neville Audeley?"

"You will say it is a wild one," answered our heroine; "but in the absence of all other hopes, I have determined to make a journey to Tewkesbury, where, perhaps, means may be discovered to effect the object upon which my soul is set."

"And does Sir Philip know of your determination?"

"He does not," replied Blanche, "nor must he hear of it till after my departure, lest he should exert his authority to prevent the task I have thus set myself."

"But surely," cried the girl, "you will never be imprudent enough to go alone?"

"Who is there," asked Blanche, "that I can ask to go with me? or, perhaps, I should say, who is there whose presence would save me from danger, supposing I am unfortunate enough to incur any?"

"I don't know that my services might do you much good," answered the attendant; "but if I might only be permitted to accompany you, I would die in your defence rather than any one should do you an injury."

"Your zeal in my service, Kate," replied our heroine, "has been too often proved to admit a doubt that your offer has been made with sincerity. I must, however, decline the proposition, as I should be unwilling to deprive Sir Philip of the only one in the household who possesses any influence over him. You must, therefore, remain with him, and should he be angry at my leaving his house without giving an intimation of my design, it will be your task to appease him till my return."

"I'll do my best for you," replied Kate; "but tell me my dear young lady, have you carefully considered all the dangers you are about to expose yourself to, and the distance that Tewkesbury is from hence?"

"I have," replied her mistress; "but nothing deters me from my project."

"Yet even should you reach your place of destination," continued Kate, "it it still hardly likely you will be able to procure the release of Master Neville Audeley. If they have made a prisoner of him, as you seem to suspect, they will not part with him quite so easily as you imagine."

"That, at least, remains to be proved," answered Blanche. "I am inclined to think that men's hearts may be moved by the tears and supplications of a helpless female; and should my hopes prove true, I shall ever look back with rapture to the hour when this idea first occurred to me."

"And if you should be discovered," exclaimed Kate, "what tales and evil reports may they not spread abroad against you."

"Innocence never need fear the slanders of the wicked," answered Blanche. "I have well and carefully considered every point, and am now resolved that nothing shall deter me from the venture I have proposed. Had it been possible to consult Sir Philip Warrenne ere the step is taken, I should have been glad; but since that may not be, I must depend upon you, Kate, to make the best excuse for me in your power."

"I'll tell him you were love-sick," replied the attendant; "and even then, I suppose, he will think you have not adopted the most prudent course, since the danger you run will be sure to rouse his anger and make him deaf to everything in the shape of an excuse."

"Nay," cried Blanche, "his anger will vanish almost as soon as it is kindled. He loves Neville Audeley, even though their acquaintance has been but a brief one; and will, therefore, easily pardon the zeal that has induced me to take this means to release him. You can tell him also, that there is but too much reason to fear that Hugh Laneret entertains a deadly project against his rival, and that even the slightest delay might prove fatal in its consequences."

"I only wish, my dear lady," exclaimed Kate, "that you could be prevailed on to think the danger not so great as you say it is; for my own part I don't believe any harm will befal him; and, what's more, it don't seem to me by any means certain that Master Audeley is in trouble at all."

"There can be no doubt that treachery has been practised against him," returned Blanche, with a sigh. "The mysterious visit of this stranger, and the suddenness of their departure together at night, afford but too much certainty that villany was intended. Even Neville must have had some suspicion of it himself, or he would not have afforded the clue by which I shall be able to trace him."

"But do you think they have really gone to Tewkesbury?"

"There can be no doubt of it, since he expressly mentions that town in his note to me."

"Ay," returned Kate, "but suppose the stranger should have changed his route when they got clear of this place?"

"That is, indeed, likely," exclaimed Blanche, with dismay. "The thought struck me not; and yet if there was treachery in one respect, we must expect it in another. Still there is every necessity for exertion; and let them have taken him where they may, I will never give up my search till Neville Audeley has been found."

"And when," asked Kate, "do you intend to set forward on this dangerous journey?"

"This night, girl."

"So soon?"

"There is no time to be lost," replied Blanche. "Every moment is fraught with danger; and the sin will lie at my own door if harm should fall on Neville through neglect."

"Then you will at least take some one with you as a protector?"

"I know not any one who I could venture to take with me as a guide," returned our heroine.

"But I do, though," exclaimed her attendant; "and, what's more, I can answer for his being a man you can depend on."

"His name?"

"Tony Amblewit."

"Ay, your lover; but are you sure he will undertake the task you would impose upon him?"

"He had better not refuse me, I can tell him," answered Kate, sharply. "He has asked me to become his wife, and there would be very little chance of my ever doing so if he refused to perform my commands."

"But there is no need for his services," replied Blanche, "besides he is engaged to Master Basil Evenden, the alchemist, and, therefore, cannot fulfil the task you would thus impose upon him."

"He is only there till he can do something better for himself," returned Kate; "you forget too, my dear young lady, that Master Herrick feels a warm interest in this affair, and he will gladly dispense with the services of Anthony, when he knows that he is required as a protector during your journey."

"And may I depend on the fidelity of this man?" asked our heroine.

"If you could not, he should be no suitor of mine," replied the other. "Tony Amblewit is a silly fellow enough, but I believe he may be depended on in every instance where courage is not required."

"Then he will scarcely do for this errand," returned Blanche; "for it is likely there will be danger to encounter, and, therefore, I shall be as well without his company as with it."

"Nay, there you are mistaken," answered Kate; "for his terrors will make him cautious, and then you may avoid dangers that would otherwise present themselves. I know Tony well, and can warrant a good and faithful servant to those who treat him kindly. So try him, my dear young lady, and you will find him useful in case of interruption on the road."

"I believe it will be more prudent for me not to travel without a companion," answered Blanche, after a pause, during which she had been considering the proposition made by her faithful attendant. "Besides, I am not altogether unacquainted with Anthony, so that he will be the best guide I could have chosen. Take this purse to him, Kate, and say that I would have a couple of horses provided—one for my use, and the other for himself."

"You have not told me, madam, at what hour he is too meet you," said the girl.

"Let it be at ten o'clock to-night," replied her mistress. "By that time it will be dark, and we may take our departure without being observed."

"And where is he to wait for you?"

"At the cross road on the other side of Chertsey," answered Blanche; "bid him mind both time and place, and if I find him faithful in the discharge of his duty, I will not fail to reward him well for the trouble I am about to cause him."

Kate hurried away, and was making towards the hall for the purpose of going on her errand with as little delay as possible, when her name was pronounced by some one near; and looking round, she saw the very person she was in quest of.

"Ah, Tony," she exclaimed, "never before was I so glad to see you as I am now. I was going to seek you on an affair of life and death."

"You want some favour done, I warrant," replied Tony; "for you are never in these good humours, but when mischief's afloat. You are going to coax me, you minx; but have a care, girl, for I've been so often fooled with your fine promises, that I have made a vow never to believe you any more till I have your word that we shall be made man and wife."

"And so we will, dear Tony," she cried, "if you will only do a favour that will cost but little trouble."

"What is it?"

"To mount the horse and away."

"When ?"

"This coming night."

"And where am I to go ?" he asked.

"That is a question that must be answered another time," replied Kate. "So tell me whether you will execute this errand for me ?"

"Am I to go alone ?"

"Oh, no," answered Kate ; "you will have a rare companion, I promise you; and what's more, she will pay you liberally for the service you are called upon to perform."

"*She* ?" exclaimed Tony, with surprise ; "is it a woman, then, that I am to travel with ?"

"It is."

"And you are not jealous, Kate ?"

"There is no cause for it," replied the girl, "seeing that the person you are to attend on is my young mistress, who will keep you even at a greater distance than I have done."

"Oho ! then I foresee mischief," exclaimed Tony. "If the young lady is a going to run away in this manner, I shall get into trouble should it be known that I aided and abetted in it."

"Foolish fellow !" cried Kate; "you have nothing to fear unless it be my anger for being such a simpleton. But I suppose I must let you a little further into the secret; so to tell you the truth, Tony, my young mistress is going in search of Master Neville Audeley, who she fancies is just now in danger."

"Tell her from me, then," answered the other, "that she had better stay at home, and leave him to his chance. These are troublesome times, Kate, even for men to travel about the country; but for a woman to do so, would be downright madness."

"And if I were to tell her so till I am tired," replied the attendant, "it would be so much good time thrown away. She has made up her mind to it, and if you don't choose to bear her company, why I know somebody else that will, that's all."

"Ah ! that's meaning Guy Addlepate," exclaimed the other, in a tone of vexation. "You always bring up his name when you want me to bend to your own will; and I've promised myself the pleasure of giving him a sound thrashing the first time I have a good opportunity."

"Or rather say," returned the laughing girl, "when you can pluck up courage enough to do so. Why you know, Tony, that you are afraid of him in more ways than one ; for if I find you rebellious or disobedient to my will, you shall be sent about your business like a good-for-nothing fellow as you are."

"Here's a pretty coil about nothing," exclaimed Tony, who began to see the necessity of submission. "As if I had a thought of refusing to go with the young lady on this mad errand of her's !"

"You agree to be her guide and companion, then ?"

"Most assuredly I do."

"In that case, we are friends again, Tony," returned the girl. "Nay, say no more about it, my good fellow, for my wrath is at an end almost as soon as it is excited ; and you know if I did feel a little angry, it was because I fancied you didn't care whether a favour was done me or not."

"Upon my life," exclaimed Tony ; "you women seem to think you may turn and twist us men folks just as you please. However, we'll let that drop now, so tell me when and where I am to meet Mistress Blanche Heriot, and I promise to be in attendance."

' Why now, that's something more like what every lover ought to be," returned Kate ; "and so as you have returned to your duty, sirrah, you must know that ten o'clock to-night is the time appointed, and the place of meeting is at the cross-road on the other side of the town."

"Humph ! and where will our walk end ?"

"Walk ?" exclaimed Kate; "who said anything about walking, I should like to

know ? a couple of horses are to carry you to the end of your journey, and to you is entrusted the duty of buying them."

"What! without money ?"

"Hold your tongue, simpleton, and take this money," said Kate, putting the purse of gold into his hand. " This will be more than sufficient to purchase a couple of steeds, and what remains over you may keep, towards setting us up in housekeeping when we got married."

" And when shall that be, good Kate ?"

" When you become a wiser man," she replied ; "and I fancy my chance of getting a husband very distant if I see not reason to alter my present determination. However, Tony, you have only to exert yourself in this instance and ι promise that the day which makes Blanche the wife of Neville Audeley, shall see me bestow my hand upon the man who appears to be worthy of it."

"And that will be me, of course?"

"No doubt of it, good Anthony Amblewit," she replied; "though I could have wished the name had been a prettier one."

"At any rate 'tis as good as Addlepate," retorted her lover, tartly.

"Why, so it is," answered Kate; "but then Guy is not a bad-looking man, you must confess, and whilst one is choosing a husband, it's natural enough to give the preference to a smart, comely youth."

"Which I am sure Guy Addlepate is not."

"That is a matter upon which we may happen to differ," said the provoking girl. "I'll admit he's rather clownish in his manner, but a wife may soon effect a great change in that respect."

"If Guy is such a favourite," muttered Tony, "why didn't you go and ask him to accompany Mistress Blanche Heriot on her journey?"

"Because I always give the preference to you dear Tony," she replied. "So, come, clear that moody brow, and tell me, once for all, whether you may be safely depended on to perform this errand."

"I may, if you promise never to mention the name of Guy Addlepate again."

"Nay, that is more than I should like to promise," answered Kate. "You have heard me say, however, that all depends upon this duty of yours being faithfully discharged; and if my young lady speaks well of your services, I shall not forget the promise I have made."

"But there may be danger in this affair," observed Tony, "and though I may have my own fair share of courage, I never liked running a risk merely for the purpose of obliging other people."

"It will be obliging yourself," she replied; "since the service will be handsomely paid for."

"But if I should lose my life, what then?"

"Why then I should cry my eyes out to be sure," answered the laughter-loving girl, "and if ever I should get over my grief for your loss, perhaps I might console myself by accepting Guy for a husband."

"Guy again," exclaimed Tony wrathfully; "his name's always on your lips, and——"

"Hush!" interrupted the merry maiden; "let me hear no evil wishes, or I shall be frightened to stay in your company, and, after all, Tony, I've only been joking with you, to see if you really loved me enough to be jealous."

"Oh, if that's all, there's an end of the matter," he replied; "so suppose, Kate, we kiss and make it up."

"The kiss must not be spoken of before matrimony," answered Kate; "unless indeed I hear a very good account of you from my young lady, and in that case it's possible that—but I'll make no promise, Tony, so you must trust entirely to my generosity. And now, away with you, for we may be overheard, and there is, besides, but little time for you to make the necessary preparations. Remember the time and place, for Mistress Blanche will be punctual, and even the least delay might prove fatal to the scheme on which she so much relies."

As she spoke, Kate bounded away with the speed of an antelope, leaving Tony to reflect upon the business which had been so unexpectedly thrust upon him. Had there been any way to escape from it, he would gladly have availed himself of it; but the affair was now undertaken, and, come what would, he must fulfil the task that had been imposed on him.

CHAPTER IX.

THE LETTER.—THE RESCUE.—THE DISGUISE.

BLANCHE did not see Sir Philip Warrenne on the day of her meditated journey till dinner time, and then she met him with a sad and cheerless countenance that did not fail to attract his notice. He, however, attributed her grief to the uncertainty which at present hung over the fate of Neville Audeley, and for some time he refrained from speaking to her upon a subject on which he was unable to offer any consolation; but finding at length that she was not likely to break the silence which had been thus long indulged, he inquired whether she had any suggestion to offer by which a discovery of her lover's place of sojourn might be effected.

"The opinion you entertain of his having proceeded to Tewkesbury is, I fear, altogether unfounded," he added, as our heroine listened to him in thoughtful silence. "I have been considering the matter carefully, Blanche, and really the more I think of it, the less probable it appears that any search after him will be successful."

"Yet surely, Sir Philip," she replied; "you would not leave him to his fate, when there is but too much reason to fear he has fallen into bad hands."

"Assuredly not, my love," he replied; "for the young fellow has suddenly become a favourite of mine, and I am ready to adopt any plan for his advantage that you may suggest. I, however, do not think quite so despondingly of the matter as you appear to do, for I have a notion that he is at this time a prisoner in the hands of the Yorkists, and if that is all, he will no doubt be at liberty before long."

"I fear not," answered Blanche, with a sigh, "for report says they have already slain many persons who have been unfortunate enough to fall into their hands."

"But report is not always to be believed," he replied, "and to speak my mind —though I am sorry for the young man—I believe your fears have greatly magnified his danger."

"I pray Heaven they may," cried our heroine; "but, alas! I can find no consolation, even though I have tried to convince myself that hope is not yet altogether lost. Hugh Laneret, it must not be forgotten, has much interest with Neville's enemies, and he will not fail to use it when so good an opportunity for revenging himself is thus offered."

"And think you, then, they are to be swayed by the villain you have named?" asked Sir Philip, with surprise. "You forget too that a few days will decide which party shall be victorious, and should the Yorkists lose the battle, those who become prisoners will be at the mercy of the conquerors. That one fact is alone sufficient to deter them from any act of cruelty to those of our people who are now in their hands, and, therefore, Neville Audeley is not in so much danger as your terror has imagined."

"You speak but as you hope, dear sir," cried Blanche.

"Nay, I speak as I really and conscientiously believe," he replied. "However, if you think that by going in search of him I may do any good, I will do so with all my heart."

"I would not impose a task upon another that I can myself perform," returned Blanche, anxious to try the effect of such a hint upon her guardian. "In such a cause, my dear sir, I have courage and resolution enough to carry me through the severest trials, and if I could not effect my object, I should be well content to perish in the attempt."

"Surely you have not thought of taking such a step?" exclaimed Sir Philip, with surprise.

"Such a thought has crossed my mind," replied Blanche, timidly, "Dangers like these are not to be met without incurring fresh dangers, and I would cheerfully encounter them rather than leave Neville to his fate."

"Nay," returned the knight, "this is the very madness of love, and must be repressed. Remember, Blanche, you were placed under my care by a dying friend, and I should ill discharge the duty I took upon myself were I to yield to such a proposition as this. So think no more of it, but if, at the end of a few days, we hear nothing of Neville Audeley, I will take such steps as may appear necessary for his safety."

"And by that time your good intentions may be of no service to him."

"If I thought that," answered Sir Philip, "I would take steps for his safety without delay. There seems, however, to be no such pressing danger as you imagine, and I will, therefore, wait with patience in order that we may know for certain whether he is in the hands of these parties or not. At present we have only conjecture to guide us, and it would only bring scorn upon us were we to make a great stir when there was no occasion for it."

"You seem to have forgotten," said our heroine, "that Hugh Laneret as much as acknowledged that his rival was a prisoner; and if such be the case, no dangers that we can picture to ourselves will exceed the dreadfu. reality. I would gladly console myself with the assurance that they will not injure him, but images of terror constantly rise before my view, and I can only think of Neville Audeley being pressed with danger, whilst those who should be his friends, sit down and quietly await the doom that snatches him from us for ever."

"Come, come, my dear Blanche, you must not give way to this despondency," exclaimed Sir Philip. "I have told you I will do all that lies in my power to rescue him should it appear his life is hazarded. But you must promise to take no share in it, or whatever I may effect will be undone through your own anxiety."

"You would ask me then," said Blanche, "to sit down calmly when I know that it requires the utmost exertion to save him?"

"There you do me an injustice," replied her guardian, "for I am almost as anxious in his behalf as yourself. I would not, however, interfere before we are quite certain that it is necessary, because I feel convinced that a single rash step would do more injury than we should ever be able to repair."

"What injury can we do him?" she inquired.

"So much," replied Sir Philip, "that we should never cease to regret it afterwards. At present, those who hold him in captivity are quiet, because they know not that we are aware of what has become of him. But once give them an idea that we know the situation in which Neville Audeley is placed, and they will not scruple to put him out of the way in order that they may not be deprived of a prisoner."

"And these are the men who hold over him the power of life and death!"

"Unfortunately it is so," answered Sir Philip, "and I see no way of rescuing him without running a risk that may plunge him into the very danger we are most anxious to avoid. My opinion may not exactly agree with yours, Blanche, but I believe, in the long run, you will find it perfectly right."

"I can give you the credit for good intentions," she exclaimed, "but it must be confessed my own opinion is not in the least altered by anything you have said. I can see nothing but that the life of Neville is threatened, and yet not a single step has been taken for his preservation."

Sir Philip Warrenne paused, scarcely knowing what reply to make; and whilst he was still wondering how he could best satisfy her, a page entered the room with a letter, which he placed in the knight's hand, and then retired a few paces to await any orders his master might have to give him. Sir Philip tore open the silken band with which it was secured, and having read its contents through, said—

"This letter, Blanche, relates to the business we were just talking about; it is from an anonymous writer, and warns us to take no steps for the discovery of Neville Audeley, and giving an assurance that his life will be safe as long as no attempt is made to rescue him from the custody in which he at present remains."

"Methinks the provision of this nameless correspondent is but a poor warrant for the life of a fellow creature," answered Blanche Heriot. "To me it seems that the writer wishes to stop all inquiry into the subject in order that the victim may be sacrificed without the deed being made public. Hugh Laneret, if I mistake not, is the writer of that letter, and his motive for it may be judged by the vindictiveness of his previous conduct."

"Who brought this letter, sirrah page?" demanded Sir Philip, addressing himself to the boy.

"A man that I never saw before," answered the youth.

"Is he now in the house?"

"No, Sir Philip." returned the other; "he put the letter into my hand desiring that it should be delivered to no one but yourself, and then hurried away before I could ask him any questions."

"Well, there's nothing particularly strange about that," observed the knight to Blanche. "The fellow acted, I suppose, according to his instructions, and, having performed his errand, he wisely took his departure so that he might not be tempted to say more than he had been desired."

"It is to be regretted that no one was near to detain him," cried our heroine. "Had he been brought before you, something might have been extorted from him to satisfy us as to who had sent him here."

"That would have been but sorry consolation, my dear girl," answered the knight, "for, even admitting that we had discovered Hugh Laneret to have been the writer of the letter, we should have known very little more than we do at present. We are already pretty well satisfied that Neville has been trepanned into the hands of his enemies; but, much as we may regret the circumstance, it would be madness to exasperate his captors, who would be but too well pleased at having any excuse for putting him to death. All, in fact, depends upon our observing the utmost caution, and you will, therefore, see the necessity of following the advice of one whose heart is warmly interested in the fate of this young man."

"He will perish," cried Blanche, "and yet no hand is put forth to save him."

"Your fears carry you beyond the bounds of reason," exclaimed her guardian. "Neville Audeley has not been taken prisoner whilst fighting against the persons who have deprived him of liberty, and, therefore, no plea presents itself for committing any violence. Indeed, except the temporary inconvenience he may suffer, he will have nothing to complain of; and when the struggle between these two parties is at an end, he will, no doubt, be restored to freedom."

"Not if Hugh Laneret has any voice in it," replied our heroine, despondingly.

"He can have none," answered Sir Philip, "for the captors of Neville Audeley will not suffer any private quarrel to influence their decision. So banish that melancholy look from your countenance, my pretty Blanche, and let me once more see the smile that used almost constantly to settle there."

"How can the face show smiles when the heart is full of sadness?" asked Blanche. "Till now I have never known what sorrow is, except by name; but since it has fallen upon me so heavily, I cannot but sink under the afflictions with which I am oppressed."

"You do not believe me, then, when I say there is no danger to be apprehended?"

"I would willingly do so if I could," replied Blanche; "but seeing, as I do, nothing but a dreary prospect before me, I cannot flatter myself that danger is so far distant as you would fain persuade me."

"At all events," returned Sir Philip, "you will promise me not to take any steps till we have spoken together again upon this subject?"

"I will make no promise, since I should be too apt to break it, should a favourable opportunity present itself," replied Blanche. "My own life I now regard as being valueless, and willingly shall it be sacrificed if I see that it could produce freedom and safety for Neville Audeley."

"And where did you pick up these romantic notions, my dear Blanche?"

"My own heart has ever taught me that it is a duty to pity and assist those who are in need of it," she replied. "Neville has been betrayed into the hands of cruel and ruthless men, and if he cannot be saved, I will at least not survive him."

"Psha! these are the notions of a young and inexperinced girl," exclaimed her guardian.

"It may be so," she replied; "such as they are I shall abide by them. Hitherto you have known me meek and submissive to your will, and if I now prove disobedient, it will be from no want of respect for yourself, but from a conviction that all my energies are required to prevent a catastrophe that I cannot think of without shuddering."

"Upon my life, Blanche," exclaimed the knight, "I could almost find it in my heart to rate you soundly for this waywardness of yours; but I give you credit for all good intentions, and so we will let the subject drop with an understanding that you will take no further steps in this affair till you have first of all consulted me about it."

"I will not shackle myself with any promises that I may hereafter find it necessary to break," she replied. "You are confident in the present security of Neville Audeley, and he is thus left to his fate; I, however, think, that there is not a moment to be lost if we would save him; and it shall be my task to snatch him from destruction."

"And what, I prithee, can you do, foolish girl?"

"More, perhaps, than you may dream of," she replied.

"Humph! you would not be rash enough to leave the shelter of my roof to throw yourself among strangers, whose honour may be all moon shine?"

"I will not explain the wild thoughts that have entered my mind," she replied. "You may rely on it, however, that I will do nothing rashly or without due reflection, and that whatever step I take shall be with a tolerable assurance of the success, for which I have fervently prayed the assistance of Heaven."

"Nay, let me entreat you to leave this task to better and more able hands," exclaimed Sir Philip. "You will involve yourself in trouble, Blanche, and thus add bitterness to the life of him who would make any sacrifice to secure your happiness."

"Happiness can never be mine whilst Neville's existence depends upon the fiat of those who would be but too glad to gratify their revenge by dooming him to a fate I dread to think of."

"You really think, then," exclaimed Sir Philip, "that he is in more danger than I have imagined?"

"There is but too much certainty of his peril," answered Blanche, "or I should not be thus anxious to take means for his liberation. The treachery that betrayed him I am certain was plotted by Hugh Laneret; and knowing, as I do, the fiendish vengeance that lurks within that man's heart, I see every reason to dread the most fatal consequences."

"If that be the case," returned Sir Philip, "I will instantly hasten myself to see what can be done for restoring your cousin to liberty without loss of time. I will despatch a letter to the nobleman who is in command of the Yorkists troops, and by representing the treachery that was practised in the arrest of Neville Audeley, it is likely I may prevail upon him to set the captive free. So make yourself easy, Blanche, and I promise you this affair will turn out better than you expect."

Sir Philip now rose from his seat and quitted the room, leaving our heroine to ponder over the events which had cast so sad a gloom over her happiness.

The proposition made by her guardian at the latter part of their conversation afforded her but little hope that the condition of Neville would be bettered; for she felt assured that the opposite party would rejoice at having secured the person of one who was well known to be warmly attached to the cause of the King Henry: and it was therefore hardly likely they would give him his liberty, even though they might spare his life, till after the final struggle for supremacy was over. It was also but too certain that Hugh Laneret possessed great influence among the partizans of the other side; and should he artfully represent that there was danger in sparing the captive, an order might instantly be given for his execution, not only to prevent any mischief from himself, but to strike terror into those who had placed themselves under the banner of the reigning monarch.

These and a thousand other wild and alarming thoughts passed in rapid succession through the brain of Blanche, as she sat mournfully contemplating the probable termination of an affair that had already caused her so much uneasiness. She was more than ever, however, resolved to carry her first-formed project into execution; and, proceeding to her own chamber, she was almost immediately followed thither by Kate Paynet, who carried in her arms a large bundle, which she threw down upon the floor, exclaiming—

"Your are surprised, I dare say, my dear young lady, to see me come loaded in this fashion; but the more I have thought this business over, the more I feel afraid that you will not pass through this adventure without difficulties, so I have made bold to borrow a page's suit without saying a word to anybody; and if you will only disguise yourself in it, I think you will pass very well for a youth; and if any one should interfere with you on your road, you can make any excuse you think proper so as to pass on without hinderance."

"And what will be said," asked Blanche, "should it be hereafter known that I donned this unseemly garb to run half over the country in search of a lost lover." .

"The world will not blame you, depend upon it," replied the girl, "for most people admire romantic adventures; and if the thing should ever be spoken of, it will rather be in admiration of your self-devotion than blaming you for making so great a sacrifice."

"But I dread lest my doing so should incur the anger of Sir Philip Warrenne," exclaimed Blanche. "He has just expressed his disapproval of my taking any share of the risk upon myself; and should he know that I have left his house in male attire, it may bring upon me his just anger."

"He shall never know it from me," said Kate; "and though, of course, you will be missed soon after leaving the house, it shall be my part to make the best of it, and soothe his anger. Besides, when he knows you are accompanied by Tony Amblewit, he will be satisfied of your safety, and the rest may be managed comfortably enough when you return home in safety."

"But all this may be done," answered our heroine, "without assuming the disguise you speak of."

"Ay, but not with so much security to yourself," returned Kate. "This is no time for women to go, almost unattended, through the country; but if you be supposed to belong to the other sex, extreme youth will prove your best safeguard, and you will be suffered to proceed on your journey unmolested."

"If I thought so I would make the experiment," answered our heroine, after some little deliberation.

"Why, there can be no doubt of it," exclaimed the attendant; "and as I have been at no little trouble to obtain this suit, which belongs to one of our pages, I hope you will not refuse to wear it as a protection against insult during this journey that you are going to take."

Thus urged, Blanche offered no further opposition to the project, and being assisted by her attendant, she was soon transformed into an excellant imitation of a smart and dapper page. Being thus attired, a dagger was added by way of completing the equipment, and with the still further addition of a handsome beaver and feather, Blanche Heriot might easily have passed undiscovered even by those who were most intimately acquainted with her.

"Now, my dear young lady," said Kate, as soon as the toilet was finished, "I think you have a fair chance of going through this adventure of yours successfully. Tony, I dare say, will prove a sufficient protection; but should any one molest or alarm you on the way, you have only to draw your dagger, and bluster a little, and I'll warrant they suffer you to pass on."

"But suppose I should be too much frightened to follow the counsel you have given?"

"It would never do to show any alarm, even if you should feel it," answered the girl. "Bluster does a great deal in this world of ours, and you will find the good effect of it in the event of any interruption. Just show people that you are not afraid of them, and it soon brings down their courage marvellously."

"At any rate I'll try to follow your sage counsel, good Kate," returned her mistress, who could not forbear smiling at the advice she had been giving. "It is as well to be prepared in case of an emergency; but, to speak the truth, I have very little opinion that any obstruction will be offered to my progress."

"That's more than any one can say," replied Kate; "for the country swarms at present with armed men, some of them belonging to one side, and some to the other. They, however, only molest those that they think they are going to fight against ; and as they'll take you for a mere stripling, it will be hardly worth their while to offer any interruption."

"And even if I believed there was any danger of it," answered our heroine, "it would not deter me from the task I have set myself. At any rate I should be carried into the quarters of the enemy, and there I should be likely to hear intelligence of Neville Audeley, that would enable me to discover what has been done with him, and whether he is in danger."

"And even if there should be anything to fear on your account," added the attendant, "you have only to let them know that you are a damsel in disguise, and that will be enough to secure you from harm."

"That is by no means certain," replied Blanche ; "for if Hugh Laneret happened to hear that I was a prisoner in the hands of his party, he would take effectual means to prevent my release. Not, however, that such a thought shall deter me from my project, for it has been resolved upon, and no selfish consideration shall induce me to abandon it."

"Well, this love is certainly all powerful," exclaimed Kate. "I have known you to be frightened if the wind blew a little louder than usual, and yet, for the sake of this young gentleman, you are willing to run a risk, the thought of which would frighten almost any one out of their senses."

"Neville is deserving of all the sacrifice I make in his behalf," replied Blanche, warmly. "He is generous and kind to all who need his assistance, and were I in danger, he would fearlessly throw away his own life to save me."

"But that, you know," said Kate, "is nothing more than a duty that men owe to our sex."

"And since all persons do not mind their duty," answered our heroine, sharply, "it is ours to give credit to those who do. Neville Audeley once saved my life when I was on the point of being drowned, and if there were no other consideration in the case, that alone would be amply sufficient to rouse my utmost energies when peril threatens him."

"Well, there's a great deal to be said in such a case as that, certainly," replied Kate. "I have always thought Master Neville Audeley to be such a man as I should like for a husband ; and—but I see the subject is not very pleasant to you, so there's an end of it ; and now I think as it's pretty well dark, the sooner you leave the house the better."

"What time is it ?"

"The curfew rang about an hour and a half ago," answered Kate ; "so that by the hour we reach the appointed place Tony Amblewit will be there with the horses."

"What mean you by we, girl ?"

"Merely that I will walk with you to the place," replied Kate ; "for the night is rather dark, and as you are not used to being out of doors at this hour, I should not like to let you go without a companion."

"Good girl !" cried Blanche ; "how can I ever reward the generous zeal you have constantly displayed in my behalf ?"

"By not saying anything about it," replied the attendant ; "for my own part I don't look upon it as any favour ; and if it only add to your safety, I shall be more than rewarded for the little trouble it occasions."

"I will accept your offer," said Blanche, "because I feel that it is made in all sincerity. Upon you, also, will devolve the task of explaining the course that has led to my taking this step. He will be angry, I fear, when he discovers that I have acted so contrary to his wishes ; but he will not refuse to hear reason, and you may perhaps be able to convince him that the course was a necessary one."

"You may depend upon it I'll not let him be angry with you for any long time," replied Kate. "He may be a little bit cantankerous at first, maybe, but I can manage him ; and if he should be very much put out, I'll remind him of the days when he was in love himself, and that will bring him to his senses, I'll warrant you."

"Have a care how you speak to him," observed her mistress, "for he has ever

been kind to me, and I would n ot wish that his anger with me should be per-manent.   However, it is now dark enough for our purpose, and we will take our departure."

Taking up a small wallet that was to be committed to the care of Tony Am-blewit, the attendant now softly left the chamber, followed by her young lady, whose alarm was now visible, though she strove as much as possible to conceal it.   Without meeting any obstruction, they at length reached the garden, and hurrying along they passed the gate which led to the high road.

The terror of Blanche now began to return ; and, keeping close by the side of Kate, she ventured to inquire whether their place of destination was far off.

" You shall reach it in a few minutes," whispered the girl ; " but speak not a word going along, for we may be overheard, and in that case all the trouble we have been at will be thrown away."

Blanche saw the necessity of caution, and they now proceeded in silence, occasionally turning round with alarm as they fancied some sound met their ears.

Fortunately, however, they were deceived in every instance, and taking a circuitous route in order to avoid passing through the town; they at length approached the place where Tony was already waiting their arrival with impatience.

He stared when he saw Kate, and, as he imagined, a stranger advancing towards him; and, addressing himself to the girl, said—

"Why, how is this, thou foolish wench? I was waiting here for Mistress Blanche Heriot, and thou hast brought me a young page, as if my time were to be thrown away in waiting upon a boy that is well enough able to take care of himself."

"If you have done railing, Tony," said the maiden, "I'll explain this matter to you. The truth is, these are no times for females to be away from their homes, and so to avoid danger I have persuaded my mistress to disguise herself as you see her."

"Odds! who would have thought I could have been deceived in this manner!" exclaimed Tony.

"Take care you are not deceived more than this another time," murmured Kate. "This is a mere innocent deception that will do you no harm, and perhaps may teach you more caution with our sex in future. But we have no time for further parley upon this subject at present; so mount, dear lady, and away; and ere morning dawns Tony, if he do his duty faithfully, will have taken you many a long mile from this place."

With the assistance of her guide, Blanche was speedily seated upon her horse; but ere she set forward upon her journey she again earnestly besought Kate to soothe her guardian in case he should feel angry at the step she had taken. This the faithful attendant promised she would do; and having committed her young mistress to the especial care of Tony Amblewit, she saw them ride off in the direction for Tewkesbury.

Kate watched them by the moonlight till they disappeared from her view, and then turned her own steps homewards to make the best excuse she could to Sir Philip Warrenne.

CHAPTER X.

THE PRISONER.—A FORCED JOURNEY.—A FRIEND.

WE must now follow Neville Audeley, who we left on his departure from the hovel, and at a time when he was a prisoner in the hands of his betrayer, Stephen Ratcliffe and his comrades. One of the men who rode nearest to him would fain have get into conversation upon various topics, which he commenced, but the young man's thoughts were too much directed towards his own misfortunes to attend to the idle conversation of a stranger; and making use of his spurs he rode up to the foremost part of the throng, and where no little consternation was caused at the moment through its being imagined that he intended to gallop forward and trust for his escape to the mettle of his horse.

"Hilloa, young fellow!" exclaimed Stephen Ratcliffe, riding up and seizing hold of his bridle, "where the devil are you going in such a hurry? Do you think to escape from us because we have put thongs upon your hands and legs?"

"I had no thought of attempting my escape," answered Neville Audeley. "Indeed, what can one man hope to do when there are so many to guard him?"

"Ay, that's true enough," returned the other; "but I fancied you were going to be mad enough to try it, and so to prevent mistakes in future, I may as well tell you that a dozen balls will be about your ears before you can get as many paces in advance of us."

"Your threat would have very little effect upon me, were I in the humour to try what speed might do for once," answered Neville. "However, to end all your fears at once, I give you my solemn word that no attempt shall be made by me to quit the very excellent company I find myself in."

"Humph! is that intended as a compliment?'

"You can take it in any light you please," returned Neville, drily; "but I should have thought there could be but one construction put upon my words."

"The young gentleman is angry at finding himself under restraint," said one of the fellows riding near them. "He don't like to find that he has bee outwitted; and I dare say if there were not quite so many of us about him, he would show some of the spirit people give him credit for."

"It is not your numbers that deter me from doing so now," answered Neville; "for had I but a sword in my hand there are some among you who should not see Tewkesbury to-night."

"Well crowed for a cockrel!" vociferated the fellow that had spoken last. "Egad! I like to see a lad of mettle, and providing I was not one that you fell foul on, there is nothing I should better like to see than a combat such as you have spoken of."

"'Tis a pity you have taken the wrong side of the question, young man," said Stephen Ratcliff, "for had you declared yourself on the side of Edward of York, there would have been certain promotion for you. We want a few spirited young fellows in our ranks, and if you think proper to change masters, why I can promise that you shall hold a post worthy your acceptance."

"I am no rebel," answered Neville Audeley, in a tone of indignation.

"Nor are we, for that matter," returned the other, sharply, "at present there are no rebels, for that is a question that will be decided only when it is known which party is to be victorious. Yet, should Edward prove to be the conqueror and gain the throne he claims, you will be likely to suffer a traitor's doom, if you don't previously declare yourself on his side.'

"And should such be my fate," answered Neville, "I can die well contented in the certainty that I have done nought to bring disgrace upon my name."

"But you may leave those behind who won't take the affair quite so philosophically," observed Stephen. "There is a young lady, for instance, who would be sorry to lose her lover; and for her sake, it would be worth while purchasing life, even though it may be at the expense of joining the opposite ranks."

"She you speak of," replied Neville, quickly, "would hold me in her utmost contempt were I to prove the villain you have hinted at. My honour is as dear to her as it is to myself, and the moment that it is forfeited, she will regard me only as one that was unworthy of her thoughts."

"Well, there's no accounting for these romantic tastes that some young ladies indulge in," exclaimed the other; "but, in my opinion, it argues very little of love if she would rather hear of your death by violence, than that you had seen the error of your ways, and at last found out on which side fortune is most likely to smile. Od ls, blood, man! you surely wouldn't throw away a good name merely because a girl might happen to think the worse of you for it?"

"I am the guardian and keeper of my own honour," replied Neville, haughtily; "and it will be my own fault if ever it be sacrificed. Death has no terrors for me, so long as it is encountered in a good cause."

"But life is worth preserving for all that."

"True, but it must be unstained."

"Upon my life, you and I differ there as widely as the poles are sundered," interposed the fellow that had before spoken. "I never could see the use of what is called honour, to any man. It neither feeds, clothes, nor lodges him; but on the contrary, very often stands in his way when a good chance offers itself. Some men have been hung on a point of honour; but I never yet heard that any one got on the better for possessing it."

"There are persons," answered Neville, "whose interest it is to banish her from their presence. *You*, perhaps, have found your advantage in following your course exactly according to your own humour."

"At all events." replied the man, " I should not hesitate about changing sides, if I could see that any good were to be got by it. At present, however, I am very well satisfied, so King Edward shall have my services till the other party makes a more tempting offer."

"Peace, thou knave!" vociferated Stephen Ratcliffe, impatiently ; "and if thou be'est a mercenary villain, publish it not to the whole world. By our Lady, if the royal Edward knew what a sordid wretch he had got among his troops, he would have thy head whipped off, an example to all others who would not fight for sheer love of his cause."

"Why, true it is!" exclaimed the other, "a man can't speak his mind a little bit freely, but what he is told his head is in danger by it ; yet I did but jest, good Stephen, so I prithee say nothing that may bring down upon me the anger of any of our noble chieftains. In truth. I am ready enough to risk my life in fair battle, but I should be loath to lose my life in what this young gentleman would call a less honourable way."

" I am no tell-tale to make mischief against an old comrade," answered Stephen, "so thou mayest consider thiyself quite safe for this once ; but I shall keep an eye on thee, Peter, and if there should be any cause for suspicion I will not fail to do that which will ensure thy harmlessness in future."

"Have you many such soldiers in your army as this one?" asked Neville Audeley.

"Pshaw! I always looked upon him as a coward," replied Stephen Ratcliffe, "and for that reason have kept him constantly at my elbow. The knave can do us but little good, even should he prove faithful, and should he turn out otherwise, we have no reason to apprehend harm from him."

" But if Edward have many such to depend on in the coming struggle," answered Neville, "the victory on our side will be even an easier one than I had anticipated."

"He'll do to swell out our numbers at any rate," said Stephen, "and if he happen to fall in battle, it may be that his death will save a better man from the same fate. Besides, we have a large body of foreigners coming over with our king, and they, you know, must fight well when they get upon our soil, for no quarter will be shown them by the people on your side."

They now proceeded some distance without any further conversation being exchanged between them. At last, however, Neville Audeley was aroused from the thoughts with which his mind was occupied, by a sudden exclamation from Ratcliffe, and looking up, be saw a party of horsemen galloping towards them. At first, the young man was not without hopes that the soldiers belonged to the Earl of Warwick, and that he had then a fair chance of gaining his liberty. But he was not long suffered to remain thus deceived; for as they approached nearer, Stephen Ratcliffe gave way to an expression of joyful surprise, and announced to his comrades that the people before them were friends, and that they were headed by Mark Evered, who was employed to lead a few chosen men in search of food and other necessaries for the army.

"By my troth, lads," he exclaimed, "I began to think just now we should have to fight for it. I mistook them for d—d Lancasterian dogs, that would not let us pass on our way with a prisoner, without first of all having a bit of a skirmish for it."

" I myself expected better fortune in my behalf," added Neville Audeley ; "but it is my evil destiny to remain a captive, and I must e'en submit to it with as much patience as I can command."

"Ay—ay, bear your troubles as lightly as you can," returned the other, "for I dare say nothing more will happen to you than loss of liberty for a little time. Had you been taken as a spy, now, the case would have been different ; for they are fellows that never meet with any quarter, unless, indeed, they think proper to turn round and tell all about the intentions of those that sent them. But our friends are here, and we shall soon know the news from head-quarters."

While he was speaking the soldiers who had been advancing at a brisk trot, suddenly halted, and the man who seemed to have the command of them, came forward alone, and having saluted Stephen Ratcliffe in military fashion, demanded whither he was going.

"To Tewkesbury," was the reply.

"And what takes you there?"

"We have a prisoner," replied Stephen, "and would place him in safe custody before we return to the main army."

"Tewkesbury is no place for a Yorkist to show his face in just now," answered Mark Evered. "The enemy is there in great force, and our leaders have been obliged to shift their ground."

"And where are they to be found now?"

"We have a strong muster at Cirencester," replied Mark Evered; "and if you have a prisoner to take care of, I should advise you to convey him there without delay."

"The very place I thought of going to from the very first," exclaimed Stephen; "but I altered my mind; and egad, it's very lucky we met, or I should have had a chance of losing my prisoner, and falling into the hands of the enemy at the same time. But how is it, Mark, that our people have been obliged to leave Tewkesbury?"

"Because the inhabitants didn't look upon us with a very favourable eye," replied the other; "and our leaders began to be afraid of treachery among them, so the troops had sudden orders to march; and as I told you before, a great part of them have gone to Cirencester, where I suppose they'll remain till the preparations for battle are nearly completed."

"And when is that expected to be?"

"How is it possible to tell?" answered Mark. "Our leaders think proper to be very secret about the matter, and all we can do is to guess. It is certain, however, that Edward has either landed already, or will do so in a few hours; and when the troops he brings with him are rested a little, he will march for London."

"But London he'll never reach without fighting his way to it," answered Stephen. "It is said the Earl of Warwick has managed to get a very large army together; and if he throw himself between our troops and the metropolis, there'll be hard blows exchanged, and many a life sacrificed, before this dispute about the throne is settled."

"And may Heaven speed the cause of good King Henry," exclaimed Neville Audeley, unable to restrain himself any longer.

"Methinks that would have been better kept to yourself," returned Stephen, "for you have no friends here, and your life might have paid the forfeit of your temerity."

"Take it now, if you think proper," returned Neville. "Deprived as I am of liberty, my arm is useless to the cause I would have served; and your taking away my life will not injure the monarch whom you would drive from his throne. Besides, I am weary of existence, and to perish now would relieve me from a load that presses heavily upon me."

"It seems, indeed, young man, that you do not value your life much," observed Mark Evered; "or you would not risk it by uttering treason against the sovereign we fight for. However, heed him not in his madness, Stephen Ratcliffe; for it will be better that you take him to Cirencester as a prisoner, since you will there find those who better know what had best be done with him."

"Is Hugh Lancret there?"

"He was not when I left," answered Mark Evered; "but he was expected hourly with the men he has promised to bring to our assistance. And so, farewell, till we meet again, which I suppose will not be till the battle is to be fought."

Mark Evered and his troops then proceeded on their way, and Stephen, giving the word of command to his men, hastened forward as if anxious to reach the place of destination as soon as possible. He now appeared to be immersed in thought, and continued so for some time; but at length checking his speed, he pointed down a beautiful valley, which, just at that moment they had entered, and exclaimed—

"Yonder, my lads, is our place of destination; once safely there, and we shall find ourselves in comfortable quarters after the rough ride we have had. I know something of the inhabitants of Cirencester, and can, therefore, speak of them from experience as being a set of jolly dogs that will not grudge a soldier a cup of good ale."

"Likely enough," observed Neville, "because needs must when the devil drives. Perhaps, however, they would rather bestow it on a Lancastrian than a Yorkist, and if that's their feeling I would have you keep a sharp watch upon them, for if they bear only half the hatred I do to your party, they will rise to a man, and clear the town of bad company."

"And get the place burned down about their ears for their pains," exclaimed Stephen.

"They would deserve to do so," replied the other; "if they came not boldly forward to prevent such an act of baseness. But it is in vain talking of what they should do, for I fear there is not spirit enough among them to get rid of those who have quartered themselves so unceremoniously among them."

"Marry, my good Master Audeley," exclaimed Stephen; "the worthy burghers are too sensible of their danger to rush heedlessly into it. We are too many for them, that's certain, and the poor fellows know it is better to endure an evil for a short time, than to bring one upon them that would last for ever. Besides they may chance to be favourable to our cause, and that, I take it, is a strong reason why, they should treat us generously to the best cheer they have to bestow."

They were now entering the suburbs of the town and the conversation dropped for the men who had formed the guard drew closer round Neville as they passed through the streets, either that he should be screened from the observation of the curious, or that no opportunity should be given for a rescue. The prisoner glanced eagerly at the few passengers that were straggling here and there in the town, and much did he envy those who, having liberty at their disposal, could wend their way here and there as suited their humour. At one time he even thought of throwing himself from his horse and claiming assistance from those those who might probably be disposed to aid him. But he knew not how far he might trust to their support, and, therefore passively resigning himself to his fate, he determined to abide the consequences, let them be what they might. At length he was roused from the reverie by the sudden halt of the party that guarded him and he perceived that Stephen Ratcliffe was engaged in conversation with a person who had just before advanced towards them. The words that passed between them did not reach his ear, but Stephen soon afterwards dismounted and followed the stranger into a house close by, where he remained for some time. From what passed among the men he gathered enough to inform him that Stephen had gone to receive instructions relative to his prisoner, and at the end of about half an hour he was seen issuing from the door of a large and strongly guarded house, which Neville perfectly understood was to be his prison till further orders were given as to his ultimate fate.

The whole party here dismounted and ranged themselves from the road to the door in two lines, through which Neville passed into the house, which he found was even more gloomy than the exterior had given him a notion of. Here a man of dark and forbidding aspect received them, and, after whispering a little while with Stephen, he led the way through a narrow passage that had many turnings, and which at length brought them to a staircase, which they ascended till they reached what appeared to be the top of the building. Here the man who acted as jailor, paused. and opening a door that turned slowly upon its rusty hinges, conducted Neville Audeley into a narrow, wretched-looking chamber, that he was made to understand would be his cell till further orders were received from head quarters. Stephen's task was now at an end, and turning to Neville as he was about to take his departure, he said—

"For the present, young gentleman, you must be contented with the lodging that has been provided for you. How long your captivity will last is more than I can undertake to say, but let me warn you to make no attempt to escape, for the place will be surrounded with a guard, and orders have by this time been given to slay you rather than suffer your departure."

"Your threat would have little effect upon me," said the other; "if I took in my head to try the experiment. You may, however, make yourself quite easy on that point, for let my destiny be what it may, I am prepared to meet it with firmness."

"Excellently resolved, indeed!" cried Stephen, "so I will now take my leave of you, and Master Robert Baldock here will take care to provide you with food somewhat better than common prison fare. Company of course you will not be permitted to see at present, but that I need scarcely tell you, since no one among your friends will know where to seek for you."

He and Badlock then left the room, and Neville, upon being left to his own reflections, turned over in his mind the various occurrences of the last few hours, and bitterly did he curse the simplicity which had prompted him to place reliance upon a stranger. It was now, however, too late to give way to these self-reproaches, and ere he had been half an hour in his new abode his mind became calmer from reflection, and instead of looking back upon the past, he tried to find consolation in the future. He then thought of the letter he had sent to Blanche, informing her of the route he was going to take, and, though it was true a slight variation had taken place in it, he had no doubt Sir Philip Warrenne would find means to discover the place of his retreat, and, in that case, there was every reason to believe that immediate steps would be taken to procure his release.

He had been about an hour occupied in these reflections when he was roused from them by hearing the key grate harshly in the lock, and as the door opened he perceived Robert Badlock, who came loaded with a tray full of provisions, which he placed upon a table, and then addressing himself to the captive, he said—

"I have brought you something to eat, sir, because I thought you must need it after your journey. To be sure this is a sad melancholy place, but I hope it won't take away your appetite for all that."

"Your words are those of kindness," exclaimed Neville, with surprise; "may I hope I am not without one friend in this cheerless abode."

"I am your friend if you will allow me to be so," whispered the other. "But I must speak low, sir, for if it should be known that I have a spark of compassion in my breast, they would hold me unworthy to fill the office they have thrust upon me."

"You do not belong," said Neville Audeley; "to the party that is at present is at present in possession of this town?"

"Heaven forbid!" exclaimed the man. "They believe, however, that I am zealous in the cause, or they would never have trusted me as you see they do. In fact, I thought it best to play the hypocrite as it would enable me to do a friendly turn should any of King Henry's people be placed under my care."

"It was wisely done," said Neville; "but tell me, friend, is there any chance of my escaping from hence, to join those who are about to draw their swords in behalf of their lawful sovereign?"

"I'm afraid it is not in my power to help you there, sir," replied Baldock; "because it would only be running my own life into danger without really doing you any good."

"Perhaps you are right," answered the young man; "and yet there is another point in which it may be in your power to serve me. It is not unlikely my retreat may be discovered by some of my friends, and if so, I would gladly see them, that means may be adopted for obtaining my release from here."

"That I'll do, sir," exclaimed Baldock; "because I think it may be managed without anybody being the wiser for it. Those that come to see you may pass as friends of mine, and I'll take care you shall see them. But they must be careful, for should any suspicion be entertained, ruin will be sure to fall on all of us. So, for the present, sir, I'll leave you lest my staying here any longer should give rise to conjecture among the people below."

The old man left the room as he finished, and Neville felt his heart lightened already of half its weight; for the despair in which he had been inclined to indulge had given place to hopes that his imprisonment would soon be at an end

CHAPTER XI.

TONY AMBLEWIT'S TROUBLES.—THE HALT.—THE HAG.

WE left Blanche Heriot at the moment when she had just set forth on her self-imposed journey, accompanied by Tony Amblewit, who had undertaken to be her 'squire and guide, in a task that promise no little difficulties, even with all the caution they might use. Tony would fain have drawn her into conversation in order to dispel the more gloomy thoughts that haunted his mind; but Blanche was too much occupied with her own reflections to heed anything he said; and the consequence was, that they journeyed on for miles without her making any answer to the numerous attempts he made to break into the silence that was so disagreeable to him."

"Confound these women," he muttered to himself; "there's no telling what to make of them. Sometimes their tongues run so fast that it's impossible to stop them, try all one can; and now, because I want her to speak for company's sake, she's as dumb as a stock fish; but never mind, if she won't do anything else, she shall hear me sing, and that will be some consolation, for I've scarcely heard the sound of my own voice since we left Chertsey."

Thereupon he raised his melodious voice to such a pitch that the very welkin rang with it again, much to his own gratification, but to the no little annoyance of Blanche, who was thus disturbed in the midst of the conflicting thoughts that perplexed and troubled her. Tony felt a secret satisfaction at the power of teasing that he possessed, and had put into practice; and greatly did he exult at the idea that he should presently force her into saying something, if it were only to rate him soundly for making such a hideous noise. But even in this case he was doomed to be disappointment; for Blanche, instead of chiding him, contented herself with putting spurs to her horse, and at such a smart pace did she now pursue her journey, that Tony, in order to follow and keep up with her, was obliged to break off in the middle of his song.

"Well, hang me if I know what to make of the wench," he thought to himself as soon as their pace slackened a little. "I've tried every way that I can think of to get a word from her, and I might as well have held my tongue. Women that talk too much are bad enough to be sure, but I never thought to see the time when I should meet with one that says too little. She is a marvel of a girl, that's certain; and if she only keep in this humour all her life, her husband and she will pass a very quiet humdrum sort of life. But no, no, she can talk fast enough when she likes, and this is only done to vex me, because she finds I don't like it."

Again he tried to bring her into conversation, but Blanche, partly because she had no wish to break into her own reflections, and partly from an inclination to excite the ire of her attendant, still maintained an imperturbable silence, not even deigning to look round upon him, or giving any other token that she was aware of his presence. Tony could now have been delighted to receive a good sound lecture had it been possible in any way to excite her anger. That, however, seemed to be quite out of the question, and again they rode forward in utter silence, except the monotonous sound produced by the clattering of their horses' feet. As time wore on he grew restless and fidgetty, and then the daylight began to break in upon them, which was a great relief to him, as he could now make use of his eyesight if his tongue were of no use to him. The sight inspired him with joy; and though he expected no reply to his exclamation, he directed the attention of Blanche to the circumstance, exclaiming—

"Thank Heaven we have got so far safe on our journey, and now that we have

NEVILLE AUDELEY VISITS THE OLD ALCHYMIST.

got daylight to guide us. I hope we shall soon get to Tewkesbury, for this is sad prosing work for a man that never could be silent ten minutes together in his life."

"Nor have you been so now, Tony," replied his mistress, who had no inclination to hold out any longer. "I have heard you talking almost ever since we have been travelling, and yet you complain of not having had anything to say."

"It's no use talking to oneself," answered Tony, "for that's but dull work, as you must allow. Had you scolded me I could have been satisfied, but to be doomed to such pennance as this, is more than the patience of any one could bear."

"The truth is," answered Blanche, "I have had much to think of, and many plans to arrange, in order to render our present journey a useful one. But my tongue is now loosened, and perhaps you may hear more of it than you like during the remainder of the time that we are companions together."

"Oh, never fear that, good mistress of mine," returned Tony Amblewit; "for I can bear scolding as well as any one, because Kate Poynet has for a long time past made me tolerably used to it. So now, young lady, pour forth your anger, and I'll endure it with all the patience of a martyr."

"You forget, Tony," exclaimed Blanche, "that for the present I must not be addressed otherwise than as belonging to your own sex. Any departure from that caution will bring us into danger, and may perhaps ruin the design which has induced me to make this somewhat hazardous journey."

"I'll remember it whenever there's a chance of being overheard," replied the other, "and to prevent mistakes, I'll call you master Theodore. It's a good sounding name enough for a page, and will, I dare say, answer the purpose intended. And now miss, or *master*, I should rather say, to bring my tongue in, where do you propose staying to rest, for our horses must be pretty well tired by this time, and it may be as well for our own sake, to avoid travelling by daylight lest we should fall into company that would serve us as they have Master Neville Audeley."

"We will tarry at the first house of public entertainment we meet with," answered Blanche. "I am myself somewhat weary of the ride, and a few hours' rest will enable me to proceed the remainder of our way.

"And do you really expect we shall be able to do Master Neville any good service?"

"I at least hope so," returned Blanche. "Woman's wit, you know, sometimes works wonders, even where 'tis scarcely to be expected, and should we discover the place he has been conveyed to, I do not despair but some method will suggest itself to me by which he may be rescued from danger."

"Humph! and it seems not at all unlikely that you may run yourself into it."

"And if I do so I can endure all rather than abandon my plan," replied Blanche. "At any rate, perseverance shall not desert me, and if you be but faithful, Tony, I have no doubt all will turn out according to my most sanguine expectations."

"Oh, I'll be faithful enough, I'll warrant," answered the other. "Kate Poynet lectured me pretty well upon that subject, and if I should fail in giving satisfaction to you, there will be an end to our love affair, and I shall have the mortification of seeing her become the wife of Guy Addlepate. Some women, it must be confessed, have very little taste, or in my opinion Guy would have looked about him a long time before he found a woman foolish enough to have him."

"Yet as people do not all think alike," said Blanche, "the person you speak of is as likely to meet with a wife as anybody else. There may be some females, for instance, who would think Tony Amblewit a very foolish, self-opinionated fellow."

Poor Antony felt himself a good deal lowered by this latter remark, and as he could not venture a reply, he rode on for some distance without hazarding another remark. At length, however, he managed to pocket the indignity, and upon once more recovering his good nature, he said—

"I was for a long time wishing you would say something, and now methinks you have done so with a witness. But I thank you even for that, and will prove that I can take a jest as well as any one."

"A jest you call it!" cried Blanche; "nay, truly good Anthony I was never more serious in my life. In truth, I have too much upon my mind just now to give way to idle raillery."

"But as giving way to melancholy never did any person good that I have heard of," replied Tony, " I can't see the use of indulging it. But yonder I see something to make the heart glad; so let us boldly onwards, and we shall soon have the rest we both of us so much require."

" What mean you, good Tony ?"

" I mean that I see a comfortable looking hostelrie," he replied. " If it please you we will put up there; and after partaking of the necessary refreshment you can retire up stairs to one of the chambers; and then when night comes again, we will set off, and I hope a few hours' ride will bring us to Tewkesbury."

" And forget not, sirrah," she exclaimed, " that you call me Theodore; and should anybody make inquiries respecting me, you can tell them I am travelling on my master's business."

" I'll not forget your caution," said Tony; " and should there be need for it, I'll be as silent as you were during the first twenty miles of our journey."

"There will be no need of your silence," answered Blanche Heroit. "Indeed, too much of mystery would be almost as bad as speaking more than need be, for people would be apt to suspect something wrong, and thus we should be involved in difficulties, from which it would not be very easy to escape."

" In that case," replied the other; " the best way will be for you to go and lay down for a little while, under the excuse of being fatigued from the journey. The people of the house may then ask me as many questions as they please, and I'll warrant they'll get nothing out of me."

The short distance they had to go was passed without anything more being said, and having reached the public-house, towards which the attention of Tony Amblewit had been directed, they gave their horses to the care of a man who was in attendance, and then entered the house, where they were greeted with hearty welcome, by the host; and, after a short time, Blanche, under the assumed name of Theodore was ushered to a chamber where she could rest herself till the period again arrived for continuing their journey.

During her absence, Tony was plied by a number of questions by his inquisitive host, all of which he continued to answer in such a manner as to afford satisfaction' without giving the least clue as to the real object they had in view, or the place to which they were proceeding. At length, however, when he bagan to find that the questions multiplied too fast from for him, he left the house, with the intention of strolling about till it was time to take their departure. This indeed was the only way to avoid committing himself; though, on the other hand, it had the effect of giving rise to suspicions in the mind of the host, who, being a warm Yorkist could not believe his guests were partizans on the other side. He was still pondering upon the subject, when Blanche once more entered the room, to whom he was about to continue his questions, when she abruptly quitted the house, under the plea of having to search for her attendant. This had the effect of rather increasing than diminishing the suspicions of the host; and he even began to debate in his own mind whether it would not be proper to retain his two guests, till he had ascertained who they were, and whether they belonged to what he considered the right side of the question.

In the mean time, Blanche, who had vainly tried to find her attendant, strolled towards a thicket which she saw at no great distance from the house, and scarcely had she reached the place, when a female of wild and forbidding aspect suddenly stepped before her. Alarmed at this circumstance, our heroine would have fled, but the hag laid her hand upon her arm, and having first looked round to see that no one was near, pronounced her name.

" You know me," cried Blanche, shrinking back with surprise and terror.

" I do."

" Art thou a friend or an enemy ?"

" A friend."

" How am I to be convinced of it ?"

" By my future actions," answered the woman.

" Your name ?"

" I am called Maud."

"And have we ever met before?" demanded Blanche.

"We have, and you then saved my life."

"Indeed, I remember it not."

"That is likely," returned the hag; "yet it scarcely four years since I fell into the hands of the mob at Chertsey, and I should have perished but for your interferance."

"I recollect the circumstance you allude to," replied Blanche. "The ignorant peasantry had had seized upon you as a supposed witch, and were dragging you to the river, when I fortunately reached the spot."

"Ay, and saved me from their violence," answered Maud. "From that time I have not had it in my power to serve you;—but now my counsel may not be thrown away. You are in search of your lover, but will fail to meet with him unless you heed my words."

"How know you that?"

"Because you are on the way to Tewkesbury, and the enemies of Neville Audeley have conveyed him to Cirencester, which, at present is one of their head quarters."

"Alas!" cried Blanche; "then all, I fear is lost!"

"You are mistaken," answered the woman, "for he is now placed under the care of one who will not prove a severe jailor."

"You know him, then?"

"Ay, Robert Baldock is my brother," replied Maud, "and will not be very strict in his watch over one who is dear to Blanche Heriot."

"Will he connive at his escape?" demanded our heroine.

"Nay, I will not promise quite so much as that," replied the woman, "but the release of Neville Audeley may be more easily effected than you imagine."

"How?"

"Visit Colonel Morton, who is in chief command at Cirencester," answered Maud, "and you will not find him deaf to your entreaties. There are reasons why he should comply with your request, and take my word for it, the attempt will not be without the success you are most anxious for."

"You seem anxious in my behalf," cried Blanche, after a pause, "and I will not reject your counsel, though, it must be confessed, I feel no little surprise at the accuracy of the information you seem to possess."

"Your surprise will vanish when you know how I became acquainted with these things," answered the woman. "Let it suffice for the present that gratitude alone has prompted me to the step I have taken, and should this meeting between us prove of advantage to yourself, I shall be happy at the chance that threw us in each other's way."

"And you believe that Colonel Morton will listen to my request in behalf of Neville Audely."

"I do."

"Will he set him at liberty?"

"At any rate it is likely he will," replied Maud; "and even if he should hesitate to go quite so far as that, he will take the young man under his own special protection, and then your lover will be placed beyond the malice of a foe, who, for some time, has sought his destruction."

"You speak of Hugh Laneret?"

"I do, maiden."

"Know you where he is now?"

"Not exactly," answered Maud, "but where the prey is, the hawk will quickly follow. Neville Audeley, I have told you, is now at Cirencester, and thither will Laneret pursue him. You have no time to lose, therefore, and I will no longer delay you from a task that requires the utmost promptitude. Return, then, to the place where you rested, and lose no more time than is necessary to prepare your horses for the journey, which must be instantly commenced. If there is need for it, I will see you again; but should my presence be unnecessary, it is likely this will be our last meeting."

Thus saying, she instantly darted into the thicket, and Blanche Heriot, remembering the caution she had received, retraced her steps and finding that Tony and the horses were ready, she mounted her steed, and once more pursued her journey.

CHAPTER XII.

A FRIEND.—THE SUPPLICATION.—TABLES TURNED.

It is unnecessary to trace the progress of the travellers, as no incident of any consequence occurred till they reached Cirencester, where, having made cautious inquiries, they soon succeeded in discovering the house of Colonel Morton, who had fortunately just returned home when they reached it. The first care of Blanche was to send a message, requiring an immediate interview upon business of importence; and this having been acceded to, she left Tony to take care of the horses, while she proceeded to the room in which the officer was waiting her arrival.

Colonel Morton received her with far more kindness than she had anticipated; and, emboldened by the courtesy with which he had addressed her, Blanche at once made him acquainted with the business that had led to the interview; and having confessed the disguise she had been induced to assume, she informed him of her real name, and the purpose which had forced her to put on a disguise, of which she felt ashamed.

"Mistress Blanche Heriot scarcely need offer an excuse for that which, in my opinion, does her so much honour," answered Colonel Morton. "I can respect her motives; and the daughter of my old friend, Arthur Heriot, may rest assured I will do my utmost to obey the request she has made."

"You knew my father, then?"

"We were sworn companions," answered the Colonel, "and have fought in many a battle side by side on the commencement of this fatal civil strife. I saw him perish beneath the swords of his enemies; and though it was not in my power to save the life of my friend, his daughter shall have reason to know that I still remember him with kindness."

"And you will set Neville Audeley at liberty?"

"I see no obstacle to my doing so," replied Colonel Morton, "because it appears the young man was not made our prisoner whilst bearing arms against us."

"He was basely trepanned by one who seeks his death," replied Blanche; "and nothing but your interposition can save him from destruction."

"Who is his enemy?"

"Hugh Laneret."

"Indeed!" exclaimed the colonel; "and may I inquire the motive that has led to this enmity?

"He considers Neville Audeley a rival for my affections," answered Blanche, with hesitation, "though, Heaven knows, I have ever given him reason to see that my heart never could be his."

"I understand," replied Colonel Morton; "and so, for not other cause than the one you have named, Hugh Laneret has been base enough to seek the life of him for whom you have come here to plead?"

"That," answered our heroine, "is the only ground he has to complain upon. You have already heard to what an extent he has succeeded; and had it not been for my having followed him thither, there is too much reason to believe Neville Audeley must have perished through the designs of a cruel and vindictive foe."

"He shall be disappointed, at any rate," exclaimed Colonel Morton; "and it is even likely that this incident may serve to render this young Audeley the more secure in future; Hugh Laneret has transgressed one of the orders that were given with respect to prisoners, and that circumstance has put it into my power to order him into confinement till commands have been sent from head-quarters."

"My purpose," replied our heroine, "was not so much to seek for a punishment upon Hugh Laneret, as to save Neville Audeley from the danger into which he has fallen. You have promised liberty to the captive, and I seek not the revenge you have spoken of."

"That is generously said, at any rate," said Colonel Morton; "and doubtless your word will hereafter weigh with me. At present, however, he must submit to the confinement to which he has subjected another; and, perhaps, after a time, he will learn the duty that one man owes to another."

"I fear the contrary," sighed Blanche; "for his disposition is ferocious in the extreme, and any punishment he may endure will but serve to increase his hatred against Neville Audeley."

"But you forget," said the colonel, "that Neville Audeley will now be on his guard against him, and that consequently he will be well able to guard himself against the evil designs of his enemy."

"I am aware of it," returned Blanche; "yet, when I know the disposition of Hugh Laneret, I cannot but feel alarmed at the mischief he will meditate. The death of his rival will alone satisfy his boundless hatred, and there is but too much reason to believe he will find means to carry into effect the revenge he so much desires."

"Well," exclaimed the colonel, "it must be admitted there is some ground for your fears: and I will, therefore, see to the release of Neville Audeley without delay. You perhaps will accompany me to the place of his captivity, and since there is some fear of a pursuit from Laneret, you will thus gain a fair start before the news is spread about."

To this proposition Blanche eagerly assented, and a few moments afterwards, under the protection of Colonel Morton, she left the house; but, to her great surprise, neither Tony Amblewit nor the horses were to be seen anywhere near the place. She, however, after a little reflection, supposed he was exercising them at no great distance off; and, following her conductor through the principal streets of the town, they at length turned down a dark and narrow one, which presently brought them before the house which had been converted into a temporary prison. Here they observed Tony Amblewit, with only one of the horses; and, in answer to the inquiries of Blanche, he informed her that he had found the means to effect the escape of Neville Audeley some few minutes previously, and there was every reason to believe he was by this time safely on his way back to Chertsey.

Delighted at the zeal which had been thus manifested by her faithful attendant, Blanche would have immediately followed; but Colonnel Morton was anxious to satisfy himself whether the jailor was in fault; and, taking her arm, he proceeded towards the door, when he was encountered by Baldock, whose looks testified the alarm he felt at the escape of his prisoner.

"It is all over with me!" he exclaimed, on perceiving the colonel; "yonder knave prevailed on me to let him have an interview with the prisoner, and taking advantage of my brief absence from the room, he has contrived to effect the escape of Neville Audeley."

"And for which he is rather to be praised than blamed," observed the colonel.

"Then you are not angry with me?" exclaimed Baldock, with surprise.

"On the contrary," returned the other. "Your prisoner was unfairly trepanned by a trick of Hugh Laneret's; and as all honour has been violated in this instance, I came hither with this lady to order his instant release. Yonder fellow it seems has deprived me of a pleasure that I contemplated; but the service he has done is so important. that I can easily pardon him as well as yourself, for the disappointment I experience."

"Nor shall your conduct go unrewarded," added Blanche; "for I will myself bestow upon you a sufficient sum of money to release you from a situation for which you seem to be ill adapted."

"And shall I receive no punishment, when I expected death at the very least?" cried Baldock, with astonishment.

"You shall receive your deserts, villain!" exclaimed Hugh Laneret, who at that instant rushed furiously towards him with his sword drawn. The deed he meditated, however, was frustrated by the interposition of Colonel Morton, who having struck the weapon from his hand, exclaimed—

"It is fortunate, Hugh Laneret, that I have been the means of saving you from a heinous crime, the punishment of which must have proved fatal to yourself. Leave us, sir, and henceforth learn the respect that a soldier owes to his own character and honour."

"Colonel Morton," said the other, fiercely, "you have made an enemy of one who never endures an insult without seeking immediate vengeance. For the present, you may boast of having obtained an advantage over me; but beware of him who now speaks this warning to you, for his retaliation shall be as speedy as it will be certain!"

"Your threats are unheeded," answered the colonel; "or I might, perhaps, ask in what way I have given the offence you complain of?"

"By taking part with those you know to be my enemies," he replied. "I have already heard enough to know that Neville Audeley has been suffered to escape; and, instead of punishing the villain who has neglected his duty, you have commended him for doing that which should have insured his death."

"Your own conduct in this affair has been marked with treachery and deceit," answered the colonel, in a tone of displeasure; "Neville Audeley is at present only suspected to be in favour of the party we are opposed to; and yet, for no other reason than your own hatred, he has been betrayed into our hands, and brought hither as a prisoner. He has fortunately escaped; but had it been otherwise, I came here to set him at liberty."

"He shall not escape me," exclaimed Hugh Laneret, passionately. "I will myself pursue him; and should he be overtaken, Neville Audeley shall perish by the hand of his mortal enemy."

"Nay, then, in that case," returned Colonel Morton, "it shall be my care to prevent the fulfilment of your murderous designs. You shall remain here as my prisoner for some little time to come, and your liberation will depend upon your giving a promise that this quarrel shall not be carried any further."

"Colonel Morton," exclaimed the infuriated villain, "you dare not carry your threat into execution; nor will I submit to become the prisoner of one whose power over me I deny."

"You have heard my order, Baldock," cried the colonel; "and in your custody I shall for the present leave this rash and misguided man. See that he escapes not, for should he elude your vigilance, the consequences will fall upon your own head."

"And who will dare lay hands upon me?" exclaimed Hugh Laneret, glaring fiercely upon those by whom he was surrounded.

"I will!" cried Tony Amblewit; and ere the other could defend himself, he sprung forward and pinioned him tightly in his arms, while Baldock passed a cord round him, so as to prevent further resistance. Laneret struggled violently to unloose himself, but against the united efforts of Tony and Baldock he could do but little; and thus secured, he was forced to ascend the stairs and enter the room which had so lately been occupied by Neville Audeley. There they left him, after having carefully secured the door; and on returning to the room where they had left Blanche and Colonel Morton, they found the latter urging her to commence her journey homewards without delay.

"You have nothing to fear now," he said, "since Hugh Laneret is rendered powerless for a while; and the pass I have written will render your journey safe from molestation, should you chance to meet any of our people. Away, then! lose no time, and may Heaven speed you!"

He led her to the door as he spoke, and committing her to the care of Tony Amblewit, hurried away in the direction of his own house. Blanche and her companion then returned to the hostelrie, where another horse was procured in the place of her own that had been taken by Neville, and together they commenced their return towards Chertsey.

CHAPTER XII.

THE MEETING.—INTERRUPTED FLIGHT.—A DELIVERANCE.

AFTER his unexpected meeting with Hugh Laneret, which has been briefly alluded to, Neville pursued his way for some little distance ; but recollecting the uncertainty which involved the fate of Blanche Heriot, he once more determined to return to the town he had left, and to seek her who had shown so generous an interest in his behalf. On his way, however, he was stopped by a party of the Yorkists, who would not suffer him to proceed till they had questioned him as to the business he was on, and the side he espoused in the strife that agitated the country. These questions Neville answered with caution, and at length was suffered to depart, as nothing could be drawn from him that proved him an enemy. This delay was vexatious, since he was most anxious to seek after Blanche ; and no sooner did he find himself at liberty, than he retraced his way to Cirencester with as much speed as the darkness of the night would permit.

At length, having nearly reached the town, he heard the sound of footsteps advancing towards him, and drawing up his horse to the road-side, in order to see who it was that approached, he recognised Tony Amblewit by the voice, as he was engaged in conversation with his timid companion ; and then riding towards them, he greeted Blanche, and having assured her that he had thus far escaped the dangers she dreaded, he inquired by what means she had passed through the difficulties, which, he feared, would terminate in her being made a prisoner, through his having escaped from the custody in which he had been placed.

"There is but little time for explanation, dear Neville," she replied, "for there are many parties belonging to the enemy on the road ; and should you fall in with any of them, it may not be our good fortune to satisfy their inquiries quite so well as we have hitherto done."

"Would that Hugh Laneret might chance to challenge us in our way !" exclaimed her lover.

"And wherefore," demanded Blanche, "should you desire a meeting that might terminate fatally for us both ?"

"It is that I may render the serpent harmless in future," replied Neville. "He has proved himself to be a villain ; and this last trick of his to get me into the meshes of my enemies will never be forgiven, till I have called him to a severe account for the injury he sought to do me."

"Take a fool's advice for once, sir," interposed Tony Amblewit, "and depend on it your sword will soon be better employed than with a villain like that. Besides, Mistress Blanche, here, can tell you a good reason why we are not likely to fall in with him to-night."

"You know something of him, then ?" said Neville, addressing himself to our heroine.

"Why, that can scarcely be denied," she answered ; "for to tell you the truth, cousin, I left him in such good hands, that we are scarcely likely to see him again for the present. Nay, I see you are impatient to know all, so the truth is, Colonel Morton has thought proper to order his arrest, and he is now a prisoner in the very same chamber that you have but lately escaped from."

"And has this been done, say you, by the command of Colonel Morton ?"

"It has."

"They have quarrelled then ?"

"Why, the truth is," answered Blanche, "the colonel professes a little too much honour to admire the treachery that has been practised ; and as a few words arose between them, he ordered Hugh Laneret into arrest ; and so now, I believe, you know as much about it as I do mysslf."

"The occurrence, it must be admitted, is a fortunate one for us," returned Neville ; "but we are still surrounded with danger, since, should any of the Yorkist party happen to meet us, we should be conveyed back to the place from whence we have contrived to escape."

THE COMBAT BETWEEN HUGH LANERET AND NEVILLÈ AUDELEY.

" Nay," answered Blanche, " ever against such an accident as that I am provided ; for Colonel Morton was perfectly aware of the difficulty, and has given
me a slip of paper which will enable us to reach Chertsey in safety."

" The colonel seems to have taken a great interest in providing for yor con-
venience."

" And for which, I suppose, you are jealous ?"

" I—I merely thought, my fair cousin——"

" That a stranger could not do a good turn, like this, without having some
unworthy motive for it !" interrupted Blanche. " You grudge him the favour
it was in his power to do, even though I must otherwise have run the risk of
falling into the power of his lawless people."

"The thought was a selfish one, I own," replied Neville; "yet, under the circumstances, I hope my fair cousin's anger will pass away as suddenly as it arose. I remember this Colonel Morton, and am much mistaken if he bears not an honourable character, though I could have been better satisfied had he joined our side, instead of leaguing himself amongst traitors to their king and country."

"But he sees it not in the same light, Neville," answered Blanche; "so that we must allow him the privilege of having an opinion as well as ourselves. We must, therefore, pray for a speedy termination of this most unnatural war; and when peace again blesses our country, it is to be hoped Colonel Morton will renew his acquaintance with my guardian, and I shall then have an opportunity to evince my gratitude for the kindness he has this night shown to those he might have immured within the walls of a prison."

"Hist," whispered Tony, riding in between them; "unless my ears deceive me, it will not be long before we meet another party of the enemy. I can hear the clattering of mounted men some distance before us, and it would be as well to avoid meeting them, in case they should take it into their heads not to pay any attention to the colonel's pass."

"I hear the sound you speak of," replied Neville; "but let the danger be what it may, we must proceed onwards fearlessly, since it would be madness to retreat now that we have got so far on our journey. You will, therefore, leave it to me when we come up with them, and no doubt we shall find the difficulty a less serious one than you seem to have pictured it."

"And you will promise," interposed Blanche, "not to involve yourself in a dispute with these men whose wrath, if once kindled, may destroy all hopes of escape?"

"For your sake, Blanche," he replied; "I will be careful to give no occasion for any quarrel. There may, perhaps, challenge us ere we are suffered to pass on; but it will only require the exercise of our coolness to render everything perfectly safe."

"I am not easily terrified," answered Blanche, "as the events of the last few hours ought to convince you. I can be firm when there is need for it, and you shall by and by have to confess that Blanche Heriot was not the greatest coward in the party when her prudence was required."

"And if matters should come to the worst," said Tony, "I can lay about me pretty stoutly; though, to confess the truth, I can't take much credit to myself for bravery, unless it may be when there is no chance of getting away without coming to blows."

"Which it is to be hoped will be avoided," observed the young man. "However, Blanche," he continued, addressing himself to his cousin, "should you find that any altercation takes place between us, ride off with all the speed you can, and I and Tony will keep these fellows so well engaged, that there shall be no fear of overtaking you."

"There I believe you will find me rather inclined to rebel," answered Blanche; "for if danger should threaten either you or our faithful Antony, I shall remain to share it with you, let the consequences be what they may. But we must now be cautious, for the horsemen, whoever they are, seem to be close by; and it would scarcely be prudent to give them the advantage of overhearing our conversation."

"And you really feel no apprehension?"

"Not while you are by my side, Neville."

"But their numbers are most likely far superior to our own," replied the young man, "and in that case I scarcely need remind you there is some danger to be apprehended. They may think proper to doubt the validity of our passport, and in that case we should have to return to Cirencester, and thus again become prisoners after the prospect of escape had appeared to be so certain."

No reply was given to this, for the tramping of the horses was heard close to them, and by the moonlight which was reflected on the armour of those who were approaching, they could see that the party consisted of seven or eight men, and no doubt remained that they were out to collect the assistance of those who might feel inclined to join them, and to make prisoners of all those who thought proper to withold their aid from the cause of Prince Edward. As they approached, the man who seemed to be the leader suddenly checked his speed, and motioning for his men to remain a short distance behind, he rode up, and in a voice of authority, demanded of the others who they were, and which side they belonged to.

"With our names," answered Neville; "you can have nothing to do, and as for the side we take in these unhappy troubles, I believe none of us have yet made up our minds which side we shall take, since it is to be hoped there will be no need of Englishmen to draw their swords against those whom they ought to regard as brothers."

"A cautious answer, at any rate," exclaimed the other; "but it is one that will not satisfy me, you must make up your mind to be more explanatory. So now, to show that I ask nothing more than I am willing to do myself, you must learn that my name is Mark Evered,—that I fight on the side of Prince Edward, and ready to do instant battle with any traitor who dares dispute the right of England's lawful king."

"This is neither a time nor place, sir, to enter into a dispute upon the subject you hane mentioned," answered Neville. "We are merely travellers making our way from Cirencester to Chertsey, and you will therefore do well to let us pass on."

"I should do ill to let you pass on were it afterwards to appear that you are an enemy," returned the other. "So, since you refuse to afford us a more satisfactory answer, you and your companions must go back with us that our colonel may himself question you upon the subject."

"You allude to Colonel Morton, I suppose?"

"In good truth do I."

"Then I believe I can spare you all further trouble upon the subject," exclaimed Neville Audeley, producing the pass and handing it to Mark Evered. "This, as you may perceive, is in the hand-writing of Colonel Morton; and we have his word for it, that no interruption should take place during our journey homeward."

"And why the devil didn't you show me this before?" said Mark, who could see enough by the moonlight to convince him that the writing was indeed that of his colonel.

"Perhaps it's a forgery," observed one of his men.

"Thou art right, Peter," exclaimed the other, glad of any excuse to show his power. "It must be a forgery, for Morton would never have given a protection to people that he knew nothing about. But this knavery shall not answer your purpose, so you must be content to return from whence you came; and if it should prove after all that I have been mistaken, it will then be time enough to make an apology for it."

"I don't know whether my master intends to submit quietly to you," said Tony Amblewit; "but for my own part I can't see what business you have to stop us on the highway, when you've seen the bit of paper that was given us for a protection."

"Then let your master say he belongs to our side, and there will be an end of the business," replied Mark Evered.

"I will yield to the commands of no man," answered Neville Audeley; "and though there may be a considerable difference in our numbers, we are prepared to decide our right by an appeal to the sword."

"Psha! it would be madness to throw away your lives thus," exclaimed Mark Evered. "Our side counts more than two to one against yours, and, if I mistake not, yonder youth would rather run away than engage such odds."

As he spoke thus, he pointed towards Blanche Heriot, whose alarm for her lover's safety had been most terribly excited, and in whose countenance might be observed the paleness which apprehension had there depicted. Neville could only glance towards her in token of his earnest wish that she would preserve all her firmness in this moment of peril; and then addressing himself to Mark Evered, he demanded, angrily, whether their time was to be any longer wasted, after the explanation had been already given.

"Why, the truth of it is, young gentleman," said the other with an expression of triumph, "the paper you have just shown me is certainly in the handwriting of Colonel Morton; but there is one thing about it that you seem entirely to have overlooked. The pass is only for *two* persons, and yet it appears that your party consists of *three*."

"Granted," replied Neville Audeley; "and you will, therefore, suffer my companions to pass on their journey, and in that case, I will return with you to Cirencester till you have seen Colonel Morton upon the subject."

Blanche could not speak for fear of being betrayed by her voice, but her gestures assured Neville that this was an agreement she would never consent to; and so perplexed was he at the impediment thrown in his way, that he knew not what course next to pursue.

"I don't profess to understand the signals that are passing between you," said Mark Evered, who had been narrowly watching them; "but it's pretty certian that there's something wrong, and it will therefore be my duty to take all three of you back with me. If there's nothing to be afraid of, you can have no objection to such an arrangement, and should I have made any mistake, why I'll convey you back in order to make reparation."

"To tell you the truth, we would rather be excused the honour of your company," said Tony, who had made up his mind to have a fight for it, rather than run the risk of being taken again to the town they had just quitted. "We are all of us peaceable travellers, and I should like to know by what right you would make prisoners of us?"

"That you shall know another time," answered Mark; "but at present we have little leisure to enter upon explanations that can be of no benefit to you. So now fellows advance, and let it be understood, that if one of them is suffered to escape it will be at your own peril."

Neville Audeley raised his sword to cut down the ruffian who had advanced to seize upon Blanche; but, at the same instant, another of the men was preparing to slay the lover of our heroine, when a female figure rushed frantically among them, and ere the fatal blow could be struck, a poniard was plunged into the bosom of the soldier, and he sank with a heavy groan from his horse. This incident so unexpected on all sides, struck terror among the followers of Mark Evered, and in spite of all the oaths and imprecations heaped upon them, they gallopped rapidly away, believing that it was a fiend which had thus interposed to prevent the capture of the prisoners.

Mark Evered was thus left to himself, and as he saw that both Neville and his companions were preparing to resist all attempts to capture them, he set spurs to his horse, and rode off with all speed to join those who had already made good their retreat. As no time was to be lost, the others were about to resume their journey, when the female, who had played so conspicuous a part in the rescue, advanced, and addressing herself to Blanche, said—

"It has been my good fortune, lady, once more to save you from danger, and I would now warn you to return home with all the speed you can. A pursuit will ere long be commenced, and should your enemies once more come in the night, I may not again have it in my power to aid you as I have now done."

"You are the woman I saw on my journey yesterday?" cried Blanche, with surprise.

"I am."

"And you are in danger should the pursuers you speak of return?"

"Ay, if they were to find me, I should have little chance of saving my life," replied Maud. "However, it will be my care to prevent the danger, and when I have removed this wounded man to a place where he will be attended to, I shall look to my own escape, which will be effected more easily than you imagine."

"At least," interposed Neville Audeley, "you will accept this purse as a small token of my gratitude for the service you have done us, and ere long it may be in my power to offer a reward that shall be better worth your acceptance."

"I will accept no reward for what I have done," answered the old woman. "The life of a fellew creature has nearly fallen a sacrifice to my anxiety to preserve this maiden when I saw she was in danger ; and as some slight recompsnse, I will now exert what skill I possess to heal the wound my hand has inflicted. Away, then, and leave me to the task I have thus set myself."

It was in vain that they tried every argument to prevail on her to quit the place; and at length, finding her firm in her determination, they hastily bade her farewell, and proceeded on their journey at a rapid pace.

CHAPTER XIII.

THE HALT.—A FRESH START.—THE RETURN.

SCARCELY venturing to speak a word, they continued their onward way, at a speed that promised to carry them far beyond reach of pursuit, though still there was considerable danger of meeting other parties belonging to the enemy. Fortunately, however, nothing occurred to create any alarm, and on reaching the house where Blanche and her attendant had rested the day before, they again stopped, and giving their jaded steeds to the care of an ostler, they entered the place, intending to remain there till the return of daylight should enable them to resume their journey with more confidence.

The people of the inn seemed to eye our heroine as if half suspecting the disguise she had assumed, but Neville Audeley so managed the conversation as to make them believe they had been mistaken in their surmises ; and as Blanche shortly afterwards retired to rest, he called for a flask of wine, and having invited the host to partake of it, succeeded in putting an end to the various hints that had begun to grow rather troublesome. But the landlord was not without his fair share of curiosity, and having observed the disordered attire of his guests, he inquired if they had travelled far.

"Merely from Cirencester," was the reply.

"And is there much stirring in that town?" inquired the inquisitive host.

"About as much as in other places, I believe," replied Tony, who began to be afraid lest there was some motive for these inquiries. "The Yorkist troops are assembled there in pretty good numbers ; and they have set the town astir by their presence."

"Humph! and there'll be a fight, I suppose, before very long?"

"I dare say there will," was the brief reply.

"And may I ask which side is likely to gain the day?"

"The one that's strongest, I suppose," answered Tony, with some impatience.

"You seem to be rather sharp upon me, my good friend."

"Which is hardly to be wondered at," replied Tony Amblewit, "since a man hardly knows what to say in these dangerous times. For ourselves, neither this gallant nor myself care much about how the affair turns out; but there are people that like to make a great deal out of nothing ; so the wisest plan is to keep a quiet tongue."

"Why you surely don't suspect a poor fellow like me?" said the host, who was not best pleased with the answer he had received ; "I'm like yourself, indifferent as to which side gains the day ; but when guests come into a house, it's the duty of a landlord to know something about them, for fear he should afterwards get in o trouble."

"If you feel any alarm upon that score," exclaimed Neville, whose attention had been called to the conversation, "we will at once confess that our wishes go neither one way nor the other. The motive that induced us to take this journey is a private one, and you will therefore rest satisfied with knowing that at present we can offer no further explanation."

"How *very* mysterious!" ejaculated the host.

"The mystery, as you term it, is entirely the result of your own imagination," replied Neville Audeley. "A few travellers have merely entered your house for rest and refreshment, and because they refuse to make you acquainted with their business, you must take it in your head that something requires explanation."

"Well," returned the host, "for the life of me I never could see the use of people keeping their affairs so very secret. For my own part, everybody knows my business; and I cant't see why I shouldn't know other people's. Not that I care much about the matter, only it looks so very odd when strangers are riding about the country at a time that all quiet folks, such as myself, prefer keeping safe within their houses."

"Confound the fellow's impudence," muttered Tony to himself; "he'll do us some mischief after all, if we don't contrive to say something that will satisfy him."

Then, nudging Neville's arm, he whispered that another flask of wine might do them some service; and when this was placed upon the table, and a cup of it put before him, he began to praise the quality of the liquor, and spoke so earnestly of its merits, that the thoughts of the host were turned into a new channel, and for about an hour afterwards he did nothing but speak of the excellence of his own wines, and mention the names of those who had paid him similar compliments to those he had just heard. At length, however, his thoughts reverted to the former subject; and, with a wink to Tony Amblewit, he inquired if he might be bold enough to ask how much further they had got to travel.

"As far," replied the other, "as will take us till after sunset before we find ourselves at home."

"Ha! and where may your home be?"

"At Chertsey," answered Neville, impatiently.

"Humph! and the roads you will have to travel are none of the best."

"You know the place, then?"

"Why, to be sure I do," replied he of the spigot; "I once lived there, and know some of the people. By-the-by, are the Morleys still in the town?"

"No," answered Tony, "they left two years ago."

"Ah! run away I'll be bound;—they were extravagant folks, and I suppose when they couldn't get into debt any further they were obliged to leave."

"Upon my life I don't know anything about it," replied Tony, "for, to tell you the truth, I never interfere in matters that don't concern me."

"Nor I," returned the host, "for if there's one thing that I detest more than another it's interfering with matters that don't concern you. By the way, I was struck with the countenance of your friend that came with you, and for some time I couldn't make out where I had seen him. But I have it now;—I know him!"

"Indeed!" exclaimed Neville with alarm.

"Yes,—I'm quite certain about it."

"And pray, my friend," said Tony, "who may you take him to be?"

"Why, the brother of a young lady at Chertsey," answered the host.

"Her name?"

"Blanche Heriot," replied the landlord. "The likeness between them is wonderful, and the thing would have struck me at first only that I don't happen to recollect that she ever had a brother."

"No more she had," replied Tony, "and so that shows how much mistaken you have been. The person you speak of is the ward of Sir Philip Warrenne, and has no relation living that can bear so great a likeness as you say."

"Then for once in my life I have been most confoundedly mistaken," replied the host.

"I should say it's not the first time," observed Tony Amblewit, "and as you have made such a mistake I should advise you to say no more about it."

"Tush, man," exclaimed the host, "I'm not quite certain yet that I have made a mistake, and as the youngster will be down presently, I shall take the liberty to ask him a few questions for my own satisfaction."

"And why should you do anything of the kind?" asked Tony, "when it can't be any concern of yours, let it be which way it will?"

"I shouldn't have thought anything about it if you had answered my questions fairly," replied the other;—"but as I told you before, I hate mystery, and particularly in times like these when we all make each other's business our own."

"You are quite determined then to make the inquiry you spoke about?" said Neville Audeley, who now began to take up the matter more seriously.

"Why, to be sure I am," replied the landlord;—"that is to say, unless you can tell me any good reason why I should not do so."

"And if need be I can give you a very sufficient reason why you should not ask impertinent questions," answered the other with emphasis.

"Indeed!—perhaps you'll produce it, sir."

"It is here," answered Neville Audeley, drawing his sword a little from its scabbard. "I am the friend of the person you propose annoying with your impertinent questions, and will not sit quietly by whilst you make inquiries that no one can have any business with. You now understand me, and I hope it will not be necessary for me to have any further dispute on the subject."

"You make use of so sharp an argument that I certainly shall not attempt to dispute it," exclaimed the host, who now began to find it necessary to act with more caution. "I thought," added he, "we were all friends together, but as a sword is a weapon that I don't understand the handling of, I shall allow that you have got rather the best of me for once in a way. And now, sir, may I be so bold as to inquire when it will be your pleasure to shift your quarters from my house?"

"When my young friend is sufficiently rested to proceed on his journey," was the only reply given.

"And that will not be long first," exclaimed Tony Amblewit. "He is, like ourselves, anxious to be off; and with the first appearance of daylight, you will have the pleasure of seeing us take the road that leads from hence towards Chertsey."

"The day is already beginning to dawn," said the host, rising from his seat, and throwing open the window-shutter. "There is the prospect of a fine day before you; and, to tell you the truth, I care not how soon I get to bed; for this sitting up all night ought to be well paid for, to make it altogether pleasant."

"You will find sufficient in this purse to recompense you for any trouble we have given," said Neville Audeley, handing to him a small bag of silver coin. "It will more than pay you for what we have had, and let that console you for the loss of two or three hours' bed."

"And you may also congratulate yourself," added Tony, "that my young master here has not made a hole through your body, for the impertinent curiosity you have been guilty of. He is not apt to be very cool in such cases as this; and I only wonder you have not brought upon yourself the whole weight of his indignation."

Any further reply that the host might have been inclined to make was here interrupted by the sudden appearance of Blanche, who, having observed to her companions that it was sufficiently light to proceed on their journey, urged that they should resume it with as little delay as possible. No persuasion was, however, necessary for those who were as anxious as herself; and the horses having been quickly got in readiness, they were again in the saddle, and on their way towards the place of their destination.

"Well, if there ain't some mystery in this, I'm uncommonly mistaken," exclaimed the host, as he saw them gallop off. "There was no getting an answer from any of 'em; and if I had only got two or three people about me, just now, they should not have rode off so jauntily as they did. But never mind; if any inquiries should be made about them, I know who they are, and where they come from, and I won't say that a good bribe would not tempt me to give a clue to them, though they were not bad customers to the house, considering the time they were in it."

He returned to the house while he was thus speaking, and seating himself in a chair before the fire, he was soon dreaming of the past, and imagining a thousand improbable things for the future. He had not, however, been thus resting himself above an hour, when a loud knocking at the door roused him from his slumbers, and starting up, half asleep, he presently gave admittance to four men, who had just dismounted from their horses, which were fastened by their bridles to the trees that grew in front of the house.

"So ho, master host!" exclaimed he who appeared to be the principal man, "you are late this morning before you begin business. Some roysterers in the house, I dare be sworn, that knew the value of comfortable quarters too well to take their departure from your goodly company, till long after the time when honest men ought to be in their beds."

"I don't rightly understand you, Master Mark Evered," replied the host, who seemed to be well acquainted with the last speaker; "but you, at any rate, ought to know that my house has got the character of being a well conducted one, and, to speak the honest truth, I know not that it ever gave shelter to a worse character than yourself."

"Humph! the fresh air of the morning seems to have sharpened your wits."

"And to have made you somewhat insolent," returned the host. "However, I'm in no cue for quarrelling, so sit you down, and if you have any money to spend, I have as good liquor to give in exchange for it, as you'll find between here and London."

Upon this hint, a couple of flagons of ale were ordered to be brought in, and whilst this was being quaffed, Mark Evered, with as much unconcern as he could assume, inquired if any travellers had happened to call during the night.

"A few," answered the host, "but that's no rare occurrence, you know, in a house like this."

"True; but how many were there in the party?"

"Have you any reason for asking the question?"

"I have."

"Then you can afford to pay for any information I may give you?" replied the host.

"Knave!" exclaimed Mark Evered, "dost thou not know I can enforce an answer from thee?"

"How?"

"By first beating thee with the flat part of my sword," replied the soldier, "and then taking thee as my prisoner to the next town, where thou wilt be made to sit in the stocks till thou hast come to thy senses."

"Your threats will not stand in lieu of coin," returned the host sullenly; "and so, if you have no better offer to make, you had better go on your journey without loss of further time; for no word will you get of me unless I can turn my information into ready money."

"You forget then how soon I could force you to give that which you absolutely withhold?"

"I know you can either beat or slay me, without fear of being punished for [it afterwards," replied the host. "There is no one about the place but the ostler to give me any help, and yet, for all that, I can defy you to make me say a word more than I think proper."

"What will make you speak, then?"

"Payment for my services, to be sure."

"And that thou shalt have when I know exactly what they are worth," answered Mark Evered; "so be quick, man; and if thou shouldst be the means of putting the fugitives within my reach, I will promise thee a reward to thy heart's content."

"A bird in the hand is worth two in the bush," replied the host, "and as I always like to see the way clearly before me, you had better give me the gold at once, and

HUGH LANERET BRIBES THE FERRYMAN TO FRUSTRATE THE RETURN OF EVENDEN.

then you will know who has been here, and which road they took upon leaving the house."

"And these are the only terms upon which you will obey my commands?"

"They are."

"Then take that for thy pains, caitiff!" exclaimed Mark Everet, striking the host with the scabbard of his sword, and sending him reeling half across the room. "I tell thee, villain, thou art a traitor to the good cause, and thy carcase shall hang from a gibbet for daring to dispute the orders of one that bears the king's commission."

"Of which king speak you?" asked the host, upon recovering a little from the blow he had received. "At this time it so happens there are two claimants to the throne, and a man is therefore rather puzzled in his loyalty to know which is the one that ought to be obeyed."

"None but a traitor would have asked such such a question," returned Mark Evered ; "for though there are two claimants, there is but one that men ought to acknowledge."

"And who may that be ?"

"Edward."

"Humph ! and the next person I see may perhaps tell me that Henry the Sixth is the monarch that all men ought to reverence and acknowledge. For my own part, I don't pretend to have any opinion about it ; but I suppose neither the one nor the other would think himself much honoured by having in his service an officer who has no better command over his temper than you seem to have."

"You are an insolent fellow," exclaimed Mark Evered; "but beware, for I am not used to parley much in affairs of this kind, and perhaps another word or two may excite my rage, that you will perish by my sword, as a warning to all other persons who know not the duty they owe to the king's officers."

"You talk bravely," returned the host with a sneer, "considering I am an unarmed man, and you have three or four at hand ready to help you in case there should be need of their assistance."

"We are losing time here, lieutenant," interposed one of the soldiers, "and if the people we are in search of have really been here, I can see very little chance of this fellow to acknowledge it, unless you first of all pay him for what he may have to tell."

"He shall perish by my hand, if he refuses any longer," exclaimed Mark Evered, furiously. "I have already been fooled enough by him, and since he now knows his fate, he will perhaps think it worth his while to save his life by giving the information I have demanded."

"If you come here to murder me in cold blood, I have no means of defending myself," answered the host. "I, however, am not to be frightened by the blustering of a fellow because he happens to wear a sword by his side ; and so, Master Mark Evered, we understand each other by this time, and you can now either put your threat into execution, or take your departure from this place as soon as you please."

"This is cool, at any rate," exclaimed the other ; "and pray, thou scurvy knave, what dost thou take me for ?"

"A bully, and a coward !"

"Hah ! have at thy heart, then !" exclaimed Mark Evered, and springing forward he would have carried his threat into execution, had not one of the men at the moment thrown himself between them, and striking the sword from his hand, sent it flying to the further end of the room.

"Come, come, Master Lieutenant," said the man, "fair play's a jewel, and it don't become a man that calls himself a soldier to turn cut-throat and assassin."

"Villain !" roared the other ; "are *you* against me too ?"

"I am not against you," replied the soldier, "and upon growing cool you will acknowledge that I have done nothing more than right in preventing what you would afterwards be sorry for."

"Had you been of my own rank this interference should have been punished with instant death," answered Evered ; "as it is, however, I shall let it pass for the present, though you may be assured I will not forget the insolence you have been guilty of to a superior officer."

This sudden change in Evered's manner had been effected less by compassion for the man than by the determination he saw expressed in the countenances of the others to defend their comrade in case their assistance should be needed. He also pretended some little show of sorrow for the violence he had been guilty of towards the host, and throwing upon the table a few pieces of gold, he inquired if that would be sufficient to purchase the information he had been so desirous to obtain.

"Why this," said the landlord, as he deposited the coins in his pocket, " is an argument that most people are willing to listen to. There's reason in it; and now I don't mind saying that three travellers arrived here in the course of the night, and that they took their departure soon after the appearance of dawn."

"And why could you not have told me as much before?" demanded Mark Evered.

"Because you were so confoundedly obstinate, and wouldn't come to the terms I proposed."

"And did you happen to know any of the persons you gave shelter to?"

"I did not; but one of them I took to be the brother of a girl that I once knew at Chertsey."

"At Chertsey? And did you hear whether that is the place they were journeying to?"

"I believe it is," answered the host; "but, to tell you the truth, they were uncommonly close upon the matter; and though I plied them with all sorts of questions, the devil a bit the wiser was I for it. But I am sure they are the people you are in pursuit of, and so the sooner you set off after them the better chance you will have of laying hold of the fugitives."

Mark Evered now saw that his men were still sullenly brooding over the quarrel he had had with them, and as this was no time for losing their services, he called for a fresh supply of liquor, in which to drown the animosity that had sprung up between them. This succeeded even to the utmost of his expectations, and having once more mounted their horses, they set forward in pursuit at their utmost speed.

In the meantime, Blanche and her companions had been making the best of their way, for they were but too well assured that search would be made after them, and it was of the utmost consequence that they should reach home with as little delay as possible.

At one time it was feared that Blanche would sink under the excessive fatigue she had endured during the last three days, but danger roused her to exertion; and after a brief rest at a house on the road-side, they continued their journey until within twelve miles of Chertsey, when they were met by Herrick Evenden, who, with half-a-dozen of the townsmen, had come out in the hope that they might still be of use to our heroine in the event of her returning from the errand which had taken her from home. The meeting between them was joyous in the extreme, and Blanche was the more gratified at it as she would then be enabled to learn whether her guardian was angry at the step she had taken for the rescue of her lover. Almost her first question was upon this subject, and Herrick lost no time in giving her the information she was so anxious for.

"The truth is," he said, "Sir Philip Warrenne was in a terrible way when he first discovered your absence; and your female attendant being sent for, was closely questioned as to where you had gone, and the object for which you had taken so extraordinary a step. The girl, I believe, hesitated, and showed a great deal of trepidation, when she saw what a furious storm was brewing; but Sir Philip only grew the more impatient, and at length she was forced to make a full confession, that alarm for the safety of Neville Audeley, had urged her young mistress to make an effort for his preservation, and that she was gone, accompanied by Toby Amblewit, to try and save him from the vengeance of an infuriated rival."

"And upon hearing that," cried Blanche, "I suppose he became more angry than ever?"

"At first, I believe, he was," replied Herrick, "but reflection sometimes works wonders; and having been left to himself for a little time, he again sent for Kate Poynet, and after giving her an assurance that he had forgiven the share she had in your flight from home, he inquired if she could give him any clue by which he might discover the direction you had taken. Kate, it seems, pleaded ignorance to everything; but at length, recollecting herself, she mentioned my name, and gave it as her opinion, that I could afford every information that might be required upon the subject. Thus she got the blame from her own shoulders, and I was immediately sent for, to give a full, true, and particular account of all I knew respecting the mysterious disappearance of a certain young lady."

"And did he seem to be seriously offended at my leaving home without having first consulted him?" inquired Blanche Heriot anxiously.

"Why, it must be admitted," replied the other, "that ne was rather angry when I first presented myself before him, and seemed to accuse me of being one of the principals concerned in your departure under mysterious circumstances. But I explained exactly all I knew—which you are aware was very little; and when I begged to assure him of your safe and speedy return, he began to think less seriously of the affair than he had done before."

"But does he know of the disguise I have assumed?" inquired our heroine.

"He does."

"And of course he was angry with me for it?"

"It must be confessed he was," replied Herrick; "but I saw when there was an advantage to be taken, and, with as much plausibility as possible, told him there was no alternative, and that you had, in fact acted with great prudence, since it was the only method that appeared to guard you from insult during so long a journey. Then I described to him the state in which the country was in, the number of wild and reckless scoundrels you might chance to meet, and the great peril you would have to encounter in the event of your travelling without the precaution that had given him so much offence. And, egad, I argued my point so successfully, that at last he declared, his only anxiety was to see your safe return; and it was at his request that I came out with these honest fellows, to see if we could not meet with you somewhere on the road."

"By doing which," exclaimed Neville Audeley, "you have confirmed the good opinion I already entertained of you. But now tell me, Herrick, what said Sir Philip Warrenne about the perilous situation in which I had fallen?"

"A great deal more than I have time to tell you," answered Herrick; "he deplored your misfortune as if you had been his own son, and declared that he would not mind giving any sum that might be required for your ransom."

"It is almost worth enduring misfortunes occasionally, if only for the sake of discovering who are our friends," exclaimed Neville Audeley, with some emotion; "I ever knew Sir Philip for a warm-hearted friend; but, till this moment, I felt not the deep obligation I am under to him."

"And yet," observed Herrick, "between ourselves, he has favoured you beyond all other persons of his acquaintance. You must remember that there were others besides yourself who sought to obtain the hand of Blanche Heriot; but his favour has been extended to you, and thus I have the gratification of wishing you joy upon the acquisition of a prize that was eagerly coveted by so many rivals."

"But all of them are not inclined to abandon the prize;" returned Neville.

"True," answered his friend; "there is Hugh Laneret, who still seeks to obtain by force what he has failed to get by fair means. But he is an exception that is scarcely worthy of being reckoned, since all men know him to be dishonourable, and it is only those who are equally so, that will associate with him. To be sure, he is not the less dangerous on that account, yet a little caution may still thwart his villanous projects."

"At present, I believe, we are tolerably secure from him," replied Neville, "for he has fallen into his own toils, and is now a prisoner in the hands of his own party."

"A prisoner!"

"Ay, that I can answer for," interposed Tony Amblewit, "for I had the pleasure of putting him into quarters that he won't get out of in a hurry. He wanted to show some of his consequence before Colonel Morton, but it wouldn't do there, and so he's left to his own reflections against he gets his liberty again."

"Which I dare say will not be long first," observed Neville, "for, with all his faults, he is not without his fair share of courage: and when fighting begins between the two factions, he will be set at liberty, in order to give his assistance in these unhappy wars."

" Well," replied Herrick, " at all events he will then be too much occupied to attend to his own base views ; and we may, therefore, regard all danger to Blanche as being at an end."

" But it is not so with Neville's danger," sighed Blanche, " for he has given mortal offence to his rival, and I fear the hatred will only terminate with the death of one or both of them."

A pause here ensued, during which they increased their speed till they came near the town of Chertsey ; and then, slackening their pace, they passed by the walls of the ancient abbey, just as the curfew was sounding forth its hollow tones upon the wind. From thence they rode to the mansion of Sir Philip Warrenne ; and, whilst Blanche hastened to her own chamber, to resume her attire, the two friends hastened to the knight to announce her safe return.

CHAPTER XVII.

THE BETROTHINGS.—AN ARREST.—THE CAGE.

NOTHING could exceed the joy of Sir Philip Warrenne as he saw the young men enter the room, for their presence augured the safety of Blanche, and a few brief words served to assure him that his hopes were not groundless.

" Where is she ?" he exclaimed impatiently. " Od's life, does she think I care nothing about her, that she keeps out of sight when I am so anxious to see her after being absent from home all this time ?"

" The truth is, my dear sir," answered Neville, " I believe she was unwilling to present herself before you in the disguise she thought it necessary to assume, when about to undertake a journey of some danger."

" And if the truth were known," added the old knight, " I suppose she thought it better that you should see me first with an apology for the harum scarum flight she has taken. Egad, it must be confessed I was angry enough when I first discovered her absence ; but somehow or other the jade has made me love her, and I forgave the act almost as soon as it was found out."

" The truth is," cried Neville Audeley, " the blame should, by right, rest upon my shoulders, since it was for me the journey was undertaken."

" And her mad scheme," observed Sir Philip, " appears to have succeeded beyond my expectations."

" Who would refuse a favour when asked by one who had risked so much to obtain ?" asked Neville. " The truth is, Colonel Morton claims some former acquaintance with both yourself and the father of Blanche, so that he could scarcely deny the request when made under such peculiar circumstances."

" And he set you at liberty as a reward for the heroism she had displayed ?"

" He did, Sir Philip."

" Then I only wish," exclaimed the knight, " that he had thought proper to take the other side of the question in this cruel war, and then we might have renewed our acquaintance, that was only dropped in consequence of his having to join the army abroad. However, he may yet see the error of his ways ; and, in that case, he will find that, though years have fallen upon me, I have as warm a heart as when we knew each other in our youth."

" And you have quite forgotten the little anger that was excited by the unexpected departure of Blanche ?"

" Why to be sure I have," answered Sir Philip. " The girl has got some of the spirit of her father, and hang me if I don't like her all the better for it. But here she comes, and my welcome shall prove that she is as dear to my heart as ever."

So saying, he pressed her in his arms ; and, having given way to the emotion that her return had occasioned, he placed her hand in Neville's, exclaiming—

"The perils you have undertaken in his behalf prove the intensity of an affection that I had previously observed with the greatest satisfaction. Take her, Neville, and rely upon it, my young friend, you have obtained a prize that well deserves a life of love and devotion. Had her father been living, his joy would have been as great as my own in thus giving her to one who, I believe, merits the regard in which she holds him."

"My Blanche shall never have to regret the moment which thus realizes my fondest wishes." exclaimed Neville, rapturously. "My utmost happiness is now indeed secured, and my heaviest vengeance shall fall upon those who dare seek to injure her."

"There is but one I have to fear," answered Blanche; "and even he he will not venture to injure me when my hand is irrevocably given to another."

"If you speak of Hugh Laneret," exclaimed Sir Philip, "I understand he is, for the present, safe; and by the time he gets his freedom, I trust you will have become the wife of him you have rescued from the hands of a treacherous villain. At any rate the marriage shall not be delayed longer than is necessary; and when the nuptial ceremony is over, I can bid farewell to the world without regret."

"And I suppose, Kate," whispered Tony, to the faithful attendant, "the same day that gives your mistress to her lover, will see you become Mrs. Amble-wit?"

"Indeed, sir, I don't know any reason why you should think anything of the kind,' answered the maiden, sharply; "I have not boxed your ears, it's true, when you thought proper to talk a parcel of nonsensical love to me; but it don't follow that you are to have me merely because you have taken such a notion into that wise head of yours."

"Why, you don't mean to disappoint me after all?"

"I don't know what I mean to do yet, sir," she replied. "Many lovers that I could tell you of have been content to court for years before they got as much as a civil answer; and yet here are you impatient to be married though we've scarcely had six months to find out whether our tempers are likely to agree."

"The truth is, my dear Kate," said Tony, "my temper is so good a one, that I'm sure you will never have any reason to find fault with it, and as for yours—"

"It can be as hot as any one's when people put me out of sorts," answered Kate, tartly; "besides, sir, I don't choose to be annoyed upon this subject just at present, so you must take some other opportunity; and mind, sir, that it's when I'm in a very good humour."

"What's the matter now, Kate?" exclaimed Sir Philip, who had chanced to overhear some of the foregoing conversation.

"Nothing, sir," she replied; "only I was telling Tony that it's impertinent to be whispering to me in the presence of our superiors."

"In other words, my good girl," returned the knight, "you would rather have these little billings and cooings where there are not quite so many persons to listen to them. And you are perfectly in the right, Kate, for lovers are apt to talk so much nonsense, that I believe the less that's overheard by other people the better. However, let me persuade you not to be too severe with poor Tony, for many a good marriage has been spoilt by a sharp word; and old maids, you know, are seldom the most enviable people in the world."

"Tony understands me well enough, sir," replied Kate; "and I don't suppose he'll take any heed of what was said more in jest than in earnest. Besides, he knows well enough that I never scold anybody but him; and if that ain't a proof of my regard, I don't know what is."

"Then, of course," laughed the old knight, "you will not object, after all that's been said, to his naming your mistress's wedding-day for your own?"

"If it is your command, sir, certainly," simpered Kate; "but we can hardly make up our mind upon that subject, when I believe even Miss Blanche herself has not yet determined when her marriage is to take place."

"Why, that's a question that cannot be settled, I believe, at this moment," replied Sir Philip; "but as it will take place immediately after the close of our political disputes, you can find no difficulty in saying whether you will then permit Tony to call you his wife?"

"Perhaps, I may, sir," replied Kate; "but he must understand that it will entirely depend upon his good behaviour, as he knows I could have half-a-dozen good offers directly, if I pleased; but as I believe him to be an honest, worthy sort of fellow, I've given him the preference."

"Upon my life, Kate, I'm much obliged to you for it!" exclaimed Tony; "and so now, since you have confessed so much, suppose we go down into the old hall, and make our own arrangements for the happy day."

"Ay, and look smilingly upon him, Kate," said Sir Philip Warrenne, as they were leaving the room; "for Tony is not a bad-looking fellow, you know; and there are other girls in the parish who may step in and take your place in his heart before you are aware of it."

"Poor Tony is aware of the advantage he has gained," exclaimed Neville; "and I am much mistaken if he does not make the girl confess her love for him, before she is an hour older. And now, since they are gone, tell me, Blanche, whether you can endure a parting till the disputes that distract our island have been settled?"

"You would leave me then?" she sighed.

"It is my duty to advocate and support a just cause," answered Neville; "and I am much mistaken if you would not urge me to the performance of a certain task, which, if left unperformed, would subject me to the eternal reproach of cowardice."

"You have done me no more than justice, Neville," she replied, "in believing that no selfish considerations should ever bring upon you a blot that nothing could ever remove from your name. My woman's fears, however, are not to be controlled; and something seems to assure me that if you enter into these wars, it will lead to almost certain death."

"Nay," he answered; "I have less serious forebodings on the subject, my dear Blanche, though I will not conceal from you the fact, that there are many dangers, some of which I may not be able to avoid. Yet, with your bright image constantly in my remembrance, I shall never be deficient of that courage which is so necessary in those who draw the sword in favour of justice."

"Would that I had the same opportunity of ranking myself on the side of good King Henry," he exclaimed Herrick Evenden; "but somehow or other my father has taken it into his head that my evil star is against me, and all the persuasion I am master of would fail to obtain his consent to my drawing a sword, even though it should be to save my country from ruin."

"And perhaps he is in the right," answered Blanche, "for, as his only son, you are the sole stay of his declining days, and it would be a poor solace to him hereafter to reflect that his last remaining child had perished by what the world calls a death of honour."

"Yet is Herrick's wish to fight for his king!" exclaimed Sir Philip Warrenne "and for my own part I can see no reason why he should remain idle, when all who are able to draw a sword will do so on either one side or the other. For my own part, I am rather too old to come into contact with the tough young fellows that have belted on the sword, or I would not remain here in idleness, when there is life and liberty to fight for."

"Are you an advocate, then, for shedding human blood?" asked Blanche, with a shudder.

"No, but I am for sustaining human honour, though," answered Sir Philip, "and I am only sorry that Master Basil Evenden has suffered his superstition to interfere in such a case as this. But he has suffered astrology, and all other sorts of nonsense, to get into his head; and, as I suppose, it would be useless for me or anybody else to try and talk him out of it."

"I will seek to do so no more," exclaimed Herrick, "because I am already but too well convinced that all would be in vain. I may not, however, be able to resist the srong temptation that is within me ; and if it should happen that I prove disobedient to his will, he must blame himself for it hereafter.''

"You have an intention, then, to go without his permission ?" said Sir Philip.

"I have some thoughts of so, sir," answered Herrick ; "but perhaps I was incautious in saying so before one who may consider it his duty to put him on his guard against the meditated disobedience of his son."

"Tush ! tush ! you have nothing to fear from me, Herrick, you may depend on it," returned the old knight. "I like to encourage rather than depress spirit ; and if I had a dozen sons of my own, I should love them all the better for disobeying me where their own honour was concerned. So consider the matter well, my dear boy, and should you want any one to act as a mediator hereafter, be sure you will find a zealous one in old Sir Philip Warrenne."

Before any reply could be given to this, Tony Amblewit came bustling into the room ; and after eyeing Blanche, as if he wished her anywhere else, he sidled up to Sir Philip, and whispered in his ear, that there were persons below who desired to speak with him immediately.

"Speak out, man," exclaimed the knight, "and let's have no secrets before friends. Who are these people that you say want to see me ?"

"They are soldiers, Sir Philip."

"How many of them ?"

"Four."

"And what is their business ?"

"That's more than they thought proper to tell me," replied Tony ; "but I happen to recollect that he who appears to be their principal is one of the fellows that stopped us as we were coming homewards last night."

"Ho, ho ! then there's mischief a-foot," exclaimed the knight ; "send them up, Tony, and we'll soon find out what brings them on a visit to me."

"Shall they all come, sir ?" asked Tony.

"To be sure," replied the knight ; "and yet, now I think of it, one will be enough : so send up the fellow that can best act as spokesman ; and do you send my servants to keep watch over the rest, to prevent their coming here, in case their comrade should give a signal for them."

Tony hurried out of the room ; and before Blanche could be conveyed out of it, Mark Evered strode into their presence ; and, by the haughty insolence of his bearing, seemed to declare that he bade defiance to any force that might be used to expel him.

"I perceive, Sir Philp Warrenne," he exclaimed, "that my errand here is not a vain one. I came hither in search of a prisoner, and find him concealed in your house."

"Indeed !" returned the knight ; "I was not aware that there was any one here that you have any control over. Perhaps you will be kind enough to name the person you have alluded to ?"

"Neville Audeley."

"Neville Audeley is my friend," answered Sir Philip ; "and therefore has a right to be beneath my roof."

"He is my prisoner," replied Evered, "and I demand that he instantly surrenders himself."

"And what if I refuse obedience ?" asked Neville.

"Then I have brought those with me who will assist in the duty I am entrusted with."

"I am no prisoner of yours," exclaimed Neville Audeley, "and will perish rather than submit."

"Do you deny having been a prisoner in the hands of the Yorkists, only two days since ?"

"I was betrayed into their hands," answered Neville ; "but when Colonel Morton heard the method which had been used to entrap me, he ordered my instant discharge, and even came down to the prison himself to see that no delay was suffered to take place."

"And Colonel Morton will have to answer for it, before his superiors," replied Evered. "He exceeded his duty, and I have been despatched in pursuit, to convey you back without loss of time."

"Then, you had better return," interposed Herrick, "and tell those who sent you on this errand, that Neville Audeley had friends about him who would rather die than suffer him to be dragged away by ruffianly violence. You knit your brow in anger, sir; but having heard our answer, I would advise you to take your departure before we are compelled to use force."

"I am not here alone, as you are perhaps aware," returned Evered, "and if violence is used on your side, I may be obliged to retaliate."

"In mercy—I implore you, do not disturb the peace of our house!" cried

Blanche, recovering herself from the alarm which had at first seized her. "I myself sought the interposition of Colonel Morton,—he listened to my entreaties, and not only did he give liberty to Neville Audeley, but he, whose treachery I exposed, was given into immediate custody."

"I know it, madam," answered Mark Evered, "and my friend will not forget the obligation you have placed him under, when an opportunity arrives. He regarded you with love, and it has been repaid with hatred and imprisonment."

"My love he had no claim to," replied Blanche, "and any imprisonment he may suffer has been produced by his own base conduct. By villany he succeeded in entrapping his rival, and it was my fortunate chance to defeat the diabolical plot he had formed and partly executed."

"I came not here to talk with women," exclaimed Mark Evered, turning upon his heel, and directing his looks towards Neville Audeley—"you, sir, were the object of my visit to this house, and as I possess the means of enforcing my demands, I shall not quit the place till you accompany me."

"You must take back my breathless corse, then," exclaimed Neville, "for never will I yield myself whilst I have life to resist those who possess no right over my liberty. And you see, sir, I am not quite so friendless as you imagined, for there are those present who will aid me in protecting myself against the efforts of a ruffian and a villain."

Mark Evered took from his pocket a silver whistle, upon which he blew a long and shrill note. The signal, however, was not answered; and he was hastening from the room to ascertain the cause of the delay, when Herrick, rushing past him, took possession of the door, and resolutely kept him back.

"I'll tell you what, Master Mark Evered, or whatever your name may be," he exclaimed; "I keep watch and ward here, and no one either comes in or goes out without my permission. You came here to bluster my friend into submission, and it shall now be seen whether you make your exit by yonder window, unless you think proper to apologize for your insolence, and give us a promise to take your departure from hence without giving us any further trouble in the matter."

"This inolence shall cost you dearly," muttered Evered, through his clenched teeth. "Remember, sirrah, I have been opposed in the execution of my duty."

"Indeed! and pray under whose authority are you acting?"

"Under the authority of a man who supports the rights and sovereignty of King Edward," answered Evered.

"Humph!" retorted Herrick; "then as we happen to acknowledge no other authority than that of King Henry the Sixth; there can be no treason in disobeying the servants of one who designs to usurp the throne to which we do not allow he has a rightful claim. He comes to deluge our land in blood; but let him beware, for he will not find that all Englishmen are traitors, like Mark Evered and his worthy colleague, Hugh Laneret!"

"This insolence shall be no longer endured!" exclaimed the infuriated Evered, and he was rushing towards Herrick, when Neville Audeley, interposing himself between them, exclaimed resolutely—

"If blood is to be shed in this quarrel, it shall be mine, and mine alone. I am the object of your search, and having found me, you shall learn that I am not to be made your prisoner without a vigorous effort in my own defence. Beware of me, then, for by the Heaven above us, I will not yield whilst I have life enough to wield a sword for my own protection."

For an instant Evered glared upon him with a look of intense hatred; and then, rushing towards him, their weapons clashed, and they commenced a combat that was for some time uncertain in its results. At length, however, it became evident that Neville's greater coolness gave him an advantage over his antagonist; and in proportion as that advantage became more and more manifest, the rage of Mark Everard increased. This decided the fate of the strife; and as the infuriated Yorkist fell to the ground, he was about to receive a mortal wound from his antagonist, the door opened, and three or four of Sir Philip's domestics rushed in, to put an end to the affray. This interruption was sufficient to save the life of

Mark Evered, who was, however, seized and disarmed ere he could make a suffi-cient effort to extricate himself.

"The fellows that were left below are all in safe custody," exclaimed Tony Amblewit, who was among the foremost of those who had come to the rescue. "We had a hard matter to keep them from running up here when they heard their leader's signal; but we took the liberty of binding their hands with cords, and they are now in the town cage, where this gentleman shall follow them before he is half an hour older."

"Villains! ye shall dearly rue this," exclaimed Evered, whose rage was beyond all control. "I have been foiled, but your triumph will be short-lived, and then all shall be made to feel the vengeance that boils within my heart."

"Let it boil away, and then it will the sooner be done," returned Tony, as he passed a cord round the arms of his prisoner, so as to make him quite secure. "For my own part, I'm not much afraid of what you'll be able to do after this, and if you only get your deserts, the rope will soon be round your neck instead of serving to keep you in order."

"I would recommend that no more violence be used than is absolutely neces-sary for his safe custody," interposed Neville Audeley, who had been occupied in restoring Blanche to composure. "He has, it is true, done little to demand our compassion, but the advantage is fortunately on our side, and we will, therefore, teach him the virtue of humanity in case an opportunity should hereafter occur for him to exercise it toward others."

"But what shall we do with him next?" asked Tony.

"Let him be taken to the cage where you say his companions have gone before him," said Sir Philip Warrenne; "he will there have time to reflect on the evil of his ways, and if it should make him a better man, her will perhaps hereafter thank us for the useful lesson we have taught him during our bref authority."

"At present I must submit to your will," exclaimed Mark Evered, gnashing his teeth with rage; "but it will not be long before my own turn comes, and you shall then find that I do not forget the violence I have this night received. You, Neville Audeley, are in particular the object of my undying hatred, and I will satisfy my vengeance, even though the next moment sees me the victim of my own fury."

"Take him away," cried Sir Philip, who saw with concern the terror with which his presence inspired Blanche Heriot. "Let him be placed with his com-panions, but remember, though we consider it necessary for our own safety that he should be kept in close confinement, we do not wish that any unnecessary cruelty be inflicted. Food they shall have in plenty, and should they think fit to promise that no further violence shall be attempted against us, they may have their liberty, on expressing their contrition for the past."

"I, for one, will die, ere I submit to any terms that you may seek to impose upon me," exclaimed Mark Evered. "I have now sufficient cause to take this quarrel upon myself, and let Neville Audeley beware of the vengeance that is in store for him, for he has now got me for an enemy as well as Hugh Laneret."

He would have proceeded still further with these threats, but at this moment he was forced from the room by those who had taken charge of him, and as he was dragged down stairs, those who were left behind could hear the fearful denunciations that he poured upon all those who had taken part against him.

"I tremble," cried Blanche, "lest he should find an opportunity to escape, and fulfil the dreadful threats he has given utterance to. Even Hugh Laneret was fierce and vindictive in his wrath, but this man's vindictive hatred is still more to be feared."

"Nay, I rather think there is not quite so much to be alarmed about as you imagine," answered her guardian, "for his passion will cool after a night's con-finement, and I am much mistaken if he does not before long come to the terms that have been offered."

"And ould you give him his liberty upon his own promise to think no more of this quarrel?"

"Why, I see no other way that remains open to us," replied Sir Philip. "In these grievous times the laws run wild, and we must be content to let him loose upon the best terms we can make. But we will talk over this subject another time, so get thee to bed, my child, and to-morrow I dare say you will see less cause for apprehension than you do at present. Away, Blanche, and may the saints protect you from the machinations of those whose ways are evil."

Blanche Heriot bade an unwilling good night to her friends, and accompanied by Kate Poynet, retired to her own chamber—not to sleep, however, but to ponder over the various misfortunes that still continued to rise in her path.

CHAPTER XVIII.

A DISAPPOINTMENT.—THE FOREWARNING.—SEPARATION.

THE next morning, after having seen Blanche, and assured himself that she had in some degree recovered from her terrors, Neville Audeley betook himself to the house of the astrologer, in order to see Herrick, and learn from him whether he had yet had an interview with his father to obtain his concurrence with his own wish of joining the troops that were assembling under the renowned Earl of Warwick, who was intrusted with chief-command in King Henry's army.

But Herrick's countenance betrayed what had been passing almost as soon as he met his friend on entering the house, for he could not endure the disappointment he had sustained, and when the first brief greeting was ever, he said in a tone of deep mortification—

"It's all over, I believe, Neville; the old man will not hear a word of reason, and I will either submit to the disgrace he would thus bring upon me, or forfeit his parental regard for ever."

"This is vexatious enough it must be owned," exclaimed his friend; "but I suppose he gave you sufficient grounds for his continued opposition to what appears to me to be a very reasonable request?"

"Had he been able to do that, I might have been better satisfied," replied Herrick; "but the worst of it is he treats me like a child, and refuses his sanction on the grounds that the planets bode me evil in such an enterprise; and then he most pathetically describes the grief that would cloud the remainder of his days were I to fall in the strife that is every day expected to commence."

"And what answer did you make to all this?"

"What could I say?" demanded Herrick. "It's true I told him that disgrace and shame would cling to me for ever afterwards, but he only smiled at what he called my foolish enthusiasm; and as a proof of his regard bade me ask any other favour that he might show how ready he is to honour me where it can be done without involving myself in danger."

"Which favour you, of course, declined?"

"I did, Neville; and he then told me that I knew his mind upon the subject of our conversation, and cautioned me not to disobey him, as such an act would for ever drive me an exile from my home."

"And that, by-the-by," exclaimed Neville, "would be carrying your military ardour beyond the bounds of prudence. I regret as much as you do that Master Basil Evenden should have laid such a restriction upon the generous motives of his son; but filial duty is not to be broken for slight causes, and I would therefore advise you to yield obedience to him, and I dare say the world will not be quite so harsh in its censures upon your conduct as you have imagined."

"Then you reckon nothing for my own anxiety to aid in a cause that I feel deeply interested in?"

"Indeed, Herrick, I feel deeply concerned for you," replied his friend, "and would have done anything in my power to forward your wishes. I am, however, almost a stranger to your father, and any argument I might use in your behalf would, most likely, only serve to confirm more strongly the notion he has been induced to form."

"My father entertains a very high regard for you," answered Herrick, "and would listen to anything you may have to say, even though he might not feel inclined to yield to your opinion."

"If I rightly understand," said Neville Audeley, "you would have me see him, and try the effect of what arguments I may be able to produce?"

"That is exactly what I wish."

"But in doing so," asked Neville, "shall I not bring upon myself the character of a busy meddler, who encourages a son in his disobedience, and then tries to convince the father that he has laid down injunctions which it would be tyranny to enforce?"

"My father's worst fault is obstinacy," replied Herrick; "but I have known that sometimes to yield, when his arguments have been fairly met. Perhaps you may wonder why I do not undertake this task myself; but the truth is, he has somewhat high notions of parental authority, and would not listen to a son who had temerity to dispute his sovereign commands."

"Well, Herrick," answered the other, "my friendship would indeed be a shallow one, were I to refuse so trifling a request as this; and I will, therefore, comply without raising any more obstacles about it. I will see your father, and if my humble efforts should have a favourable result, it will be but some poor recompense for the service you did me last night, when that villain, Mark Evered, would have used violence to carry me a prisoner to the stronghold of the enemy."

"Psha!" exclaimed Herrick; "a trifling service like that is not worth a second thought. You, however, have it in your power to do me a very essential one; and if you will remain here a moment, I'll run to my father, and inquire when it will be convenient to see you."

Upon this he left the room, and Neville had not been more than two or three minutes by himself when the door was cautiously opened, and Tony Amblewit approaching on tip-toe, exclaimed in a whisper—

"I've been waiting ever so long to see you by yourself, sir, for I've been down to have a look at the prisoners, and the one they call Mark Evered—who seems to have come a little to his senses—has sent word that he wishes to see you as soon as possible."

"Humph! and what occasion, Tony, was there for all this mystery and caution?"

"Why, sir," replied the other, "if Master Herrick happened to know what's going on, he would want to accompany you, and then the old gentleman would fly in a passion, and a pretty rumpus there'd be in the house!"

"In that case you have acted prudently," exclaimed Neville; "and it shall certainly be no fault of mine if your young master knows anything about it. And so, then, it appears that Mark Evered is so little satisfied with his place of confinement that he is ready to make terms for his immediate release?"

"He didn't say anything about that, sir," replied Tony; "but as it's pretty plain he don't like the place, and has sent a message to you, it's likely enough he will promise not to interfere with you again on condition of being set at liberty."

"Well, I'll see him at any rate, and hear the proposition he has to make."

"But you surely won't venture to trust yourself there alone?" exclaimed Tony Amblewit.

"And why should I not?" demanded Neville; "he has been disarmed, you know; and as, in that respect, I shall have an advantage over him, there is very little danger to be apprehended."

"Very true, sir," answered the other, though in a tone that showed he was not half satisfied. "If it's your determination, of course it's not for me to say anything more about it. Only take care of yourself, for there's a spice of the devil in this Mark Evered; and if mischief were to be done, he wouldn't throw away the opportunity."

Tony Amblewit hurried away as he uttered this, and before many seconds had elapsed, Herrick returned with a message from his father.

"I have seen him," he exclaimed, as he entered the room, "and though he appears to have a notion that you intend to urge him upon this subject, he is anxious to see you without delay."

"In order, I suppose, that he may get rid of me again as soon as possible ?"

"No," replied Herrick, "I rather think it is that he may make you a convert to his opinions. He entertains a very high regard for you, Neville Audeley, and perhaps imagines that your influence may curb the disobedience of his somewhat impetuous son."

"Which, between ourselves," laughed Neville, "is about as unlikely a thing as he could have taken into his head. However, I must be grateful for the good opinion he has formed of me; and if I do not absolutely try to prevail on my friend to abandon his own notions, I will not give utterance to a word that might serve to urge him in a course opposed to his father's wishes."

"And that is all he can expect of you," said Herrick Evenden; "so now follow me to the lion's den, for he is too much occupied in his own mysterious studies to leave his room, even as an act of courtesy towards those he calls his friends."

Neville Audeley immediately followed his guide towards the chamber, in which it will be remembered he formerly had an interview with the astrologer. At length they reached the apartment in which they found Master Basil Evenden intently poring over his musty cabalistic volumes; and so deeply was his attention occupied, that he heeded not the presence of his visitor till the voice of his son roused him from his studies.

"My friend waits your pleasure, sir," said Herrick, after they had been standing a minute or two unnoticed at the table. "You would speak with him, I believe, or, if you are too busily engaged at present, he will call at a more convenient time."

"I will not trouble him to do so," said the old man, raising his dim and heavy eyes towards them. "Young gentlemen, you are welcome, and I pray you be seated, that is, if Herrick can find a stool unoccupied, for I believe they are mostly occupied with books and parchments that I use in my studies."

The old man spoke truly, for there was not a seat to be found in the room till Herrick turned up an old and empty box, which was then made to answer the purpose of a more luxurious resting place. By this time the astrologer was again consulting his books, and so absent was he in mind that he forgot any one was present till once more reminded of it by his son.

"I believe," he then said, addressing himself to Neville, "you are the confidant of Herrick in most things, and you are, therefore, aware that he has a desire to mix himself in these unhappy wars that distract the country, instead of following the more peaceful life that I desire him to pursue."

"I have heard him express such a wish, sir, certainly," answered Neville, "and you must admit it is a very natural one for a young man who has fame and name depending upon his own conduct."

"Fame is but an empty sound," exclaimed the astrologer, "and as for name, what better one need he carry with him to the grave than I shall leave him? Ambition, sir, I fear is his guiding star; and it is here written in these books that if indulged in, it will lead him to an early and untimely end."

"You would have him, then, abandon his design of drawing his sword in the support of a just cause ?"

"There is no cause so just that it should deprive me of an only son," answered the old man. "You may deem me an old fool, perhaps; but I have seen all my boys, save him, laid beneath the green turf, and surely he may spare a father's griefs, by yielding to the wish he has so often heard expressed."

"Do not mistake me, sir," exclaimed Neville, "by supposing that I would say aught to make a son disobedient to his parent. Herrick, I am sure, will bow to your commands with submission; and, though the world is sometimes apt to charge people with cowardice under such circumstances, I hope, in such a case as this, people will attribute it to his anxiety to obey the commands of a father."

"They will—they will," returned the old man hurriedly; "you hear what your friend says, Herrick; and its just what I have been telling you myself. Yield, then, to my wishes. Again I warn you that an evil destiny awaits you in the field of strife, and death lurks there though you little heed how near he is to you."

"You believe, then, in some planetary influences that I have always regarded with contempt?" said Neville.

"I do," answered the astrologer; "and the opinion has not been hastily formed, I can assure you. It has cost me much wearisome thought and study, and therefore demands some respect even from those who think proper to differ from me in opinion. I have carefully watched the destiny of my son, and for years past have foreseen, that should he ever draw the sword, his death will happen in the first battle he is engaged in."

"And what if he adopts a more peaceful career?" demanded Neville Audeley.

"Then happiness and length of days will be his reward," answered the old man.

"And he will die quietly in his own bed?"

"Nay, that I am not quite certain of," replied the astrologer; "for sometimes I have seen reason to fear that after all he will perish by the sword. That, however, may be many years hence; or it is even possible I may have been led away into error by my fears."

"Well, at any rate, my stars don't seem to show me much favour," laughed Herrick; "for whether I make war my profession or not, my death is to be caused by the sword; and the only advantage I can see in following a peaceful life is, that my days may be prolonged to a somewhat greater length."

"You deride that which you understand not," exclaimed his father, in a tone of anger. "I would guide you aright, and yet, in the self-sufficiency of your heart, you scorn the counsel that age gives you."

"Nay, there you wrong me," answered Herrick, "for my friend here can bear witness that it is my intention to bow with submission to whatever commands you may lay upon me."

"Yet your own heart prompts you to seek glory where it will mock your pursuit?"

"I would gladly lend a hand where I know my services would be acceptable," replied Herrick; "but when I find you so strongly opposed to it, I will yield my own inclinations to the duty I owe you."

"'Tis well," answered Basil Evenden; "and it would also be better for you," he continued, addressing himself to Neville Audeley, "to abandon for awhile the profession in which you are engaged; there is danger in it that I fear no prudence or foresight can avert."

"In other words," exclaimed the other, "I am to understand that I shall be one of those who are fated to perish in the coming struggle?"

"I will not venture to say quite so much as that," replied the astrologer, "but a mystery hangs over your destiny, which I am at present unable to penetrate. Danger there certainly is, and the result, I grieve to say, will in all probability be fatal."

"For my own part, I care not," said Neville, "so that I do not perish ingloriously. But it is well Blanche Heriot hears you not, or she would, more than ever, give way to the alarm she feels for me."

"If your life is saved," returned the old man, "it will be through the means of Blanche Heriot."

"Indeed! then she must follow me even into the field of strife and bloodshed."

"Nay, I know not that she will do that," replied the astrologer; "but should you survive, mark my words, and you will acknowledge that there is more in my art than you at present give it credit for. But enough has now been said—you have heard me, Neville Audeley, and it now only remains for you to beware of a deadly foe ; avoid him as you would a serpent, or you will fall beneath his burning hatred.   Farewell, and should we ever meet again I hope it will be in my power to predict better for the future."

Neville and his friend then withdrew, and upon returning to the room they had left some little time before, Herrick said despondingly—

" So you see my chance of gaining an honourable name among my fellow men, is now at an end.   To be sure, I might still follow my own course in defiance of what my father has said, but then I know how much] he loves me, and so I suppose I must yield myself to his will, however unpalatable the sacrifice of name and fame may be."

"There is no alternative that I can see," answered Neville, " and therefore it only remains for you to endure the disappointment with the best grace you can."

" But his predictions respecting yourself," said Herrick, " will, I suppose, make no alteration in your views ?"

" Not the slightest," he replied.   " In fact, I am sceptical in this said science of astrology, and nothing shall ever tempt me to abandon a career which both duty and honour have called upon me to adopt."

" That's rather a hard rub, my good friend," cried Herrick, " considering the situation I am placed in."

" It was not intended to be so, at any rate," answered Neville Audeley; " and, indeed, it would have been most undeserved, for I know you are with us heart and soul, though circumstances prevent your affording all the assistance you would wish."

" And when," asked Herrick, " is it expected the first trial of strength will take place between the two parties ?"

" It is looked for daily, almost hourly," replied the other; " for the Earl of Warwick is now prepared for battle, and by this time, I suppose, Prince Edward and his followers have made their landing upon the eastern coast, where he will speedily be joined by those Englishmen who have forgot the loyalty they owe to him who now occupies the throne of these realms.   The rebels will doubtless march for London, where I fear they are likely to meet with too welcome a reception, and it will consequently be the first act of the Earl of Warwick to interrupt them in their way.   This will bring on warm work, though I trust the Lancasterians will not sustain a defeat. .But I must now leave you, Herrick, for my stay in Chertsey will be brief, and there is one to whom I must devote the remainder of my time."

The two friends then parted from each other. and never did Herrick Evenden feel the bitterness of disappointment more than when he saw his companion set forth without him.

———

CHAPTER XIX.

THE HUMBLE FRIEND.—A CURE FOR COQUETS.—THE CAPTIVE.

WITH a mind intent upon the interview he was about to have with Mark Evered in his place of confinement, Neville slowly pursued his way, but had not proceeded far when he heard hasty footsteps behind, and looking round, he saw Tony Amblewit running towards him nearly out of breath with the exertion.

" How now, my good fellow," he exclaimed with surprise, " what message are you the bearer of that you come in such haste on your errand ?"

" I have not come on any message, sir," answered Tony, " only I thought to myself it was a pity you should run the risk of seeing Mark Evered alone, and so I have taken the liberty of following to ask if you would let me bear you company ?"

"There is no occasion for it, Tony," replied the other, "for he has been deprived of his weapons, and could not injure me, even if he had the inclination. Besides, his object is to obtain his liberty, and if danger is really to be apprehended, it will be when he has another and better opportunity than the present affords."

"Won't you let me go with them?"

"Not on any consideration." replied Neville. "It would look as if I were afraid to meet him alone, and as in reality I feel no apprehension, I should be sorry that he thought I feared him."

"Well, but I would stay outside where he couldn't see me," returned Tony; "and then I should be ready in case my assistance was wanted."

"I would really much rather go alone," answered Neville, "for there is no cause of alarm, except that which exists in your own imagination. However, your fidelity is deserving of all praise, and if you will accept this small sum as a reward——"

"Reward!" exclaimed Tony, stepping back, as if he feared there were contagion in the money; "and do you think, sir, I would accept payment for doing what's only my duty?"

"I do not offer it as payment," replied Neville, "but merely as a token of my regard for the honest zeal that has prompted you to make this kindly offer."

"Well, sir, you may put back your money," exclaimed the other, resolutely, "for not a coin of it shall ever find its way into my pocket. But," he exclaimed after a momentary pause, "there is one favour I would ask of you if it were not taking too great a liberty."

"What is it, Tony?"

"That you would just speak a word in my favour to Kate Poynet."

"There is no need of it," replied Neville.

"I only wish I was quite certain about that," exclaimed Tony, "but the truth is there's no depending upon her for five minutes together. Last night I thought she had almost consented to be married to me on the same day that you and Mistress Blanche go to the altar, and yet, would you believe it, we had a quarrel before we parted, and she as good as told me that I might go and look somewhere else for a wife, as she had done with me for ever!"

"A foolish speech, good Tony," replied Neville Audeley, "that I dare say was forgotten long before you had arrived at your own home."

"Well, you've got a way of comforting a poor fellow, at any rate," cried Tony. "But do you really think she didn't mean what she said?"

"I merely judge," answered Neville, "for the natural love that some people have for teasing whenever they have the power of doing so. Mistress Kate, I dare say, is not deficient in that quality, and I rather think you may cure her of it if you only follow my advice, sir."

"And what is your advice, sir?"

"That you stop away from the house and don't see her for at least a week."

"A week!"

"Ay, or a fortnight would be still better."

"She would go mad."

"On the contrary, it would bring her to her senses."

"But it would be cruel," exclaimed Tony.

"Nay," replied Neville, "it appears she has been so to you, and, therefore, deserves the less pity."

"Upon my word, sir," returned Tony Amblewit, after some little hesitation, "I don't think I can ever make up my mind to it. Kate loves me, I'm certain, and it would break her heart if she wasn't to see me for a week."

"It would break her spirit, and that's just what you ought to do," replied Neville. "The remedy, I'll admit, is rather a sharp one, but the woman scarcely deserves pity who can trifle with the feelings of one that loves her."

"Well, there's something in that, to be sure," exclaimed Tony; "and now I come to think of it, there can't be any great harm in trying it. At any rate I'll see what effect three days will have, and if that don't do, I'll try what a week will do next time."

"And the second time she will laugh at you for a simpleton," replied the other. "No, no, Tony, these things must never be done by halves, or they had better be left alone altogether. So either undertake the business properly, my good fellow, or make up your mind to endure all sorts of miseries after you are married."

"I'll do it!" cried Tony, plucking up resolution; "I can see that you are in the right of it, Master Neville, and so I'll go home, and won't see her for a week."

Tony Amblewit strode away as if fully determined to have revenge upon Kate Poynet; but he had not gone many yards on his way, when he came running back, and pulling the sleeve of Neville's doublet, said—

"My resolution's gone already, sir; I thought to have done it so nicely, and yet the moment I left your side, my courage went off like a flash of lightning."

"Then I'm afraid our case is an hopeless one," replied Neville; "the girl will find the power she possesses over you, and take my word, she'll never relinquish it."

"That's just what I'm afraid of."

"Yet you take no means to remedy it," answered Neville; "however, I can give you credit for all good intentions, Tony, and am only sorry that Kate should have rendered it necessary for me to give you such advice. The truth is, she is a bit of a coquette, and they are awkward customers for a man to have to deal with."

"I don't know what a coquette means," answered Tony; "but she is certainly rather fond of having her own way, and that I've very often noticed makes married people very uncomfortable. So as I don't want to give up Kate, who, after all is a very good sort of a girl, I'll think about what you've been telling me, and if I can only find the way to break her spirit without breaking her heart into the bargain, hang me if I don't have a try for it. So, good by, sir, and when you come back to Chertsey, perhaps I may have it in my power to say that your advice was not thrown away."

Tony Amblewit again turned away, and Neville, who, it must be confessed, was not sorry to get rid of him, hastened on towards the place where Mark Evered was imprisoned, and on application to the jailor, he was immediately ushered into the room or cell where the person he wished to see was anxiously awaiting his arrival.

"I thought you didn't intend to come at all," said Evered, gloomily, as he entered; "for when a man gets into a place like this, it's seldom his friends think it worth their while to pay him a visit."

"I have not come as a friend," answered Neville, "but in compliance with a request that you sent me early this morning. May I hope that the quarrel between us is at an end?"

"Ay, I suppose so," returned Evered. "I'm heartily tired of this cursed place, and so, if any arrangement can be made, I should be glad to turn my back on it with as little delay as possible."

"I have no wish to extort hard terms merely because you have not the power to reject them," answered Neville. "For some reason or other, you have thought proper to rank yourself amongst the foremost of my enemies, nay, my life even has been threatened; and all I desire is, that you will give me your word not to make any treacherous attempt."

"Treacherous attempt?"

"Ay, your hatred is too intense to stand upon trifles; and, to speak plainly, I have little doubt, should an opportunity offer, that you would not hesitate to rid yourself of me."

"It seems, then, I am not indebted to you for a very favourable opinion."

"Your own actions forbid it," replied Neville; "however, I have not come here to heap reproaches upon you, and, therefore, once for all, let me assure you that I shall, at all times, be ready to meet Mark Evered in fair and honourable terms. Your liberty is a thing I have no wish to deprive you of, though, but a few hours since, you sought to make me your captive, without having received provocation. But that is past, and on your promise not to seek my injury, you shall be free to depart from the place within half an hour after I quit it."

"You have no power to order it," replied Evered.

"True," answered the other, "but Sir Philip Warrenne is a magistrate, and at my request he will not refuse to give you your freedom."

"Well I'll take your word for it," returned the captive; "and now, having settled this much of our business, let me ask if it is your wish to end the quarrel that at present exists between you and Hugh Laneret?"

"Yes, if it can be effected upon honourable terms."

"And there's nothing more easy."

"When you explain yourself, I may be better able to judge."

"Well then," continued Mark Evered, "it seems you both love the same girl, though, from all I have heard Laneret was the first to make her an offer of his hand.

If so, it would only be fair to resign her to him, and then all farther enmity ceases."

"And is this proposition made seriously?" demauded Neville, with surprise.

"It is."

"Then if it has been done at the instigation of Hugh Laneret," returned the other, "you will soon have an opportunity of telling him that I will resign Blanche Heriot only with my life. She has accepted me as her future husband, and base indeed I should be to yield her to one who I know she loathes and despises as much as I do myself."

"Well," replied Evered, coolly, "here the quarrel stands just as it did. I thought to have done you a good turn, but since you are resolved to follow your own mad schemes, it's no fault of mine whatever may happen afterwards; and yet one would think you must yourself see the folly of making an enemy where the odds are so greatly against you."

"Hugh Lnneret may succeed in ridding himself of a successful rival," answered Neville, "but it can only be through exercising that treachery of which I know him to be fully capable."

"Nay," exclaimed the other, "there is a chance that you will soon meet together in battle. Edward is already in England, and both he and Warwick are anxious to bring matters to an issue by an immediate engagement."

"When did you hear that Edward had arrived?" inquired Neville anxiously.

"Just before I left Cirencester."

"It is strange, then, that I should not have heard it as well as you."

"I see nothing at all strange in it, for you were among the Yorkists, and it was hardly likely you would gain any information from them. Colonel Morton did not act with his usual caution when he set you at liberty, or——"

"Perhaps," interrupted Neville, "I have committed an equal indiscretion in promising that you should be set at large at such a moment as this."

"Why, then, I must confess you have me at close quarters," exclaimed Evered; "however, I should imagine you will hardly brake a promise that has been made within so short a time."

"I will not," replied Neville; "the cause of your being here was a private quarrel between ourselves, and I had no desire to manifest a feeling of animosity after the first flash of anger had passed away. Besides my word has been given, and even an enemy shall never have it in his power to reproach me with a breach of faith."

"But, at the same time, let it be understood," exclaimed Mark Evered, "that should chance throw us in each other's way in the field of battle, this affair is not to be remembered by either of us; I have promised that no treachery shall be practised. But it still remains for us to decide our quarrel upon fair and equal terms."

"Agreed."

"And when we meet," continued Evered, "nothing but death shall part us."

"To that I am also agreed."

"Why, then, it seems we understand each other better than was expected," said Mark Evered, with an air of unconcern that seldom forsook him; "I wish though, you could have consented to make friends with Hugh Laneret upon the terms I spoke of, and then, except in the field of battle, where we take different sides, we might have been upon as good terms as if nothing had ever occurred to ruffle or discompose us."

"Your wish is a vain one," replied Neville, "for even if I had a desire to join the friendship of the man you speak of, it never should be done upon the dishonourable terms that have been suggested. It so happens, however, that my hatred for Hugh Laneret can never be effaced, and I shall, therefore, conceive myself fortunate in having one great and overpowering reason for continuing the antipathy I bear towards him."

"Well, I must caution you to beware of him," returned the other, "for Laneret is not a man to be thwarted with impunity, and there are few who can be more terrible in their wrath than he is when once he finds these obstacles in his way. Of course, I don't say this to intimidate you, Master Neville Audeley, but as you are about to do me a little bit of service, I thought it were as well to put you upon your guard, so that I may have nothing to blame myself for afterwards.'

"I can perfectly understand you," answered Neville, "and can estimate the advice you have given at exactly what it is worth,—nothing. However, I have promised you freedom, and let it cost me what it may, you shall find I will be as good as my word."

Neville Audeley bowed haughtily to the prisoner, and having summoned the jailor, he shortly afterwards left the house of sorrow and captivity.

CHAPTER XX.

NEWS OF THE ENEMY.—THE LOVERS.—THE FAREWELL.

As Neville Audeley once more directed his footsteps towards Redwynde Manor House, he could not help feeling some regret at the haste with which he had been induced to promise freedom to an enemy; but the pledge had been given, and there was now no way of escaping from it with honour to himself. He reflected too upon the danger which still hung over Blanche Heriot, through the artifices of a treacherous rival, and for some little time he felt half inclined to remain in Chertsey that he might watch over her, and avert the designs which he felt but too certain would be put in practice. But should he remain inactive during the ensuing struggle, it would, he knew, be attributed to cowardice; and as no other alternative remained, he determined to commit her to the care of Sir Philip Warrenne and Herrick Evenden, both of whom he knew would faithfully discharge the duty entrusted to them. On reaching the garden through which he had to pass on his way to the house, he was met by the knight, who, welcoming him back with all his usual frankness, inquired if he had heard the news that had just been spread abroad.

"You mean the arrival of the usurper, Prince Edward?"

"I do; he is now on English ground, and we must therefore now expect to have some hard fighting."

"And if all go to it with as good a heart as I shall," replied Neville, "his highness will, before long, have sufficient reason to repent that he came to sow discord in our once happy land."

"But it unfortunately happens," said Sir Philip, "that there are too many who have joined the standard of the reckless adventurer, and though we may eventually succeed in driving him back to his ship, it will not be till after some of the best blood in England has been shed in the attempt."

"Has Blanche heard the news?" inquired Neville.

"She has."

"And, of course, has made up her mind that I shall not delay my departure?"

"I suppose she has," replied Sir Philip, "but, to tell you the truth, I saw her looking so melancholy that I was glad to make my escape with as much despatch as possible. But what are you moving off for in such a hurry, Neville? I have been waiting to hear what you think had better be done with our prisoner, who is hardly in safe custody while he remains in that place where a child might effect its escape."

"You forget, sir, there is more than one," exclaimed Neville; "and I had also forgotten that I am under a promise to ask you for their immediate release."

"Their release!"

"Yes, Sir Philip; the reason of their being ordered into confinement was grounded upon a private quarrel, and as I was the party principally concerned in it, I have now to repeat my request, that they may forthwith be set at liberty."

"And so give them an opportunity to join the ranks of the enemy?"

"I was aware of the objection that wou'd be raised," answered Neville Audeley "but my word had been given before I knew of Pince Edward's arrival."

"Then I suppose I have no alternative but to accede to your request ?" exclaimed Sir Philip. "However, your wish shall be obeyed, though it must be confessed I'm sorry your humanity was not exerted in favour of persons more deserving of it."

"My promise," added Neville, "even went so far as to declare that they should be at liberty within the space of half-an-hour."

"Very well, Neville, your promise shall be made good; but upon my word I don't know what will be said to it, when it shall afterwards appear that all this mercy has been shown to the enemies of the king, whose name we have adopted."

"If there be blame I will myself bear it," answered Neville Audeley; "I was wrong for having given a promise too hastily; but, since the error was committed, I must e'en be content to endure the consequences. There is, however, a consolation in knowing that I may meet this Mark Evered; and should it be my fortune to do so, I have sworn that either he or I shall never quit the battle ground alive."

"Then all I hope that it may be his chance to fall," exclaimed Sir Philip, "for we saw quite enough of him last night to have no desire to be honoured with his company again. Had he depended upon my will he should have remained long enough in prison, before he had an opportunity of showing off any more of his villanous tricks."

"His enmity to myself I have forgotton," returned Neville, "but he is a traitor to his country, which I never can forgive; and as the friend of Hugh Laneret, I am afraid he will league with him to carry off poor Blanche at the first opportunity that offers. I therefore leave her under your watchful guardianship, and should any attempt be made to take her from your roof, I will never seek rest or repose till I have hurled a terrible vengeance upon her enemies."

"They will be too much occupied for some time to think about her," replied Sir Philip; "but for all that you may be quite satisfied that I will be careful of her safety. But go to her, Neville, or she will begin to think you have taken your departure without so much as a farewell."

Upon this suggestion, Neville hurried away, but for some time his search after Blanche Heriot was without avail, and it was not till he entered the small chamber in which she used to sit, when desirious of solitude, that he at length found her wrapt in melancholy reflections at the separation so soon to take place. As he approached, however, a change was instantly visible in her countenance, but it quickly gave way again to the gloom which she had in vain sought to dispel.

"At last then, dear Neville," she said, "the hour I have so much dreaded has arrived. The fearful sound of war has commenced even within our own once happy island; and you are forced to fly from scenes of happiness and joy, to mingle in the strife that will doom so many to an early grave."

"But those who survive the storm, Blanche," he replied, "will return with honour to reap the reward which a consciousness of having performed a sacred duty will bring with it. There is at least hope left for us, and that alone is sufficient to support us even in as great perils as those you look forward to."

"And what hope have I," she asked "who know that your rash adventurous spirit will ever lead you to places where the greatest danger is to be found ? Besides, even should you be made a prisoner, there are those in the enemy's ranks who would take care never to suffer your escape."

"You are thinking of Hugh Laneret, I suppose ?"

"I am; and a more dangerous enemy I could not have to apprehend."

"Granted, but he possesses little influence in the camp, and with Colonel Morton to oppose him, I really think there is less to fear from him than you imagine; and it must also be remembered, that though we regard Prince Edward as one who seeks to usurp the throne of England, he is neither vindictive nor unjust towards those who are opposed to his claims."

"At least, so you would have me believe," she replied; "but war makes me blood-thirsty, and adversity may render our foes reckless to the voice of humanity. You see, Neville, I anticipate the worst, and though I have tried to fortify my mind, I yet feel an oppression that it is impossible to conquer."

"Yet it may be conquered when you hear of our successes against these invaders," answered her lover. "You must remember, Blanche, that we have skilful chiefs to direct our armies, and under their guidance, we may yet expect to see the victory claimed by those who have drawn the sword for King Henry."

"And I have also heard," she replied, "that Prince Edward has leaders fully equal to our own both for skill and bravery. They are as ardent too in the cause they have adopted; and when the two factions, thus similarly circumstanced, meet in deadly strife, who shall say on which side the advantage shall be declared? You will think me a weak, foolish girl, Neville, for thus giving way to my terrors; but the times are fearful, and I shrink aghast from a contemplation so full of horrors."

"You will at any rate have your guardian always present with you," answered her lover.

"Ay, but you will be absent, and for your sake I shall bitterly curse the war that leads you forth to scenes of massacre and danger.'

"Nay, then, you must think of it as little as you can," he replied; "or if it does occasionally cross your mind, Blanche, let it not be without the accompanying reflection that my life may be spared, even though the battle rages hot and fiercely. It must not be forgotten, too, that all men have a duty to perform towards their country; and if they neglect to fulfil it, they deserve the execration of all those who have liberties worth contending for."

"Yet women cannot be expected to look so calmly upon these fearful events," answered Blanche; "their minds are not so busily occupied as those of men, and they are, perhaps, but two apt to see dangers where they do not in reality exist. For this there is no help, nor are they to be blamed for it."

"Blame there certainly must be," replied Neville Audeley; "but it is to be regretted that they sometimes give way to unnecessary alarm. You, dearest Blanche, I hope will prove an exception, if it is only to be an example to those who yield to their terrors without knowing that any cause for them exists."

"I will, at least, endeavour to prove myself worthy of your confidence," exclaimed Blanche. "That I am not without some little share of firmness I believe, and, since it is your wish, I will exercise it to the utmost of my power. Yet, in spite of all this, I shall tremble at each report of a battle, and my mind will be distracted with fears until I have ascertained that you are not among the hapless persons who have fallen."

"You shall hear often from me, if it will be any solace to you," answered Neville. "Couriers will be frequently passing to and fro through the country, and by their means I will contrive to let you know how our cause is proceeding. I have, however, for my own part, little doubt that the war will soon be at an end, and when that happy period arrives, I shall once more be enabled to return home, where the remainder of my life will be passed in the society of her whose love is my chief blessing in this world."

"Ay," she replied, "could I indeed be certain that all would be as you have said, there would be little effort required to await with calmness the issue of this most unfortunate quarrel. The parting I could endure, were I to know it is but for a time; but to believe that it is eternal, lays a weight at my heart that no effort of my own can remove."

"At all events your guardian will be able to inform you how the war goes on," said Neville; "and no doubt a short time will serve to afford him a clue as to the side on which it is likely to terminate favourably."

"But he will not tell me," answered Blanche, "if he should see reason to fear that it may be against the party to which you belong."

"Nay, he will have more reliance in your firmness than to practise a deception that must, sooner or later, be known to you," exclaimed Neville Audeley. "Besides, even if we should happen to be unfortunately on the losing side, I might chance to escape the death you so much fear, and in that case we must make up our minds to pass the remainder of our days in another country. The world would still be open to us, and, doubtless, there is some place where we may find a home till circumstances permitted our return to England."

"And who knows that things are going to turn out so badly as all that?" demanded Sir Philip Warrenne, who at that moment entered the room. "For my own part, I never let hope forsake me, even when matters look most black and threatening; and at present I see no reason why you should be anticipating evils that may never happen."

"I would fain have prevailed on Blanche to think so," replied the lover, "but she can see nothing but danger in the coming strife; and to you, therefore, I must leave the task of supporting her during the period of my absence."

"Ay, that I'll cheerfully undertake," exclaimed the knight, warmly. "Blanche, I trust, has ever found me anxious to supply the place of her father; and she may confidently rely upon it that she will never want a friend while Sir Philip Warrenne lives."

"I am well assured of it my kind, my generous friend," cried Blanche Heriot; "and happy should I indeed be were it not for the peril in which this war involves the life of Neville. I know his ardour in the cause he has adopted, and there is but too much reason to fear it will lead him into the dangers I apprehend."

"Ah, my dear Blanche," exclaimed Sir Philip; "this love, I fear, has made a terrible coward of you."

"It must be confessed in that I do feel alarmed," she replied; "but surely that should not subject me to your reproaches. We have ever been dear to each other, and now that I know he is about to risk his life, it is scarcely to be wondered at that I feel those apprehensions at which you have expressed your surprise."

"Well, well," exclaimed Sir Philip, "it must be acknowledged I was rather unreasonable in supposing that lovers can part without sorrow, but it is so long since I felt the tender emotion myself, that you must pardon me for feeling a little hard-hearted when I witness the grief of others. However, I will not stay to be a witness of your adieus; and so, Neville, when you have taken your farewell of Blanche, I will see you in the blue chamber to give you a letter to the Earl of Warwick, who will not fail to patronize the protege of his old acquaintance, Sir Philip Warrenne."

So saying, the knight quitted the room, and Neville used every argument he could think of to banish from the mind of Blanche Heriot the grief to which she had given way. But it was in vain that he strove to afford even the slightest consolation, and when at length he was compelled to tear himself from her presence, he left her weeping and disconsolate in the care of Paynet. He then hastened to Sir Philip, and having received from him the promised letter, mounted his horse, and set forth for the head quarters of the Lancasterian army.

CHAPTER XII.

THE MARCH OF THE INVADER.—THE BATTLE AND ITS CONSEQUENCES.

In those days, however, news did not fly quite so fast as in the present, and ere Neville Audeley left home to join the party whose cause he had espoused, a bloody battle had taken place between the two armies, and the Earl of Warwick with many other nobles, had perished in the cause they bravely arose to defend. But that this part of our narrative may be the better understood, it is necessary that we briefly relate the events which had hurried on a crisis that drove Henry from the throne, and placed Edward the Fourth there in his stead.

About the period to which the commencement of our narrative belongs, Edward appeared with a fleet off the coast of Suffolk, having been assisted in secret by the Duke of Burgundy, who played as double a part in this business as might have been expected from a man of his restless and ambitious character. He had issued a proclamation forbidding any of his subjects to join Edward, but underhand he sent him a large sum of money, furnished him with three or four great ships of his own, and hired secretly fourteen or fifteen more.

As Edward's troops, however, did not exceed twelve hundred men, he was deterred from landing in the Wash, on the shores of which he well knew was assembled a Lancasterian army; but, bearing to the north, he sailed into the Humber, and landed at Ravenspur. Finding the people there not very favourable to his cause, he veiled his actual designs, and even at York he only engaged the citizens to recover

his title and estate as Duke of York, solemnly swearing not to attempt to recover the crown. A few oaths cost nothing to a man without principles, and in the present case, the necessity for dissimulating soon passed away.

At Pontefract, Warkick's brother, the Marquis of Montague, treacherously opened a correspondence instead of fighting, and permitted Edward's weak column to march within sight of his quarters, where a great force was collected. As soon as the Yorkists crossed the Trent they were on their own ground, and the people flocked from all sides to the standard of Edward, who then reassumed the royal title. In the neighbourhood of Coventry he found himself in the power of a Lancasterian army, under the command of the Earls of Warwick and Oxford, and the Duke of Clarence: now was the moment for the latter to act, and making his men put the White Rose of York over their gorgets, he went over with colours flying, to his brother Edward. Upon this sudden manœuvre Warwick found himsels compelled to decline the battle which was offered to him, and Edward fearlessly marched towards the capital, where he was received with enthusiasm.

The reception he then met with in London may be attributed to three things especially :—the first was the great number of his partizans in sanctuary within the walls, and the recent birth of a young prince ; the next the great debts which he owed to the richest of the merchants, who could only hope for payment through his being placed upon the throne ; and the third was, that the ladies of quality and rich citizens' wives, whom he had formerly delighted with his gallantries, forced their husbands and relations to declare themselves on his side.

But whatever were the motives it is certain that the White Rose of York was hailed with delight, though the citizens took good care not to declare themselves openly until they saw which way the campaign was likely to turn.

But Edward had short time to enjoy those demonstrations—the Lancasterian army was not inactive, and Warwick was advancing upon the capital by the north road. After passing only two days in London, Edward took the field. He found Warwick's force drawn out in order of battle on Barnet Common, only twelve miles from the metropolis. About forty thousand Englishmen prepared to draw the sword and bend the bow against each other, the two armies being nearly equal in numbers.

At an early hour on the following day the battle commenced. Both sides fought on foot, and the king's vanguard suffered extremely in this action; the earl's main body advanced against his, and so near, that the king himself was engaged in person, and behaved himself as bravely as any officer in the army. The Earl of Warwick's custom was never to fight on foot ; but when once he led his men to the charge, he mounted on horseback himself, and if he found victory incline to his side, he charged boldly among them ; if otherwise, he took care of himself in time, and provided for his escape. But now, at the importunity of the Marquis of Montague, he fought on foot and sent away his horses. The battle raged with great fury on both sides, and in the end the Earl of Warwick, the Marquis of Montague, and several other brave officers were killed. The slaughter that took place was terrible, for Edward had resolved to give no quarter, as he had conceived a mortal hatred against the commons of England for having favoured the Earl of Warwick so much in the dispute respecting the crown. The result was that the Lancasterians were completely beaten, and on the king's side alone fifteen hundred men were slain.

Neville Audeley heard the report of this disastrous battle from a party of the fugitives, who were hurrying to seek concealment in the southern parts of the country. He also gathered from them sufficient information to assure him that another struggle would take place in the neighbourhood of Tewkesbury; and unappalled by the horrors that had already been acted, he rode forward determined to afford what assistance he could in the last effort that was to be made in behalf of the unfortunate King Henry.

It is unnecessary to follow him throughout his rapid journey, and it will therefore be sufficient to observe that after encountering some few obstacles in the way, he at length reached the army, which he found prepared for the ensuing contest. Here he learned that King Henry had been taken in London, and that he was then a prisoner in the Tower, at the mercy of a rival from whom he had no favour to expect.

Margaret of Anjou, whose activity and resolution are well known, called the victorious Edward again into the field only five days after the battle of Barnet. Many circumstances had detained her on the continent, and it was her future fortune to land at Plymouth with her son, Prince Edward, and a body of auxiliaries, chiefly French, on the very day on which Warwick was defeated and slain.

On the 4th of May, King Edward (for he had now taken the sovereign title), with his brothers Clarence and Gloucester, fell upon her near the town of Tewkesbury. Her troops had thrown up some retrenchments from which they had repulsed the Yorkists; but the Duke of Somerset had the folly to quit his position, and, sallying forth, he ordered the mass of his troops to follow him, which some did and others did not. Those who sallied, were driven back with dreadful loss, and those who staid behind were suspected of treachery, for no general was now sure of his officers. The banner of the audacious Richard, Duke of Gloucester (afterwards Richard the Third), was already within the Lancasterian lines; Edward and Clarence now followed, and the battle of Tewkesbury terminated in panic, confusion, and slaughter.

Margaret of Anjou, who had survived so many catastrophes, was made prisoner, and with her was taken her son, the Prince of Wales, who was now only in his eighteenth year. He was shortly afterwards taken to the tent of King Edward, where, after undergoing the most cruel taunts, he was cruelly murdered in the presence of the vindictive conqueror.

We have thus given a brief but circumstantial history of the events which, within a week, changed the monarchy of England, though not without a dreadful sacrifice of human life. In the latter contest Neville Audeley behaved with remarkable courage, constantly defying danger, and setting an example to the troops by his own gallantry. At one period of the battle, and that too when all hope was utterly at an end, his attention was attracted towards a part of the field where five or six of the Lancasterians were attacking a person who appeared to be of high rank; and having been thrust from his horse, one of the soldiers was about to slay him with his dagger, when Neville rode forward, and striking the weapon with his sword from the fellows hand, he leaped to the ground and resolutely declared that though the stranger was an enemy, he would protect him against the cowardly assault of so many upon one. The men shrunk away, and the stranger, who was quickly assisted to rise by his deliverer, said in a voice of deep emotion—

"Stranger, you are a foe, and yet I owe my life to you; say then, how can I repay the deep obligation you have placed me under?"

"I require no other reward than the consciousness of having performed my duty," replied Neville Audeley; "you were attacked unfairly by men belonging to our party, and my life should have been sacrificed in your defence."

"Will you return with me to my tent?"

"That I cannot do," replied the young man; "for I belong not to the side you do."

"You are afraid, then, to trust yourself to the honour of the man you have saved from death?"

"Fear I know not," answered Neville; "yet as I acknowledge not the rule of he who has this day proved victorious, I cannot accept hospitality from one who has fought for him."

"Have you forgotten then that it will be almost impossible to leave this scene of carnage without falling into the hands of some of the victorious party?"

"I know my danger and am prepared for it," replied Neville. "It is but too likely I shall be pursued, but whilst my sword remains to me, I will defend myself to the last extremity."

"Yet I would rather spare you the risk, young man," exclaimed the stranger.

"The Yorkists have been commanded to show no quarter to the enemy, and should you fall into their hands, certain death will be the consequence."

"But not, perhaps, before I had avenged myself upon them," answered Neville Audeley. "I know what to expect at their hands; and now that our cause is lost, death is rather to be desired than avoided."

"Nay, hear me," returned the other, "and accept the terms I am about to propose. Accompany me to the camp, and on condition that you swear fealty to the new sovereign, I will undertake to procure your pardon."

"At present I am in no humour to accept the offer you have made me."

"Indeed!" exclaimed the other; "then though the kingdom has been fairly won in this day's battle, you still remain the enemy of the conqueror?"

"I do."

"You are somewhat rash, methinks," returned the stranger; "and yet there is an honest bluntness in your manner that pleases me. May I inquire the name of him who has preserved me from death?"

"Ay, 'tis Neville Audeley."

"The name is familiar to me," exclaimed the stranger; "your father died in honourable battle, and left a character unblemished by a stain?"

"He did," replied Neville; "but now, having answered your question without hesitation, may I not ask who it is that —"

"You may," interrupted the other. "Edward of York is gratified at having it in his power, then, to thank his gallant deliverer."

"Prince Edward!"

"Ay, call me *Prince* Edward, if you please," exclaimed the conqueror; "but England will now have to acknowledge me for her lawful sovereign. However, we will not differ about trifles; you have saved my life, Neville Audeley, and I would return the obligation by preserving you from an almost certain doom. Return with me to the camp, and you shall have a guard to accompany you home in safety."

"Your highness —"

"Nay," interrupted Edward, "I can see you are about to object to my proposition, and I will therefore make another that may not meet with the same fate. Take this ring, and should you hereafter fall into trouble through the part you have taken, send it to the palace at Westminster, and I will repay the obligation you have this day done me. I owe you a life, young man, and in the hour of need you shall find I am not unmindful of it."

As Edward said this, he slipped a valuable seal ring upon the finger of Neville Audeley, and once more desiring him not to forget the injunction he had given, turned away and directed his way towards his own camp.

Neville felt bewildered at the adventure which had thus befallen him, and scarcely could he prevail upon himself that all which had passed was real. The ring upon his finger, however, convinced him that it was no dream; and then, as the recollection of Blanche Heriot flashed across his mind, he thought what happiness it would afford her when she learnt the fortunate chance which had thus secured him the royal pardon. Full of these thoughts, he remounted his horse and galloped from the scene of slaughter and bloodshed.

CHAPTER XXII.

THE ENCOUNTER.—A FRIEND.—CHANGE OF ROUTE.

IT was not without some difficulty that Neville Audeley rode through the scene of recent conflict, for the field was covered with the dead and dying, and the moon had scarcely yet risen high enough to assist him with her light. At length, however, he had nearly reached the outskirts, which conducted him towards the road he wished to take, when the quick trampling of a horse was heard; and on look-ing round, he perceived that some one was in pursuit. Scorning to flee from one man, he instantly checked his own steed, and as he did so the well-remembered voice of Mark Evered struck upon his ear.

"By Heaven, this meeting is well timed," exclaimed Neville, "for it was our wish to engage hand to hand in this day's fight, and even at the very last moment chance has luckily thrown us in each other's way."

"Say rather unluckily for thyself, Master Neville Audeley," replied the other with a sneer; "for thy party has been soundly beaten, and it shall be no fault of mine if thy carcase is not left here to mingle with the other traitors who have this day met their deserts."

"Thy idle boastings have yet to be put to the test," answered Neville Audeley, "and even should they prove prophetic I can yield up life without a murmur, since the cause I had at heart is for ever lost."

"Humph! and so Blanche Heriot is forgotten because thy king has lost the day?"

"She is too dear to me to be so easily forgotten," replied Neville; "but when hope is thus distroyed, life, with all its attendant miseries, is scarcely to be desired."

"Argued like a philosopher!" exclaimed Mark Evered; "and so, because matters have not turned out quite so favourably as you expected, Blanche Heriot is to be abandoned to her fate, and your rival, Hugh Laneret, will be allowed to make an easy conquest."

"Villain!" cried Neville, "and like a fiend you exult in the misery this day will bring upon her whose goodness should have been her best protection."

"Upon my word, I don't see any occasion for the miseries you talk of," answered Mark Evered. "You, it seems, have made up your mind to throw away your life, and I can see no objection to her becoming the bride of a man that it's evident loves her far better than you ever did."

"Hugh Laneret never loved her," exclaimed Neville, "or he would have acted with more honour when he found that his addresses never would be accepted. Blanche rejected him, and yet, when all other means failed, he sought to gain her by force and intimidation."

"And what other course was he to follow?" demanded Mark Evered; "he asked her over and over again to be his; she chose to be obstinate, because there was somebody else she thought proper to like better, and had I been in his place I should have taken the liberty to carry her off long before this."

"To your counsel then," exclaimed Neville, "it is likely she owes the greater part of the persecution she has been made to endure?"

"Why, it cannot be denied that I have given Laneret the benefit of my opinion," answered the other with an air of unconcern; "and where's the friend that would not do so under such circumstances? Nay, never look so fiercely man, for an excellent opportunity to revenge yourself now offers, so you have only to dismount, tie your horse to yonder tree, and then you and I can settle the differences that are between us."

Almost before these words were uttered, both of them had thrown themselves from their saddles, and having secured their steeds in the manner proposed, their swords were drawn, and both of them advanced with looks of hatred towards each other. In another moment the clashing of their weapons broke upon the silence of the night, and by the fury with which the attack was made, it became evident that they were actuated by a feeling of hatred that nothing but death could ever quell. Neville Audeley, however, maintained the greatest coolness and self-com-mand, and thus he soon found an advantage that gave him a superiority, when the other began to grow exhausted from the violence with which he had commenced his attack. At length the strife became more and more unequal, and as a last effort, Mark Evered was rushing furiously towards Neville, when he received the sword of his antagonist in his body, and fell mortally wounded to the ground.

"It's all over with me," he murmured, as soon as he could speak; "you've given me my death-wound, Neville Audeley, and I would have done the same thing by you, if fortune hadn't deserted me in my utmost need. But I can forgive you, boy, and so there's my hand upon it."

"Your repentance comes too late," exclaimed Neville Audeley, as he bent over the dying man. "Had you said as much half an hour since, your life would have been spared, and I should have been saved the future reflection of having shed the blood of a fellow-creature."

"If anybody is to blame in this matter, it's Hugh Laneret," returned the other. "He worked upon me by representing you as an enemy, and now I can see that it was all done to serve his own end. But it's not too late yet for you to profit by my advice; beware of him, Neville Audeley, for he is already in search of you at the head of a body of Yorkist soldiers. He seeks you as an enemy of the cause that now happens to be uppermost, and should you fall in his way, nothing will save you from destruction."

"Where does he seek me?" demanded Neville.

"At the old Manor-house at Chertsey," answered the other; "he was to leave the camp at nightfall, and felt confident that he should there be able to surprise and make you his prisoner."

"Let him beware lest he fall into his own trap," exclaimed Neville Audeley; "doubtless we shall meet again, and his fate may be similar to that which is now hurrying you to another world."

"But you will not meet him alone," answered Mark Evered; "he has resolved upon your destruction, and will be accompanied by others, to prevent any mischief happening to himself."

"What would you have me do then?" demanded Neville Audeley.

"I would have you avoid the Manor-house," replied the dying man.

"What! and leave Blanche Heriot to her fate?"

"A warning," replied Evered, "may be conveyed to her in time to save her, and then she can join you at any place you think proper to name. Her guardian also will do well to remove himself for a time, for he is known to be a Lancastrian in his heart, and Hugh Laneret, in his revenge for the loss of Blanche, will betray him into the hands of his enemies."

"And how am I to be convinced that this danger you are telling me of is real?"

"I can have no further interest in deceiving you," replied Mark; "my last sand is nearly run out, and though my life has been a reckless one, I would make all the reparation I can, while it is in my power."

"And you think Hugh Laneret is still bent upon ensuring my destruction?"

"I am sure of it."

"But how know you that he has taken the road that leads to Redwynde Manor-house?"

"Because I was to have joined him there," replied Mark Evered; "nay, if it had not been for the cursed mischance of meeting with you, I should by this time have been on my way to follow him."

"Do you believe then," asked Neville Audeley, "that your wound is mortal?"

"Ay, there can be little doubt of that," replied the other, "for even now I can feel life departing from me so fast, that if you remain here another five minutes, it will be to look upon the stiffening corpse of poor Mark Evered. Yet why should I care about quitting a world that I was never upon very good terms with? I have always expected that such an end as this would come, and your hand has perhaps saved me from many a crime that has thus been spared me."

"You can forgive me then, the act which has thus abruptly closed your career?"

"I do, from the very bottom of my heart," replied Evered, "for I am not so blind but I can see that the quarrel was of my own seeking, and that no man of spirit could do otherwise than you have. I die without a feeling of resentment, Neville Audeley, and when you think of me in after times, let it be as of one that was not worthless by nature, but who was led away by his friendship for a man, that I now know to be a villain."

Mark Evered paused from exhaustion, and as the pale moonbeams fell upon his countenance, Neville could see that the convulsions of death were now racking him with torture. Presently, however, he seemed to have a slight cessation from pain, and stretching out his hand to Neville Audeley, he said—

"The last struggle is come, and in a few moments all will be over. It is in vain that you stay longer here to watch over a dying man, for here you are in danger; the victorious party will show no mercy should you happen to fall into their hands, and even now they are seeking round in every direction, to take any of the straggling Lancastrians that may be near the scene of strife. Fly, then, and save yourself before it is too late."

Neville Audeley looked round him, but no one was within sight; and while he was still gazing in the direction of the town from whence came sounds of strife and discord, he was startled by hearing a heavy groan from the wounded man; and hastening towards him, he saw that the spirit had just left him, and that his countenance had settled in the rigidity of death. Having thus witnessed the end of this unfortunate victim of his own rashness, he once more mounted his horse, and set off at a brisk gallop, in order to quit a place where there was but too much reason to know that he was surrounded with danger.

With a mind still intent upon the scene he had just witnessed, and thinking over the warning he had received respecting Hugh Laneret and his intentions, he rode forward, revolving in his own thoughts a thousand schemes for his own preservation and that of Blanche Heriot. For himself he cared little, except that his own safety might be essential for that of her he loved; and would his own death have been the means of rescuing her from the power of a relentless persecutor, he would have willingly sacrificed himself in such a cause. He, however, knew that she needed his protection, and resolving to defend her at all hazards to himself; he was about to urge his horse to greater speed in order to reach Chertsey without delay, when a figure suddenly emerged from the road-side and seized hold of the bridle, and the next moment he became aware of the presence of Maud, who had presented herself before him on a recent occasion.

"Hold!" she exclaimed, "you are in danger, and to proceed further on this road will be to encounter certain destruction."

"I am aware of my danger," he replied; "yet even death has no terrors for one who is flying to save another from the peril she is threatened with."

"If I mistake not, your journey is to take you to the Manor-house of Redwynde?"

"It is."

"And there your worst enemy will arrive almost as soon as yourself."

"Ah!" exclaimed Neville Audeley, "how know you that he seeks me?"

"Even from his own lips."

"And he told you that he was in pursuit?"

"I have not spoken to him," she replied; "but he and his people rest at a house hard by here, and from the conversation that took place among them, I gathered quite enough to know that they intend to take you by surprise."

"Of that I have already received an intimation," replied Neville. "They were to set off at dusk, and my present object is to reach Redwynde before them, in order that I may protect Blanche from the peril with which she is threatened by this heartless ruffian."

"The attempt would be a vain one," exclaimed Maud; "for you will be assailed by numbers, and what can one man do against so many?"

"Then you would have me abandon Blanche Heriot to her fate?"

"You wrong me," she replied. "I would save you from the violence of those men, that your own may still be reserved for Blanche, when you may better aid her than you can at present. Remember, the defeat your party has sustained from the Yorkists render you an outcast; and ere this time a price has been set upon the heads of all those who joined the cause of King Henry, who is now a prisoner in the Tower of London. Hugh Laneret knows his advantage, and should a meeting unfortunately take place, he will not fail to rid himself of an enemy, especially as by so doing he will obtain the approbation of his monarch."

"Nay, my condition is not quite so desperate as you imagine," answered Neville Audeley; "I have this day saved the life of Edward when it was placed in imminent danger, and was offered any boon I thought proper to ask for it."

"Of course you demanded pardon for yourself?"

"I made no demand," replied Neville, "because I cannot yet reconcile it with my conscience to acknowledge him as my sovereign."

"Then you are lost!" exclaimed Maud; "for Edward will forget the debt of gratitude he owes you, and no man will incur his displeasure for seeking the death of one who is well known to have taken the other side in this fatal battle of Tewkesbury."

"But I have a token," replied Neville, "which he has promised to recognise at any time that I send or take it to him. He gave me a signet ring which I am to make use of should any danger overtake me."

"Depend not on it, lest you should be deceived," cried Maud, earnestly. "Should you fall in the way of Hugh Laneret, instant death will be certain, and then of what avail will this ring be to you? or, even supposing they should throw you into a prison, who would be found to convey the signet to his majesty? I therefore warn you to place no reliance upon it, but to seek safety in concealment, when you may be able to send a message to the king and obtain his pardon for the past."

"And whilst I am there securing the past," exclaimed the young man, "Blanche Heriot will be exposed to danger from a vindictive enemy. I know the villain Hugh Laneret too well to trust anything to his mercy, and will therefore repair with all speed to Redwynde Manor-house to thwart his projects."

"If there be no persuading you against it," said Maud, "you will at least follow my advice and pursue a different road to the one you are now taking. It is less frequented than this, and will enable you to reach Chertsey before your foes."

"That is a suggestion that I can have no objection to," answered Neville Audeley. "I am not so wilfully blind as to run into danger needlessly, and in order to reach Chertsey with certainty, will follow any other route that you think will be more safe."

"Then turn your horse and I will lead you to a road that you passed about a quarter of a mile from hence," exclaimed Maud. "You will meet with no difficulty in tracing your way, and as Hugh Laneret and his companions are not likely to set out just yet, there is a good opportunity for reaching Redwynde Manor-house before them."

Whilst she was thus speaking, Neville Audeley had began to retrace his steps, and on reaching the cross-road she had spoken of, Maud said—

"The way now lies strait before you, and there is little chance of your meeting with interruption, as none need know you are a fugitive from Tewkesbury field. On reaching Chertsey, let your interview with Blanche be as brief as possible, and then seek sanctuary within the abbey walls. You will be safe among the holy brotherhood, and doubtless, a messenger will there be found willing to convey your signet to King Edward. Thus you may yet be saved in spite of all the villanies practised by your unrelenting foe."

She turned away as she uttered these last words, and almost instantly disappeared from sight. No further time was now to be lost, for every moment was of the utmost consequence, and putting spurs to his horse, Neville Audeley proceeded on his way.

CHAPTER XXIII.

[LOVE'S ALARM.—THE LOVER'S RETREAT.]

THE brief interval that had occurred since the departure of Neville Audeley from Redwynde Manor-house, had been passed by its inmates in intense anxiety, that they in vain endeavoured to conceal from each other. Blanche made frequent inquiries of those about her to ascertain how matters were going on between the two hostile parties, but from no one could she hear any satisfactory intelligence, since all were desirous to conceal from her the news which had been received, of the defeat of the Lancastrians at the battle of Barnet, and the too great probability that a similar fatal result would await them in the engagement that was hourly expected to take place at Tewkesbury.

At length, unable to endure this state of suspense any longer, she sought out Sir Philip Warrenne, and having assured him that she could bear any ill-tidings he might have to communicate, rather than the uncertainty under which she was suffering, she entreated him to inform her whether anything had been heard by which the probable fate of Neville might be imagined.

"Why, at present, my dear Blanche," he replied, "I am as much in the dark in this respect as you are yourself. A thousand rumours are afloat, and yet from none of them can I glean anything satisfactory."

"I have heard," said Blanche, "that one disastrous battle has been fought, and that the Lancastrians were preparing to enter the field again in another part of England; do you know whether the two forces have yet met in deadly strife?"

"Nothing was known when I last heard the subject mentioned," replied Sir Philip; "but as both parties were anxious to bring the affair to a speedy issue, I have no doubt that before this time the struggle for victory has taken place."

"Was there any chance that the friends of King Henry would be masters of the day?"

"I am afraid the probabilities are all against them," replied the knight. "The troops of Edward are flushed with their recent success, whilst those on our side are equally depressed at the turn fortune has taken against them; still, however, I would not have you despair, for even though our cause may be lost, it is to be hoped Neville will escape the perils of battle, and in that case you may still look forward to a life of happiness."

"That I fear would be in vain," sighed Blanche; "for should Prince Edward prove to be the victor he will show little mercy to those who have taken part against him."

"So at least your fears make you believe."

"There is but too much reason to fear the worst," she replied; "and though I have tried to discover some grounds for hope, I find, alas, that all is in vain, and that the happiness you speak of is wrecked for ever."

Before Sir Philip Warrenne could make any reply to this, Tony Amblewit entered the room, and seeing that Blanche was there, he was about to hurry back again, when the knight, who saw by his countenance that he was the bearer of evil tidings, bade him speak.

"You have come to bring me news," he said, "and something assures me that it is not so favourable as I could wish. These, however, are no times for hesitation, and I therefore desire you to speak out boldly."

"And the young lady, sir?"

"Expects the worst," answered Sir Philip, "and can endure anything rather than suspense."

"Yes, Tony," said Blanche, recovering her composure as well as she could; "I already anticipate your news, and am prepared to hear it with firmness. Have the armies been engaged in battle?"

"They have."

"And fortune has again declared in favour of our enemies?"

"Right," answered Tony, "and it is said that the army of the Lancastrians is completely routed and dispersed."

"And Neville Audeley?"

"Ah! now you are asking a question that I am unable to answer," returned the other. "I've only been telling you the news that has just reached the place, but who is killed, or who escaped, no one can yet say."

"I fear the worst," sighed Blanche; "and now, Sir Philip, with a heart torn and lacerated, I shall enter the cloisters of some nunnery, and devote the remainder of my days to prayer and meditation."

At this juncture a horse was heard galloping into the court-yard, and Sir Philip, who happened to be standing near the window, exclaimed in a tone of joyful surprise, that Neville Audeley had returned, apparently unhurt. This intelligence seemed to give new life to our despairing heroine, but she was unable to give utterance to her boundless joy, and ere she could again question Sir Philip upon the subject, she was once more folded in the arms of her lover.

"Blanche—dearest Blanche!" he exclaimed; "this is a happiness I almost despaired of, yet great as it is, our separation must almost immediately follow, and Heaven only knows whether it may not prove eternal."

"You are in peril, then?"

"Our cause is for ever lost," he replied, "and those who have proved conquerors will scarcely show mercy to those who have drawn the sword against them."

"Nay, you shall remain here in concealment," exclaimed Sir Philip; "and should any of the scoundrels come in search of you, I'll warrant they none of them go back to say whether you are here or not."

"You shall be exposed to no such risk on my account," replied Neville; "for rather would I perish under the most cruel tortures than bring trouble upon those whom I love and venerate."

"Why, you surely won't go scampering over the country when there is so much danger to be apprehended?" exclaimed Sir Philip in a tone of remonstrance."

"There is but one alternative remaining for me," answered Neville Audeley; "the abbey is not far from hence, and within its walls I may claim the privilege of sanctuary, which is never denied even to the greatest criminal. There I shall be safe for a time, and it is even possible that I may obtain pardon from the sovereign who has now won this kingdom for himself."

"Why, this is better news than I expected," cried Sir Philip; "you hear him, Blanche? and yet I know not what ails the wench, for she looks as gloomy and downcast as ever!"

"And if I do," she replied, "it is because I do not see so much ground for hope as you appear to do. The privilege of sanctuary may not be respected by furious men, and should they insist upon Neville's being delivered up to them, the monks will not risk their own safety by a positive refusal."

"Then you are determined," exclaimed the knight, "to look only on the darkest side of the picture?"

"Blanche has spoken truly, I believe," said Neville Audeley; "for our enemies, exulting in their own strength, will pay little respect to the usages we have been accustomed to regard as sacred. I rely, however, upon being able to obtain the sovereign's pardon, which I believe will be less difficult than you imagine."

"But you have enemies," cried Blanche, "and will not they try to poison the king's mind against you?"

"I have but one," replied her lover. "Hugh Laneret bears me deadly hatred, and will, no doubt, pursue me with all the vengeance his fierce nature is capable of. Yet even he, I believe, will not succeed in his design, since I have already received the king's promise of protection, should it ever be applied for."

"Which you will of course do immediately?" exclaimed Sir Philip Warrenne.

"As soon," replied the other, "as I am received within the walls of Chertsey Abbey."

"Well," said Sir Philip, "I should begin to think matters began to look promising enough, if those villains, Hugh Laneret and his friend Mark Evered, had only met their deserts in the late battle."

"Laneret, it is true, still survives, to pursue me with his hatred," replied Neville; "but his friend will never trouble me or any other person again."

"Ah! he is dead then?"

"He is."

"Are you sure of it?"

"As certain as my own eye-sight can make me," replied Neville, "for my own hand slew him in fair battle; and when last I looked upon him, life had fled from him for ever."

"Excellent!" cried the knight; "then we may congratulate ourselves, Neville, upon there being one rascal the less in the world; and it was nothing but a just retribution that he should lose his life by the man he most sought to injure."

"There was less of hardened villany in Mark Evered than I expected to find," answered the young man. "He, in fact, expressed contrition for what had passed and as the only reparation he could make, cautioned me against the further machinations of Hugh Laneret, who, he said, was coming here, under the expectation of finding that I should seek an asylum beneath this roof."

"He will be here then!" cried Blanche, in accents of terror.

"There is but too much reason to fear he will," answered Neville; "I would, therefore, entreat you to keep out of sight, lest you should again be subjected to those threats which he is but too likely to carry into execution. For a time you may avoid him, and ere long I trust to be again at liberty, when he shall dearly suffer for the persecution with which he has pursued you."

"If he comes here," exclaimed Sir Philip, "I would advise him to look to himself, for a man cannot always control his passions, and as I happen to owe him a grudge, he may chance to get something that will prevent his doing any mischief in future."

"Nay," cried Neville, "an act of violence would ruin you for ever with the party now in power. Already there are suspicions that you were in favour of King Henry, and any imprudence would be certain to bring upon you the fury of your enemies."

"Well, well, in that case I must smother my rage till a more favourable opportunity presents itself," replied Sir Philip. "It must be confessed, however, that I shall hardly be able to conceal my fury, if he comes here to make any of his insolent demands."

"And there is but too much certainty that he will come," exclaimed Blanche, "for after the sad reverses that have depressed our party, there is no doubt he will make sure of frightening me into compliance with his proposals. He, however, little knows the resolution of Blanche Heriot, who would rather perish than give her hand to one, of whose villany she has seen so many proofs."

"He had better beware of what he does," exclaimed Sir Philip Warrenne, "for though I have no longer the strength and activity that I could once boast of, I am a thorough hater of tyranny and oppression, and can yet wield a sword in behalf of an oppressed female. You, Neville Audeley, must unfortunately be out of the way for a time, but you may make yourself quite easy that Blanche is not left without a protector."

"I am aware of it, my dear friend," answered Neville; "yet it does not lessen my regret at being absent when my aid may be so much needed. As I said before, however, there is every probability of obtaining the king's protection, and when that is made sure of, the task shall be mine to call Hugh Laneret to a severe account for the injuries he has inflicted upon us."

"Begging your pardon, sir," exclaimed Tony Amblewit, who had hitherto been a silent auditor of all that was passing; "but if a poor fellow like me may be allowed to put in a word, I think I know a person that wouldn't mind running from one end of the world to the other, in case you should happen to want his services."

"Meaning yourself, I suppose, good Tony?"

"Exactly so, sir."

"Well," replied Neville, "I will not promise but that your kind offer may be accepted before long, though in what way I cannot exactly tell you at present. You, however, may as well remain in this house till the arrival of Hugh Laneret, and should he proceed to violence, hasten to the abbey, and let me know of it."

"That you may hasten to our rescue, I suppose, Neville," exclaimed the knight; "and then plunge at once into the very danger it is so necessary for you to avoid?"

"And would you have me regard my own security," demanded the young man, "when those I love need my presence and exertions?"

"Why, under other circumstances," answered Sir Philip, "it must be confessed,

I should not try to persuade you to such a course. But as it is, you could do no good for us, and there is the certainty of your falling into the hands of your enemies at a moment when they are too numerous for us to oppose with any chance of success."

"The danger may not be so great as we apprehend," said Blanche, who was anxious to allay the fears of her lover previous to his departure. "Hugh Laneret has hitherto proved himself to be cruel and remorseless; but we have got the sovereign to appeal to, and he dare not risk the displeasure of one who has the power, and may have the will to punish him."

"True," exclaimed her guardian, "and if need be, I should not hesitate to lay my complaint against him even at the foot of the throne. To be sure, we know little of Edward at this moment; but we have no reason to believe he would suffer an injustice to be committed when he has the means of preventing it. So now, my young friend, let me prevail upon you to lose no time in seeking the sanctuary of our abbey; and rest assured Tony will be a frequent visiter to let you know how matters are going on."

To this request Blanche Heriot added her own earnest entreaties, and Neville, who was aware of the danger of delay, promised a ready obedience to the wishes that were thus expressed. He, however, over and over again urged Blanche to send him instant word should there be any fear of force being used to carry her away from her guardian's roof. This, though not without some hesitation, she promised; and then, having taken leave of her and Sir Philip, he left the house and hastened towards the abbey of Chertsey.

CHAPTER XXIV.

THE FOE.—THE SANCTUARY.—THE DISCOVERY.

THE ensuing night was an anxious one to the inmates of Redwynde Manorhouse, for they every moment expected the arrival of Hugh Laneret and his companions; and their apprehensions were wound up to the highest pitch for the result of an interview which there was so much reason to dread. Nothing, however, was heard of the expected visiters until the following morning, when Tony came running in with all haste to announce that Laneret and his troopers had arrived, and that the former had peremptorily demanded an immediate interview with Sir Philip and Blanche.

"Bid him come to me here," said the old knight; "and mark me, Tony, let nothing be said to indicate that we have the least fear of the business that brings him hither. Say I will see him, and be yourself his conductor."

Tony left the room, not very willingly, it must be confessed; and Sir Philip then urged Blanche to maintain all her firmness, in order that Laneret should have no advantage of their fears. This our heroine promised to obey, and in a few moments afterwards their unwelcome guest made his appearance before them.

"You are an early visitor this morning," exclaimed the knight, as soon as the other presented himself; "and I trust your business here is of such a nature that we shall not have to regret your coming beneath my roof."

"My business is not so pleasant a one as I could have wished, Sir Philip," answered the other with forced courtesy. "The truth is, I am in search of a traitor to his country, who, I have been credibly informed, has sought shelter in your house."

"Indeed! and have you any reason to believe that I would shield a traitor?"

"Why, the truth is, you regard him as a friend," answered Laneret; "and under such circumstances a man will sometimes commit himself."

"Humph! that's plain, at any rate," exclaimed Sir Philip; "and pray sir, may I now ask the name of this traitor, as you are pleased to call him?"

"Neville Audeley."

"Neville Audeley is no traitor," exclaimed Blanche, indignantly. "He took up arms in favour of a cause that has failed; but he was loyal to his king, and was ready to die in his service."

"His evil example has not, it seems, been thrown away upon you," returned Hugh Laneret, with a sneer. "It is a pity that young ladies should be thus easily led away in matters that they do not understand; but perhaps before long you may see reason to change the hasty opinions you have formed."

"Whatever observations you have to make, Master Hugh Laneret," exclaimed Sir Philip, "must be addressed to me. You are, it appears, in search of Neville Audeley, who you are pleased to term a traitor?"

"I have already told you that is my object."

"Then I have now to tell you, sir, that your hopes are frustrated; for happily, Neville Audeley is not at this moment a visiter in my house."

"That," exclaimed Laneret, "I may be permitted to doubt, since I have good reason to know that you have given him the concealment he required."

"Had you been speaking to a young man, sirrah," exclaimed Sir Philip, "you would not have dared to charge me with uttering a falsehood. Yet hear me, Hugh Laneret, I have yet strength enough to wield a sword; and by Heaven, either your life or mine shall be sacrificed, if another word of insult escape from your lips."

"You would intimidate me, Sir Philip?"

"I would teach you, sir," replied the knight, "the duty and respect that one man owes to another. You tell me you are in search of Neville Audeley, and will you say by whose authority you have come hither?"

"By my own," he replied. "A general order has been given to make prisoners all persons who are known to be rebels to the king who now reigns. Neville Audeley fought in the battle of Tewkesbury on the side of the Lancastrians; and, therefore, it is my duty to arrest him without loss of time, in order that he may receive the punishment due to his crime."

"There may be a difference of opinion, Master Hugh Laneret," answered the knight, "as to which is the greater rebel, yourself or Neville Audeley. Both took opposite sides in a struggle for the crown, and because your party happened to prove victorious, it seems that all who belonged to the other side are to be branded with the name of traitor."

"Beware what you say, Sir Philip Warrenne, or I may feel it my duty to arrest you on a similar charge."

"That you may do with all my heart," replied the knight, "since it would give me an opportunity of exposing a villain to the scorn of the world."

"Sir Philip Warrenne," exclaimed Hugh Laneret, "I came here to perform a duty, and not to seek a quarrel with a man whose years nearly treble my own. You shall, therefore, have my forbearance as long as possible; but, remember, I may be moved to wrath, and should that unfortunately happen, the consequences will be entirely of your own seeking."

"My dear sir," cried Blanche, "let me entreat you to leave the room with me before worse happens from this. A quarrel would best suit the purposes of this bold intruder on our privacy; and I would therefore pray you to abstain from giving him an advantage which he would not fail to take. Retire with me, sir, and let Master Hugh Laneret search the house, when he will perhaps be convinced that no falsehood has been uttered."

"Your coldness, young lady, will but ill serve you," exclaimed Hugh Laneret, unable to conceal the anger that her words had excited. "You, at least, might spare me, since I have thus far shown a degree of favour that it seems you scarcely deserve at my hands."

"Answer him not, Blanche," said Sir Philip. "His visit, it seems, is to me, and to me alone must he be content to address himself. I have already told him that the person he seeks is not in my house; and though I might and would resist him if I pleased, he is at liberty to rummage every corner of the house in search of a person who, I am happy to say, is in some far safer place."

"I now begin to believe that Neville Audeley is not here," answered Hugh Laneret, "since the permission—which, by-the-by, was scarcely required—would not have been so readily given had the rebel been beneath this roof. I have reason, however, to believe, Sir Philip, that you are acquainted with his place of concealment, and if you think proper to give me the requisite information, it will save you from incurring the same trouble that has befallen this fugitive."

"Betray my friend!" exclaimed Sir Philip indignantly. "Do you, then, imagine that I am equal to yourself in baseness and villany?"

"Do you still seek to quarrel with me?" asked Laneret, with assumed humility. "I offer you fair terms by which you may ensure your own safety, and yet they are rejected in such a manner that I can hardly refrain from taking offence."

"I heed but little how you feel inclined to take my words," replied Sir Philip Warrenne, "for I have no wish to obtain the respect of one whose reckless conduct has made him the foe of all who are not vicious like yourself."

"Let me then appeal to Blance Heriot," exclaimed Laneret, "for she, at least, will scarcely venture to speak as ill of me as you have done."

"Blanche has prudently enough left the room, rather than remain longer in the society of one who she has so much cause to dread," returned Sir Philip. "She has left us to ourselves, Hugh Laneret, and now, to speak my mind plainly, I care not how soon I am fairly rid of your company."

"Still, Sir Philip Warrenne, I would rather that we part not upon bad terms," exclaimed Laneret, with hypocritical humility. "I bear you no malace, and though my visit here has been an unpleasant one, it was forced upon me by the duty I owe to my king and country. Tell me, therefore, where Neville Audeley is; and, though I cannot do otherwise than arrest him on this charge, yet I pledge you my word to get him off with a punishment that shall be short of death."

"You would persuade me to trust the wolf within the sheep's fold then?"

"I have said he has nothing to fear from me."

"Well, I am inclined to think you are perfectly right, there," exclaimed the knight; "for, to confess the truth to you, Neville Audeley is now in a place where you dare not follow him."

"Ha!—I understand," cried the other; "he has sought the protection of the church?"

"He has."

"And would claim the privilege of sanctuary?"

"Right again."

"And I suppose you will not deny that he is at the present moment within the walls of Chertsey Abbey?"

"It would be useless to deny it," replied Sir Philip, "nor is it, indeed, necessary, for there your power cannot reach him, since none dare take him from it."

"We will see that," exclaimed Hugh Laneret, "for I will at least make the venture, with a certainty that the king will protect me in it. A traitor is not to be shielded by the privilege which is thus claimed by an arrogant church, and neither pope nor devil shall save Neville Audeley from the hate of the man who has sworn his destruction."

So saying he hurried from the room, and proceeding to the place where his companions were waiting for his return, he quitted the Mannor-house of Redwynde to put his desperate intentions into effect.

We must now follow Blanche Heriot, who, fearing lest further violence should be offered, quitted the room, as we have already seen, and hastening from the house with what speed she could, directed her steps towards the abbey, in order to acquaint Neville of what had occurred, and to prevail on him to flee to some distant place, where he would be more safe from the vindictive malice of his enemy. Her lover listened to her brief narrative with emotion, for he ardently wished to meet Laneret face to face, and it was with no little difficulty that she was able to prevail upon him to remain where he was till further means could be taken for his safety.

"Remember, dear Neville," she said, "you would now be entirely in his power, and, enraged as he is, I fear lest, upon the slightest provocation, he should slay you. You smile at my alarm, and perhaps deem it frivolous, but no reliance is to be placed upon Hugh Laneret; and should your death happen in the manner I have said, he would find no difficulty in excusing the act under a plea of necessity."

"But after all, Blanche," he replied, "by remaining here, I am but acting the part of a sorry coward."

"That can scarcely be," answered our heroine, "when there is so small a chance of defeating those who have thus leagued together for your destruction. Here you can scarcely be considered safe, yet how you are now to escape from the abbey I know not."

"I will not attempt it," replied Neville, "for already I have lowered myself, by hiding from an enemy, instead of boldly confronting him. Yet my honour shall be restored, for at the first opportunity that presents itself, I will seek the villain, and either sacrifice him to my vengeance, or lose my own life in the attempt."

"Again you seek to involve yourself in danger," cried our heroine, "though I have prayed and entreated you for my sake to avoid the consequences that I so much dread. Remember, Neville, you are at present a fugitive, and were you to quit this place, there are others beside Hugh Laneret who would be ready to hunt you into the snares of destruction."

"And of what value is life to me," exclaimed Neville, "when I am thus driven to seek shelter from my foes?"

"The trial is indeed a severe one," she replied, "yet I trust it will not last much longer; and should the king's pardon be obtained, there is yet a chance of happiness being in store for you. Were that obtained, Laneret would cease to persecute, and then a future life of joy would recompense you for the sharp affliction that has followed your earlier career."

"Your words are ever consoling to me, dearest Blanche," he exclaimed, "and in gratitude for your kindness, I will endeavour to believe that the picture you have drawn, may one day or other be realised."

"And that it will be so I am certain," she replied, "or hope has terribly deceived me. Sorrow and persecution have indeed been your lot, but the triumph of the wicked lasts not for ever, and we shall see Hugh Laneret foiled in his daring designs upon us. He knows how utterly I scorn him; and when all hope of forcing me to an odious marriage is at an end, he will look elsewhere for a more willing bride."

"It may be so," replied Neville, "but at present, it must be confessed I see but little chance of it. He is actuated solely by a feeling of revenge, excited in the first instance by a disappointed passion; and now that hatred has taken possession of his heart instead of love, he will never rest satisfied till his own dark purposes have been fulfilled."

"Again you are indulging in your gloomy thoughts," exclaimed Blanche, reprovingly. "I would see you abandon them, and yet it seems they increase more and more, each moment of your life."

"It is because I cannot see a fair ground on which to establish the hope which you would instil into my heart," he replied. "I know the unrelenting nature of Laneret even better than you do yourself; and judging of the future by his former acts, I cannot but foresee that nothing but his death will ever bring us the security we desire."

"And let me hope," she cried, "that, except under absolute necessity, the death of this reckless man will not be produced by your hand. I know the provocations you have received, Neville, and that circumstance increases the alarm which thus tortures me."

"Then be assured, Blanche," he replied, "that I will never seek out this man, however much my own feelings have been excited against him. Yet, on the other hand, it is to be feared he will not hide himself from me, and should he be discovered in any of his base plots, I will not promise to keep the pledge I have thus given you. I have yearned for vengeance against him, but it will now be his own fault if I hurl upon him the wrath he has engendered. He has been my direst foe, and will, undoubtedly, remain so, for the cause which produced his hatred has not a wit abated ; therefore, it is vain to imagine, for a moment, that he will forego his base designs. I know well that he will make it appear, in the eyes of the world, that he is one of the most loyal subjects in his majesty's realm, and that he pursues me from loyal and patriotic motives, while it is well known to us that he is a cowardly ruffian, devoid of honour, and only per-severing in his present purposes from a spirit of revenge."

" I have sometimes thought that, like many other villains, he is a coward at heart," said Blanche. " It has ever been his practice to surround himself with those who may assist him in case of need, and even to-day, when he visited my guardian's house, he came with a number of men, all of whom, I suppose, were ready to perform his slightest bidding."

At this period they were startled by hearing a loud hammering at the abbey gates, and from the confusion that was immediately evident among the fraternity, it was certain that something of an unusual character had occurred to fill them with the most unccountable alarm and perfect dismay.

The fears of Blanche Heriot were instantly excited, lest this was caused by a visit from Hugh Laneret and his companions, and Neville was not long before he guessed the nature of the fears with which she had been seized. He would have led her from the chapel to a more retired part of the convent, but ere he had reached half way down the aisle, the doors were suddenly burst open, and his enemies rushed tumultuously into the sacred edifice.

"Seize the traitor!" exclaimed Hugh Laneret, pointing to the object of his vindictive wrath. "Seize upon him I say, and if priest or monk dare venture to oppose us, they shall answer for it to the king, in whose behalf we are here present."

"What means this turbulence and outrage?" demanded Father Angurin, who now advanced to place himself between the soldiers and their expected prisoner.

"It means," replied Laneret, "that you have given shelter to a rebel who has fought against his king. He is now a prisoner, and let none venture to interfere between the sovereign and yonder traitor."

"I know him not as a traitor," answered Father Angurin; "but gave him, as he desired, the security of the sanctuary. It is the privilege of our church to grant it, and your king dare not violate the sanctity you have thus broken in upon."

"It will soon be seen whether we dare bring down your wrath or not," replied Hugh Laneret. "I here attach the person of Neville Audeley, and since an attempt is to be made for his rescue, I will slay him, even though it be at the very altar."

"Wouldst thou commit murder in the house of peace?" demanded the abbot, terrified at the menace. "Again I warn thee to depart; for, if violence be offered to one who has sought refuge beneath our roof, thou shalt be pursued with the vengeance due to the enormity of thy crime."

"Let me add my entreaties to those of the holy father," cried Blanche, interposing to save the life of her lover; "he you have pursued hither is under the protection of the church, and a heavy punishment is awarded to those who dare violate the sanctity of a place like this."

"It is in vain that you plead to a ruffian, whose boast it is to set all law and religion at defiance," exclaimed Neville Audeley; "I have been pursued by blood-thirsty men to the altar, and since it is my life they seek, I am willing to lay it down rather than be the cause of further strife where peace only should reign."

"My son," replied the abbot, "I have pledged myself for your safety, and force alone shall deprive you of the privilege that, till now, has never been denied to those who seek the shelter of our roof. This man knows the power I possess, and heavy shall he feel the wrath he has provoked, unless he instantly depart in peace."

"Your threats, proud monk, I can laugh to scorn," exclaimed Hugh Laneret vauntingly; "I am here on the king's business, and all those who would protect a traitor, share in the crime. The office of religion, my lord abbot, shall not shield you from punishment; and you see I have enough with me to overcome any vain resistance to the duty it is my purpose to fulfil."

"Let the doors of the abbey be instantly closed," said Father Angurin, addressing those who stood behind him. "These intruders have yet to learn that we are not so powerless as they imagine; and if a hand be stretched forth to slay or even to capture this youth who has sought sanctuary here, it shall be tried whether imprisonment in our dungeons will not teach them respect for the rights that have been bestowed upon us."

"How!" exclaimed Hugh Laneret, surprised at the boldness that he had not expected, "are we, who are acting in the king's name, to be caged up within these walls like common felons?—Hark ye, priest! there is not one among us that has more respect for a monk than for any other man, and should any restrain be put upon us, you shall be the first to fall beneath the vengeance your own presumption has called forth."

"You would murder me then?"

"Ay, if murder it may be called," answered Hugh Laneret. "We came here to arrest a traitor, and those who would protect him have no claim on our mercies or compassion."

"Hear me," said Blanche, in accents of terror; "you have, without sufficient warrant, intruded yourself upon a place dedicated to religion and peace. The privilege of sanctuary has never yet been denied, even when the suppliant was guilty of the most heinous offence; yet, in satisfaction of your own heartless hatred towards Neville Audeley, you would murder him even in this consecrated place."

"And whose fault is it, that I have formed these feelings of hatred against him?" demanded Hugh Laneret. "Have I not seen him regarded with favour and affection by her whose love I in vain sought for? and shall I coolly sit down and endure the reflections that, like a canker, are for ever gnawing at my heart? Blanche Heriot! this is all your doing; and, be the consequences what they may, you have yourself to blame for them."

"Then you deny her the right to make a free choice?" exclaimed Neville.

"You have triumphed in the disappointment of my hopes," replied Laneret; "but at length a time has come when it is for me to exult over a fallen foe. Your life is in my power, Neville Audeley, and even though the doors of the abbey have been closed upon me, and I am threatened with the anathemas of the holy church, I will see you lying dead at my feet, ere I take my departure."

"Monster!" exclaimed the terrified Blanche; "villain, as you are, you dare not violate the laws which will surely punish the crime with death."

"I tell you, girl," answered Hugh Laneret, "the king's commands have come forth to slay all who are known to have taken part with the Lancastrians, wherever they may be found. There was no reservation in favour of those who have fled to sanctuary; and whatever may be said upon the subject, I can refer my accusers to the orders given by my sovereign."

As Hugh Laneret said this, he advanced fiercely towards Neville, and was in the act of plunging his sword into the bosom of his rival, when the abbot suddenly placing himself between them presented a barrier, which for a moment had the effect of awing the ruffian from his deadly purpose. At length, however, recovering himself, he motioned Father Angurin away, and muttered his threats to slay both of them if any further opposition was offered.

"I will not move from this spot till your sword has been sheathed in its scabbard," answered the abbot. "And now, thou man of blood and discord, hear the proposition I have to make—You seek the life of Neville Audeley, and would sacrifice him to a feeling of deadly malice that seems to be almost demoniac. It must be confessed I possess not the means to shield him from your wrath, but as a boon, I would entreat you to spare him for a few hours that he may have time to make his peace with Heaven. Spare him till the curfew bell tolls to-night from our abbey tower, and if by that time your heart still remains hard and resolute to its cruel purpose, I will surrender him into your hands, even as you have demanded."

"Agreed," exclaimed Hugh Laneret; "I can wait with patience till the expiration of the few hours you have asked for; but remember, when the curfew tolls I shall return hither to claim my prisoner, and no entreaties will then prevail upon me to defer my purpose for another moment."

"And what," asked the abbot, "will you then do with him?"

"Lead him forth to a short distance beyond these walls," replied Laneret, "and then slay him like a traitor as he is. You have heard your doom, Neville Audeley; and now, as you may have a few parting words of consolation to say to Blanche, I shall leave you; but be assured, that when the curfew sounds, I shall be here to lead you forth to death."

With a grim look of hatred he now took his departure, followed by the man who had accompanied him; and the abbot then addressing himself to Neville, who was supporting the almost fainting form of Blanche, said—.

"It grieves me, my young friend, that no better terms could be made with the ruffian, whose violence I have it not in my power to resist. What I have done, however, was in the hope that something may be thought of to rescue you from the death with which you are threatened."

"Fly from this spot, dear Neville, ere it be too late," cried Blanche, catching even at the faintest hope that offered itself to her.

"That I fear is impossible," returned the monk, "for they will keep watch out of the abbey walls ; and should their victim be discovered in his attempt to escape, his death would be the immediate consequence."

"How then would you counsel us to proceed?" asked the almost distracted girl.

"Alas !" answered Father Angurin ; "shut up as we are from the world, I have no counsel to give ; I will, however, leave you with your lover ; something may yet be thought of, and though it is not in my power to aid, I will retire and pray to Heaven for succour in this great hour of peril." ·

The abbot raised his hands in benediction over them, and then sorrowfully departed from the chapel.

CHAPTER XXV.

THE SIGNET RING.—A FAITHFUL FRIEND.—THE JOURNEY.

"ALL, all is lost !" cried Blanche, as the abbot disappeared ; "you will perish, dear Neville, and the only consolation that remains to me is, that my own death will soon follow the fatal intelligence that assures me you are no more."

"Nay, there is yet one chance for me," replied her lover ; "the king's signet ring is still in my possession ; and if it can be conveyed to him in time, I may yet be saved from the doom you so much dread."

"Give it me," she exclaimed eagerly, "and I will myself take care that it shall reach its destination."

"I understand you," replied Neville ; "you would yourself convey it to London, and thus run a risk that I tremble to think of."

"I will," she exclaimed ; "and Heaven will aid me in my purpose."

"Nay, it must not be," returned Neville ; "for rather would I suffer a thousand deaths than allow you to encounter danger on my account. And now I bethink me, Herrick Evenden has often expressed the warmest regard for us both, and if you describe to him the necessity for promptitude, he will be the bearer of my message ; and upon his zeal in my behalf I can rely with the most perfect confidence."

"I will hasten to him," cried Blanche, taking the ring which Neville had presented to her. "My request will not be made in vain ; and the only fear I feel is that he may not have time to go to London and return ere the fatal curfew sounds your death-note."

"A swift horse will enable him to do it," answered Neville. "Tell him to demand an instant audience with the king, which will be readily granted upon the production of this signet ; and when he stands in the presence of Edward, he will have briefly to recount to him the adventure that befel us in the field of Tewkesbury. He will not forget his royal promise ; and if all speed be used, Herrick may yet return in time to deprive Hugh Laneret of his expected vengeance."

"I will hasten to him without delay," exclaimed Blanche ; "and so well do I feel assured of his friendly zeal, that I already anticipate the happiest results from his mission. Yes, dearest Neville, you will be saved, and in another country we may find the peace which has, alas ! been denied us in this."

"But there is yet something to fear from Hugh Laneret," answered her lover ; "he may see you quit the abbey ; and should he entertain a suspicion tha you are going to attempt anything in my behalf, he will find means to destroy even this, our last remaining hope."

"That is a danger which I believe may be easily avoided," she replied. "There are more gates than one by which I can leave the abbey; and I will not venture to quit the place till I am thoroughly convinced there are no enemies lurking near me."

"It is a cruel destiny," exclaimed Neville, "which thus forces me to be inactive whilst you, dearest Blanche, undertake a task that is full of peril. Nay, it must not, shall not be; life preserved by such means would be torture, and rather will I yield it up this moment than endure the shame and bitterness that I know will be mine."

"Would you then cruelly deny me the only favour I have ever asked?" she cried.

"Only in such a case as this," he replied; "for your sake, Blanche, I would avoid the doom that hangs over me, but it must not be done at a hazard that would attach future infamy to my name. I am now ready to die, and though it is hard to part thus from thee, I shall at least have the consolation of knowing that my days have not been prolonged at the expense of my honour."

"You reflect not, then," said Blanche, reproachfully, "on the misery to which you thus condemn me?"

"It is to preserve you from harm that I have come to this resolution," he replied. "Hugh Laneret is a foe too powerful to be thus thwarted; and, should I be saved, his first act of vengeance would be to hurl destruction upon her who had rescued a victim from his power."

"Which he cannot do without involving himself in danger," answered our heroine. "The king, who has just taken forcible possession of the throne, must gain the hearts of his subjects by acts of mercy and justice; and he would thus be compelled to punish those who practice tyranny and oppression. Hugh Laneret know this, and fierce as his vengeance may be, he will pause ere he does aught to bring upon himself the wrath he trembles to encounter."

"My entreaties, then," exclaimed Neville Audeley, "are of no avail?"

"In this instance," she replied, "I must be permitted—like a wayward child —to have my own way. For my own part, I see not so much danger as you appear to do; and depend upon it, Neville, I shall not only accomplish my errand, but you will see me back here as soon as it has been completed. Herrick Evenden will cheerfully undertake the task entrusted to him, and I will then return to this place of sanctuary, and remain with you till he comes from London with the joyful tidings of your pardon."

So saying, she slipped away from his presence, ere he could offer any further remonstrance, and maddened at the thought of her danger, he was about to follow in pursuit, when the abbot suddenly presented himself at the door through which she had just fled.

"My son," exclaimed the aged monk, "why do I thus find you resolved upon destruction when every effort is being made to preserve you from an ignominious fate? Blanche Heriot, as she passed on her way, conjured me to use my best efforts to aid her departure from hence without interruption, and, under the guidance of one of our holy brotherhood, she has ere how quitted our abbey walls. Be calm then, I entreat, and console yourself with the hope that all will terminate better than you expected."

"What hope can I indulge in?" demanded Neville, "when I know the danger she incurs on my behalf?"

"The danger is not so great as you imagine," answered the abbot, "for she is now under the care of a monk belonging to our holy order; and reckless as Hugh Laneret is, he will not venture to satisfy his wrath at the expense of bringing upon himself the displeasure of the church."

"He will not regard it," exclaimed Neville, "when he knows his own plans are likely to be frustrated."

"But the king's favour is not to be thoughtlessly thrown away," returned the abbot.

"The king's favour is not to be thus forfeited," answered Neville, "and since he will regard me as a traitor to his cause, I have little mercy to expect from him."

"Yet from your own lips I have heard that he owes his life to your generous interposition in the late battle that won for him the throne of England."

"True: but he may still remember that I took part in that very battle as his enemy."

"Believe me, my son," exclaimed the abbot, "you do him an injustice in thinking so. There are few persons who would be guilty of such black ingratitude, and why, therefore, should we expect it from the king towards whom all eyes are at this moment turned? He has to conciliate his subjects by acts of kindness, and will scarcely venture to forfeit their regard when he well knows that many of them will regard him as an usurper."

"For myself I care not what fate may be in store for me," replied Neville, "but she who has just left me must share in my downfall, and that thought alone fills me with an alarm that I cannot subdue."

"I have already said there is nothing to fear on her account," answered the abbot. "She is at present under safe protection, and from her firmness and resolution I anticipate the most favourable result. Your friend has ample time to reach London, and return ere the fatal hour of the curfew; and there is no doubt he will bring with him the pardon which snatches you from the power of Hugh Laneret. Therefore, I again entreat you to be calm and all will yet be well."

"I will at least try to follow your friendly council," exclaimed Neville Audeley, "though, to confess the truth, I shall find the task a more difficult one than you may conceive. I know the fiendish heart of him who has driven me to this fearful pass; and it is on Blanche's behalf that I regret the doom which hangs over me. With my fall she will be thrown entirely at the mercy of a reckless villain, and who will then be left to guard her against the designs that baseness has plotted?"

"Remonstrance and entreaties are I see alike in vain," returned the abbot, meekly; "and yet my duty commands that I should not abate in my zeal till you have regained your wonted composure. Follow me, then, to my study, and we will there converse upon those subjects which have occasioned you so much uneasiness. Come then, Neville Audeley, and learn from an old man's experience the duties of meekness and resignation even under the worst afflictions that can befal poor human nature."

Yielding to the abbot's entreaties, Neville Audeley followed him to another part of the building, where the reasoning and arguments of the aged priest had the effect of rendering him somewhat more reconciled to what was taking place than had at one time seemed possible.

Leaving them for the present, however, we must now follow Blanche Heriot, who, guided by the monk, shortly reached the astrologer's house without meeting the interruption which had occasioned her lover so much alarm. The interview she requested of the elder Evenden was speedily granted; and upon entering the room in which he was awaiting her arrival, she discovered to her no small satisfaction that Herrick was also there; and upon his zeal in behalf of a friend she placed the greatest reliance.

"This is an unexpected pleasure, Blanche Heriot," exclaimed the old man as she approached; "though much I marvel what can have brought you here, unless indeed it be that you would consult the mysterious science of which I am an humble professor."

"My present errand," answered Blanche, timidly, "is as much with your son, as with yourself."

"Ha!" cried Herrick, "then already I guess your errand; I have heard my friend Neville Audeley is in trouble, and you are here to ask my aid in attempting to rescue him from it?"

"You have guessed truly," she replied. "Life and death hang upon your exertions, and my last frail hope rests on the answer you give me to my request."

"Can you doubt my answer?"

"Scarcely," she replied; "yet your father may oppose an errand that is not unattended with danger."

"It will appear nothing, maiden, now that the fearful strife is over and the sword has been once more returned to its scabbard. Speak, Blanche Heriot, what is it you would demand of me?"

"Herrick must set forth without delay to ask an audience of the king," she replied. "Upon that the life of Neville Audeley depends, and should you refuse my request I shall depart hence sorrowful and broken-hearted."

"Then be happy, my child, in the certainty that my permission shall not be withheld," exclaimed the old man; "Herrick, I know, will joyfully undertake your mission, though it must needs be confessed I see but little prospect of his obtaining access to the king."

"This ring," said Blanche, "will obtain him an immediate interview and secure the boon he asks."

"The king knows it, then?"

"He does," replied Blanche; "it was given by him to Neville as a token of gratitude for having saved his life at a moment when it was in imminent peril. He will send back a pardon for his deliverer, and then Hugh Laneret will be foiled even at the very moment when he made most certain of his revenge."

"By St. Paul, and a more pleasant task could not have been entrusted to me," exclaimed Herrick Evenden. "A swift horse will serve me in the hour of need, and——"

"You know not yet the short time you have to perform the journey in," interrupted Blanche.

"Let me have six hours and I will undertake to be back again," answered Herrick; "that is provided no delay takes place when I reach the palace."

"You have more than that time," exclaimed our heroine, "since Hugh Laneret has postponed his vengeance till the curfew tolls this evening. The ring, too, will secure you instant admittance to the presence of the king, who will not delay the pardon when he learns the perilous condition of his preserver. You may thus save the life of your friend, and gain the lasting gratitude of those who have confided in you a task upon which so much depends."

"The confidence you have reposed upon me shall not be abused," answered Herrick, "nor will I know rest till the task has been successfully executed. In the meantime you may assure Neville of my zeal in his service, and bid him rely on the friendship of one who is ready to lay down even his life to preserve him from the machinations of his remorseless foe."

"Have a care, my son," exclaimed the old man, "how you incur dangers that cannot serve your friend. Remember, too, that should aught happen to you, it would imbitter the few last remaining days of my existence, and bring sorrow and despair upon him whose only happiness has been centred in the child of his fondest affections."

"Never fear anything on my account," answered Herrick, "for whilst I remember the duty I owe to my friend I shall not forget the gratitude due to a parent, whose kindness has been manifested in every action of his life. Nor indeed is there any occasion to incur danger, since the siguet I possess will give me ready access to the palace, and I shall not travel unarmed, in case of meeting with interruption on the road."

Basil Evenden would still have urged him upon the subject of his almost constant dread, but the young man knew the fatal consequences that would result from delay, and with a hasty adieu he hurried from the room, and a few minutes afterwards his horse was heard clattering from the court-yard, to commence the journey upon which depended the life or death of a human creature.

"He is gone," exclaimed Basil Evenden; "and rash and impetuous as he is, I cannot help fearing lest some terrible accident befal him."

"Nay, be not alarmed, dear sir," answered Blanche, "for your son knows that all depends upon his prudence, and the recollection of your anxiety on his account will prompt him to act with the greatest caution in the mission he has thus generously undertaken."

"I pray Heaven he may," exclaimed Basil Evenden, fervently; "and, since the errand he goes upon is worthy of him, I will try to forget my own selfishness in the honest pride that his generous conduct has called forth. Yes, Blanche, I am now more at ease; and, instead of looking gloomily on the future, I will anticipate his return with the glad tidings of his friend's pardon."

"That is indeed spoken like yourself," answered our heroine, "and rejoiced am I at seeing you thus contented. I will now return to Neville, whose anxiety to learn the success of my mission, has already been too long delayed."

With this she hastened from the room; and, having found the monk waiting for her, she left the house, and once more directed her way towards the ancient Abbey of Chertsey

CHAPTER XXVI.

STARTLING NEWS.—THE FERRYMAN.—THE COUNTERPLOT.

WE must now return to Hugh Laneret, who was watching with his troopers on the outside of the monastery, anxious for the arrival of the moment which, he doubted not, would give Neville Audeley into his power. He felt all the exultation of a fiend as he thus saw the near consummation of the vengeance he had so long meditated; and when, from a distance, he saw Blanche leave the abbey-gates, he at once guessed that she was gone to make some effort in behalf of her lover, but laughed with triumphant malice at the apparent certainty that nothing she could do would save him ere the ringing of the curfew-bell; for he had resolved to claim his victim when the first sound was heard, and he now felt as certain of attaining his object, as if the breathless corpse of his rival were already laid at his feet.

Upon consideration, however, he despatched one of his men to watch where Blanche went to; and, after pacing to and fro with feverish excitement for nearly half-an-hour, the trooper returned with information that he had seen her enter Basil Evenden's house, and that shortly afterwards Herrick had ridden forth at full speed, taking the road that led towards London. Laneret paused thoughtfully after hearing this news, and then, speaking aloud, he exclaimed—

"I see it all. They think to cheat me of my prey; but bitterly will they find themselves mistaken. He shall die, and I will now enter the convent and demand him from those who would shelter him with their protection!"

"If I may be allowed to speak," returned the messenger, "I would suggest that it would be dangerous to interfere with the privileges of the Holy Church. Besides, your solemn word has been pledged to the abbot, and to break it might bring upon yourself the anger of those whose power we cannot resist."

"Peace, thou babbling fool!" exclaimed Laneret, "and keep thy craven counsels to thyself, for I'll have none of them. Neville Audeley is a traitor; and, so little care I for the sanctuary he has claimed, that, were he even kneeling at the altar, my dagger should let forth his heart's blood."

"Again I caution you to beware," returned the man, "or this rashness will surely turn against yourself. Besides, it is not likely Herrick Evenden will return in time, and in that case you may with justice claim the victim when the curfew tolls forth his knell. Be advised by me, I say, and all will yet turn out as you have planned."

Hugh Laneret made no reply to this, but continued to pace up and down with rapid strides, as if impatient of the brief delay that had been suggested. At lenght, becoming more cool, he suddenly paused, and muttered to himself—

"Yes, I will wait the appointed time, but it shall be on condition that I take other steps to render my vengeance the more certain. Herrick Evenden must cross the ferry, and I will hasten to the boatman, and prevail upon him by a bribe

to bring no person across during the two hours previous to curfew. That, at least, will make me secure, and there is some consolation in the certainty that the anticipation of pardon will but add to the bitterness of death, when all hope of rescue shall have passed away. I hate him from the very bottom of my soul; and shall I now be baulked of my vengeance when I see Blanche still exerting herself to safe the life of my enemy ?'

"Yet, even if you succeed," said the man who had before spoken, "I see not that you will have any better chance of obtaining the maiden's hand."

"It may be so," answered Hugh Laneret; "but I shall, at least, have the satisfaction of knowing that she will not wed my rival. She has thought proper to reject me with scorn, and we will now see who triumphs in the end."

"Which, to my thinking, will be but poor satisfaction."

"Thy thinking?" returned Laneret with scorn; "and who heeds the thoughts of a coward that would rather endure a wrong than resent it? I have suffered tortures enough through this Neville Audeley, and do you imagine I will forego the pleasure of revenge from any weak feeling of pity? Have I not sworn his death, and who is there that ever knew me break my word when once it had been uttered?"

"But what I said," returned the other, "was merely that I might prevail upon you to look to your own safety in case the king should happen to take an unfavourable view of your conduct."

"My life has been perilled in his service," answered Hugh Laneret, "and he will scarcely interfere when all I seek to do is to rid him of one who is well known to have been amongst the most active of his enemies. Neville has justly forfeited his life, and why should he not fall by my hand, as well as by that of the public executioner?"

"That may be all very true," returned the other; "but so may not think our royal master when he learns that all this has taken place in satisfaction of a private feeling of revenge."

"He may think of it as he pleases," replied Hugh, "but since the proclamation was issued against all those who are known to have been in arms on the Lancastrian side, Neville Audeley has become an outlaw, and it is therefore legal for any one to take his life in case of resistance."

"Which he has not yet offered."

"He has done so by the very act of claiming sanctuary," answered Hugh Laneret. "I demanded him, and have been refused, and if that is not resistance, it must be confessed I know not what is. And even if I had not right upon my side, I may surely decide our quarrel as many a one has done before me."

"And have been punished for it, as a warning to others," observed the man.

"But all may not be inclined to take the warning," replied Laneret; "and I for one will not be deprived of my revenge, even though a king should be angered by it. Edward was glad to gain friends to his cause a month ago; let him beware, now that he is seated on his throne, that he makes not more enemies than he will know how to cope against. I am not one to be trifled with, and if he does wisely, he will make no stir, merely because I think proper to take my revenge into my own hands."

"These are dangerous words, Master Laneret."

"They are such as you can turn against me if you please," returned the other; "but if I thought there was any fear of it, my dagger should be in your heart before another instant passes away. But why do I waste words in idle parly with a poor-spirited knave like thee? I have my own purposes to work out; the return of Herrick Evenden must be prevented till to-morrow, and then my triumph will be accomplished."

"Then you are now going to the ferryman?"

"I am," answered Laneret, "and during my absence, let a careful watch be kept round the abbey walls, lest an attempt should be made to favour the escape of Neville Audeley from them. I warn you not to let him depart, for should he do so, I will never rest satisfied till all who are here present have been made to feel that I am not to be cheated of my prey with impunity."

"You would threaten us?"

"Ay, and my threats will surely be carried into execution," he replied. "You all know me, and therefore I say let your watch be strict and diligent, or my rage will be turned against yourselves."

"Ay, ay, Master Laneret, there shall be no reason to find fault with us," answered the man, assuming a different tone. "We know you don't like the young fellow, and perhaps there may be reason enough for it; so make yourself easy upon the matter, for I don't suppose Neville Audeley will attempt to escape, when he knows the place is surrounded by your people; and if he should do so, why he must e'en take the consequence of it."

"Why, that was better spoken," exclaimed Laneret, "and now that it seems we understand each other better, I can leave you to your task with more confidence. You understand my directions, and on my return from the ferry-house let me find that you have obeyed my orders, and you shall not fail to be rewarded.'

As he uttered these words, he turned haughtily upon his heel and pursued the direction that led towards the part of the river where the ferryman's house was situated. The men watched him in silence as long as he remained in sight, and then the one who had been parleying with him, said—

"There goes one of the biggest villains betwixt here and Johnny Groat's house. He seems to revel in the thought of blood, and it's my notion, he'd put his own father out of the way, if a trifle happened to put him out of humour."

"And what's all this anger against this young man about?" demanded a comrade. "It seems they both happen to have taken a fancy to the same girl, and because Hugh Laneret can't have his own way, he must needs get rid of his rival by taking away his life. For my own part, I'm sorry we have got anything to do with him, and if this Neville Audeley were to pass by me this moment, I don't much think I should put forth a hand to prevent it."

"I don't know that I should be quite so qualmish as that," replied the other, "because there's no telling what other people might say of it; but if the truth must be told, I would much rather plunge my sword into the heart of Hugh Laneret, than the other one. However, this Herrick Evenden has the character of being a highspirited young fellow enough, and if he has really undertaken to serve a friend, it ain't a trifle that will put him off from it. So who knows but he may find other means to get across the river, and in that case Hugh Laneret will be disappointed of his revenge, and we shall have the satisfaction of being spared a task that not one of us likes. But come, we must seem to be doing our duty at any rate, so now let us each take our post, for Master Laneret may soon be back, and if he finds us talking instead of watching, it may be the worse for some of us."

Acting upon this hint the party broke up, and each moving towards his appointed station, the walls of the abbey were so completely surrounded, as to prevent the possibility of anybody passing either in or out, without being seen.

In the meantime, Hugh Laneret had made the best of his way towards the place he intended to visit, and on reaching the ferry-house on the banks of the Thames, he knocked loudly at the door, and was promptly answered by Stephen Lindsey, who seeing a stranger, demanded whether he wanted to cross the river.

"I do not," was the reply, "but if you have a few minutes to spare, I would speak with you."

"Ay, ay, I have minutes enough to spare, worse luck!" answered Stephen. "There's no great deal of business stirring just now, and a poor devil like me may starve, for aught the world cares."

"Humph! you are poor, then?"

"As a church mouse."

"And would earn money?"

"Yes, if it's to be honestly come by."

"Which it may be in the present instance," answered Hugh Laneret.

"How?"

"By a very simple method; in fact, by refusing to work.'

"Indeed!—methinks that's a strange way for a man to make money."

"It will not appear strange when you hear my proposition," answered Laneret. "I suppose, if you objected to ferry a man across the river, there's no other way of his getting over?"

"None," replied Stephen, "unless he thought proper to go to the next ferry, and that's a good way higher up the river, and even there the boatman might not be at home."

"And for these three pieces of gold," observed Hugh Laneret, "I suppose I may purchase your time till to-morrow morning?"

"How mean you, sir?"

"That I would afford you the luxury of a holiday," answered the other. "You shall have rest for a night and day, and as I shall pay you well for it, there can be very little objection to it on your part."

"Why, it must be owned you have made me a tempting offer enough," returned the boatman; "but, on the other hand, it must not be forgotten that there may be many persons anxious to cross during the time you have mentioned, and if they should happen to make a complaint against me, the chances are that I should lose my situation, and then your three pieces of gold would prove but a sorry recompense."

"Hast thou prudence, sirrah?"

"Humph! my caution in this instance should be a ready answer to your question."

"Dost thou know a youth whom men call Herrick Evenden?"

"The alchymist's son?"

"The same; hast thou not seen him to-day?"

"Ay," answered the ferryman, "I took him across scarcely half an hour since."

"And know you whither he was going?" asked Laneret.

"It would ill become me to ask impertinent questions of my customers," answered the other; "but he seemed to be in a desperate hurry, and immediately upon landing, he remounted his horse and galloped up the London road as if the devil were at his heels."

"It is as I suspect!" muttered Hugh Laneret; "the busybody must needs step in and thwart the plans I have been at so much pains to form, and would have succeeded but for a lucky chance. But I am upon his track, and he shall yet find that I am not to be foiled so easily as he imagined."

"Are you in pursuit of him?" asked Stephen, who had only gathered a portion of what he had uttered.

"No," replied the other; "but I would delay his return till to-morrow morning. You can easily manage that for me, and on condition that the task is well executed, the sum I have already promised shall be doubled when I am assured you have earned it."

"And I am not to bring anybody over if I should be hailed from the other side of the river?"

"Why, since you know the person I am in quest of," replied Laneret, "you can freely ply your trade with all but him. There is life and death hanging upon your obedience, and you will therefore do well to obey the directions I have given."

"Whose life is in danger?" asked Stephen, anxiously. "Is there fear of Master Herrick himself falling into peril, if he should cross sooner than you wish?"

"There is," replied Hugh Laneret. "He would interfere in the affairs of other persons, and should he succeed in effecting his object, there is one who would not fail to seek his life."

"Poor fellow!" ejaculated the other; "and yet, after all; perhaps he has only entered upon this matter from the best of motives."

"He is a meddler in other people's affairs," muttered Hugh Laneret, "and therefore deserves little pity, whatever fate may chance to befal him."

"Well, it's no business of mine, to be sure," exclaimed Stephen, whose thoughts just then turned to the reward he was to receive. "It certainly is not right to meddle or make oneself busy in other folk's business; and so, as it's only to keep him waiting a few hours on the other side of the water, I don't mind doing as you have said."

"I may depend on you, then?"

"Of course; but since I may not bring him over to-night, what time to-morrow shall I be at liberty to do so?"

"Any time after sunrise," answered Hugh Laneret. "It will then be impossible for him to do any mischief, and the reward shall be yours."

"Well, it shall be done at any rate," exclaimed Stephen; "but if any trouble should come of it, mind I shall say who bribed me to do the business, and you must take the consequences upon yourself."

"There is no fear of it," replied Laneret. "Besides, you can make what excuse you please to this Herrick Evenden, and I suppose a man is not compelled to work unless he pleases. Tell him you have other business to attend to, and that he must be content to wait patiently till you are at leisure."

"But he is choleric," said the ferryman; "and it may chance that I get the worst of it should we get into a quarrel."

"In that case, you have but to strike him down with your oar, and he will become more tractable."

"And so slip my neck into a halter! No, no, my good sir, I am not so tired of life as all that comes to, and if the young fellow should be very resolute upon the matter, I shall forget your promised reward and bring him over. If his business be very urgent he will pay me as much for my trouble as you would."

"Villain!" exclaimed Hugh Laneret, drawing his sword and holding it menacingly towards the boatman, "swear that you will not deceive me, or this moment is your last. Swear, I say!"

"I do," faltered the trembling Stephen.

"It is enough, and I will trust you," answered the other. "You may still deceive me, as you have just now threatened, but should you do so, I will have your life before you are twelve hours older!"

"Two can play that game, at any rate," muttered Stephen; but quickly recovering his temper, he added, "there's no occasion to doubt me, sir, for your offer was the first, and having accepted it, you shall see that I will be no worse than my word. The young fellow shall not cross till the time you have said, and so there's an end of the matter."

"Then for the present we part," answered Hugh Laneret, "and should all turn out well, call to-morrow morning at the 'Crozier,' a small inn near the abbey walls, and inquire for me. I shall not leave there till mid-day, and you shall then have the gold I have promised as the reward."

He turned away with these words, leaving the ferryman brimful of wonder and curiosity at the singular visit that had been paid him.

"There goes a strange fellow at any rate," he muttered to himself. "That he's got more money than wit is very certain, for who but a downright madman would ever have thought of promising six pieces of gold for refusing to take a fare? But perhaps there's something at the bottom of all this that I don't understand; there may be villany in it, and in that case I shall get into a dilemma, and the money will be dearly earned. But psha, what's the use of meeting troubles half way? I'm a poor fellow that can't afford to throw away a good chance; and so let what will come of it, Herrick Evenden stays on the other side of the river till after sunrise to-morrow morning."

Saying this he entered his cabin with a full determination to do that which— though he knew it not—would consign a fellow-creature to death.

But the conversation which thus passed between them was not so secret as they imagined, for Kate Poynet, chancing to see Laneret as he was making his way towards the ferry-house, and suspecting that further mischief was in progress, she followed him at some little distance, and when certain of his place of destination, she hurried onwards by another path, and had just time to conceal herself behind a boat that had been hauled up near the cottage, when Hugh Laneret arrived, and had his interview with Stephen. Not a word was uttered but what she heard, and no sooner had the boatman entered his house after the departure of Laneret, than she issued from her hiding place, and ran with all her speed towards Redwynde Hall, to give intimation of what was going forward. The first person she met on entering the house was Tony Amblewit; and scarcely giving herself time to recover breath, she informed him that a terrible plot was in progress, and that he must without delay do something to avert it.

"And pray what does all this mean?" inquired Tony, who began to think that she had lost her senses. "You have been telling me a long rigmarole about somebody being in danger, but not one word have you yet said to let me know who you mean."

"Neville Audeley," she replied.

"Why, you foolish girl, don't I know that already?" exclaimed Tony; "and yet I don't know that there is so much danger after all, for Master Herrick Evenden has set off for London, and if he makes good haste he will yet be in time with the pardon."

"There is a plot to prevent his return till after it is too late," answered Kate. "I overheard it just now, and unless you will hasten down to the river side, poor Neville Audeley will perish, and then we pretty well know what will be the fate of Mistress Blanche."

"And where am I to go to?" asked Tony Amblewit, bewildered with surprise.

"To the ferry-house."

"And what to do there?"

"Learn if Stephen is at home," answered Kate Poynet, "and if possible don't let him know what you are about."

"Upon my life, Kate," he exclaimed, "I can't at all understand what you mean. What has Stephen got to do with either the life or death of Neville Audeley?"

"Everything," she replied; "he has accepted a bribe from Hugh Laneret, and if something be not done to thwart the plot, Herrick will be detained on the other side of the ferry till it will be too late to save the life of my young mistress's lover."

"But how know you this?" demanded Tony.

"I overheard it all," she replied; "I saw Laneret going towards the river side and followed him, hiding myself in a place where I could overhear all that passed. He has prevailed upon Stephen not to bring over the messenger of good news, and all will be ruined unless you will act according to my directions."

"Explain yourself."

"As I said before, you must go to the ferry-house and see if Stephen be at home," she replied. "I dare say by this time he has crossed the river, and as there will be nothing to prevent it, you must then jump into his other boat that you will find close ashore, and row over to a place either a little above or below where he goes."

"Well," said Tony Amblewit, "and having done that, what's to follow?"

"Why, then you must be waiting about till Herrick returns," answered Kate; "and as Stephen is sure to refuse to bring him, you must take him to your boat and bring him to the abbey with all speed."

"That is to say if Stephen will let me."

"He will not be able to help himself, as there will be two against him. Besides," she added, "rather than suffer him to delay you, strike him down with an oar, and I'll warrant you there will not be much trouble afterwards."

"What do I hear?" exclaimed Tony, with surprise. "Do I hear the gentle Kate recommend an act of violence that is very likely to end in the death of the unfortunate ferryman?"

"The truth is," she answered, "I heard a similar recommendation given to Stephen, in case the young gentleman should exhibit any wrath. So it's only doing by him as he would serve others; and as you needn't do more than just crack his crown, perhaps it will serve as a useful remembrance to him in future."

"In that case, I don't know but what I shall follow your recommendation," exclaimed Tony. "But this is rather an awkward business you have set me, Kate, and as we are upon the subject of business, pray what is to be my reward, if all goes off well?"

"Why, for the reward, good Anthony," she replied, "I think we had better talk about that some other time."

"There's no time like the present." he exclaimed, "so tell me what I am to expect, and I'll go to do your errand without the loss of another moment."

"Why, what do you expect, sir?" asked Kate.

"The fulfilment of your promise."

"I know not that I ever made one," she said; "but if I did, you may depend upon it I will not be worse than my word."

"Then you want reminding," exclaimed Tony, "of your promise to become Mistress Amblewit, on the same day that sees your young lady the wife of Neville Audeley."

"And my word shall be faithfully kept, Tony," she replied; "but you have forgotten that there is very little chance of the marriage taking place, unless you assist the young gentleman out of his dilemma. He is now in the greatest danger, and when the fatal curfew begins to toll, he will be demanded by the blood-thirsty monster who seeks his life."

"Ay, I am aware of all that," answered Tony; "but there's plenty of time yet to save his life for Herrick Evenden can't possibly return yet; and, when he does come, I'll take care to find a way for bringing him across the river."

"You will!" cried Kate, joyfully, "then I have not been deceived in you, Tony; and I don't know that I could do better than give my hand to an honest, warm-hearted fellow like you."

"Come," he exclaimed, "I'm glad to hear you confess as much at last, and I can now only promise you that you shall never have reason to regret your good opinion of me. It must be confessed I like to do a service when I can; and, as Master Neville Audeley was always a special favourite of mine, I shall not lack courage to assist him by helping to defeat this villanous plot of his enemies."

"With a good heart all may yet be done," answered Kate; "courage will not be required so much as prudence; and, though you are a thoughtless, giddy-pated fellow at times, I have a notion that this affair will be as safe in your hands as anybody else's."

"It will be safer in my hands," returned Tony, "because I shall be anxious to deserve your approbation when all is done and over. I am pretty skilful in the management of a boat, and I know there's always one lying in readiness on the beach; it will not be a very difficult matter to transport myself to the other side of the river."

"The greatest difficulty," replied Kate Poynet, "will be to prevent a discovery by the ferryman. He might chance to see you, and, if so, I fear he would take means to prevent the execution of your project."

"And that may easily be avoided by rowing about a mile up the river before I go across," exclaimed Tony Amblewit. "Besides, he is but one man against me, and what's that when I know I've got right on my side?"

"Very true," returned Kate; "and, as I see you are not so great a coward as I once took you for, there is no doubt you would prove a match for this Stephen, if he should be villain enough to attempt any violence against you. Besides, if he only hurts a hair of your head, let him beware how he ever comes in my way again, for he shall learn what it is to injure innocent people in the execution of their duty."

"Why, gadzooks, girl, you love me a great deal better than I thought!"

"The truth's out, Tony, and there's no going back," answered Kate, vexed with herself for having said so much. "I didn't mean to feed your vanity by such a confession; but the joy of hearing you say what you did, completely put me off my guard."

"So much the better, Kate," he exclaimed, "for now I'd go through fire and water to serve you; and it shall be no fault of mine if Master Herrick Evenden reaches not the abbey before the curfew tolls. I can pull with double strength over the river when I think of you and what I've just now heard; so never mind a little slip of the tongue for it's done no harm after all."

"Well, Tony, there's been quite enough said," returned Kate; "and now, as there's no time to lose, away with you, and be sure to return with a good account of what has been done."

Tony required no second bidding, for he knew it was time to be stirring; and, saluting the cheek of the unresisting Kate Poynet, he left the house a much happier fellow than he had entered it.

CHAPTER XXVI.

A DISAPPOINTMENT.—THE CURFEW.—THE PARDON.

UPON arriving at the ferry-house, Tony Amblewit had soon the means to convince himself that Stephen was absent from home; and then, hurrying down to the water-side, he released the boat from its moorings, and, with all the speed he could, rowed up the stream, taking care to keep as close to the shore as possible. At length, finding a place favourable for his purpose, he crossed over to the other side; and, having secured the little vessel so as to prevent its being carried away by the tide, he moved away, keeping near to the bank, in the hope that he might presently see the ferryman, who, he thought it possible, might be prevailed upon to accept a higher bribe to take no part against Neville Audeley.

Leaving him for the present, however, we must now follow Stephen, who, as much perhaps from malice as anything, was pacing up and down in the expectation of being accosted by Herrick, whose disappointment at his refusal, he thought, would afford him some amusement. But the period when he ought to have arrived passed away, and the fatal curfew hour was rapidly drawing nigh, and still the young man was not to be seen anywhere near the place. At length, however, he was approaching at a rapid pace on foot, and, pointing towards the boat, he was walking up to it, when Stephen took him by the arm, and roughly demanded what he wanted.

"To cross the river without delay," was the answer. "Quick, sir, and lose not a moment, for the life of a friend depends upon my speedy return."

"Stop a bit, young man," said Stephen, "for if you are in such a confounded hurry, I am not. Besides, I am already engaged by another party, and if you wait to go over with them, it may be an hour or more before they come back."

"An hour!" exclaimed Herrick, in a tone of horror; "ere that time, he I would save will have fallen a victim to the hatred of a scoundrel."

"It can't be helped, sir," returned the ferryman; "and as for your friend, I suppose he deserves his fate, or else he wouldn't have had to suffer it."

"'Tis false!" exclaimed Herrick, indignantly. "He has been accused of treason, and yet it is not many days since he saved the king's life."

"Then the king should have saved his in return," muttered Stephen, sarcastically.

"It is his desire to do so."

"Humph! how know you that?"

"Because I have the royal pardon in my pocket," answered Herrick. "I have myself had an audience with the king, and when he heard the danger that threatened his preserver, he granted my boon, and vowed a heavy vengeance against all those who are concerned, if my friend should perish ere I arrive."

"Well," exclaimed Stephen, "at any rate, I have nothing to fear from the king's anger."

"But you have from mine," answered Herrick Evenden, "and therefore I once more ask you to ferry me over without further loss of time."

"If you were to ask me a hundred times, I should still give you the same answer," returned the fellow. "I have already told you my boat is engaged, and surely I ought to know best whether I can oblige you or not."

"Will the offer of a handsome reward move you to hear my entreaties?"

"It depends upon the amount of the reward," returned the ferryman.

"Ten pieces of gold."

"Ten pieces of gold!" exclaimed Stephen, "that's a pretty sum for a man to earn in a quarter of an hour's work, and I begin to feel almost tempted to accept your offer. So let me have them in my hand, Master Herrick Evenden, and you shall be on the other side the river in double quick time."

"Nay, I have not so much about me," answered the young man, "but you shall

have them before the night draws to a close."

"That won't do for me," replied Stephen. "I must have the money down, or you remain here till the morning."

"You would sacrifice a fellow creature, then, to your own brutal avarice ?"

"I don't know what you mean by avarice, young sir," exclaimed the other, "but these are slippery times, you know, and if a man don't look after money, he has a fair chance of starving."

"But I have said you shall have it to-night."

"And I have said I must have it now."

"Villain !" exclaimed Herrick, furiously, "I will not suffer my friend to perish, while I have strength remaining to enforce my demands. Either consent to carry me across without delay, or I will take forcible possession of your boat, and row myself to yonder shore."

"Indeed !" exclaimed Stephen, snatching up an oar, and brandishing it resolutely; "you may think to frighten me with your threatenings, but it remains to be proved whether I am to suffer my boat to be taken away against my own inclination."

"Say, then," returned Herrick, who saw the uselessness of attempting force, "upon what terms can I prevail on you to do my bidding ?"

"You have already heard—I must have the money you spoke of, and then you shall have your way."

"I have said it shall be yours, shortly after I land."

"Ay, but that don't suit me," answered Stephen, "for, to tell you the truth, I have made a better bargain on the other side."

"You have been bribed?"

"Exactly so."

"And by Hugh Laneret?"

"Right again—Hugh Laneret knows the value of a man's services, and has offered me six pieces of gold not to take you over till after sunrise to-morrow morning. You, on the other hand, have offered me ten for my labour, and provided I have the money down, I shall take the best offer. So now you know what I mean, and if you can't do it, why, there's an end of the matter."

"And knowing that a fellow creature's life is in peril, you can refuse to put forth a hand to save him?"

"Why, the truth is, Master Neville Audeley, it is nothing to me," answered Stephen, "and that being the case, I don't care a doit whether he lives or dies. The king's pardon may be all very well, but, great as it is, it's of very little use when a poor fellow like me thinks proper to stand between it and the criminal."

"You will repent this before long," exclaimed Herrick, passionately.

"Ay, ay, you may threaten as much as you please," returned the other, with indifference, "but a man ain't to be persuaded against his will, especially when he has got good reasons for acting according to his own notions."

"Surely," cried Herrick, "you cannot mean to let Neville Audeley perish, when, by a trifling exertion, it is in your power to aid in saving him. Let me again implore you to relent; it is now fast approaching the hour when the curfew usually tolls, and even with our utmost speed, I fear there is scarcely time to arrive soon enough to avert the stroke of death."

"There you are right," answered Stephen, in a tone of cold indifference, "for I rather think if you wait here another half hour, you will hear the sound booming over the water. I've often listened to it from this spot, but never thought it would one day toll for a death knell."

"This delay drives me to madness!" exclaimed Herrick. "I can no longer endure the torture of suspense, and if you prevent me from taking possession of your boat, it shall not be till we have had a struggle for it."

Saying this, he seized the fellow in his arms, and exerting all the strength he possessed, endeavoured to throw him to the ground. But his antagonist proved to be the more powerful, and as Herrick fell heavily to the earth, the other drew a knife, and raising it aloft, was in the act of plunging it into his heart, when a heavy blow was dealt upon the head of Stephen, and, with a yell of torture, he sank insensible upon the ground. In an instant Herrick was assisted to rise, and to his mingled joy and surprise, he discovered in his deliverer, no less a personage than Tony Amblewit. Grateful for the service that had been performed, he began to pour forth his thanks, when the other interrupted him, by saying,

"This is no time for compliments, seeing that the terrible hour has almost arrived, and it's as much as you will be able to do to get to the abbey in time. So jump into the boat, sir, and I'll take you across as fast as I can, and then, if you have anything to say, you can do so as we go along."

Without making any reply, Herrick Evenden seated himself as he had been directed, and scarcely had they left the shore, when they could perceive Stephen recovering from the stupor in which he had been lying. They were now, however, in no danger of pursuit, and whilst Tony was quickly plying the oar, Herrick learned from him the circumstances to which he owed his fortunate deliverance.

"And now, sir," he added, after a pause, "may I inquire if you have got the pardon?"

"I have."

"Well, that's good news, at any rate," answered Tony, "for I dare say poor Mistress Blanche is in a terrible way by this time, and almost despairs of the pardon being obtained. However, it's better late than never, and if she's in grief now, the pleasure will be all the greater afterwards. But how is it, Master Herrick, that you have returned without your horse ?"

"He broke down from exertion, about three miles before I returned to the place where you just now found me," replied Herrick Evenden. "That unfortunate circumstance it was that made me so late ; and, to add to it, I have lost nearly another half hour in trying to prevail on yonder villain to bring me over."

"Oh, he has been bribed by Hugh Laneret to do it," answered the other. "Kate Poynet happened by good luck to hear their villanous plot, and so, knowing I would do anything at her bidding, she hurried me off to help you in case of need."

"And your generous zeal," exclaimed Herrick, "shall not go unrewarded."

"That's likely to be done in a way most agreeable to me, sir," replied Tony, "for you must know I have long had a hankering after Kate, and she has promised, if I succeed in this, to be my wife on the very same day that witnesses the union of Mistress Blanche and Neville Audeley ; which, between ourselves, will not be long first, if we only succeed in reaching the abbey before curfew time."

Saying this, he pulled harder and faster than ever, and both of them being occupied in their own reflections, the remainder of the way was passed in silence.

In the meanwhile, Neville and Blanche were watching the passing moments in a state of mental torture that it would be impossible to describe. Still, however, the lover strove to support his mistress with expressions of a hope that he himself felt not ; he reminded her of the well known zeal of Herrick Evenden, and though the time had passed when he might have been expected to return, he assured her that his own confidence in the friendship of their messenger was still undiminished.

"I have still the same confidence in him that you have," she replied ; "but I can no longer anticipate his return with the same hope that I did. He must have failed in the purpose that took him from home, and I am doomed to see you the victim of a treacherous villain."

"Nay, dearest Blanche, there is yet time enough for his arrival."

"It is but brief," she replied, mournfully ; "and much as I wish to think the best, dear Neville, I dare not now look forward with the faintest hope."

"Yet it has never abandoned me even for a single moment," answered Neville Audeley ; "and though all certainly looks blank enough at present, I still feel assured that all will yet end well."

"From Hugh Laneret," she replied, " we have no mercy to expect."

"Nor would I ask it of him," exclaimed Neville. "He has ever been a vengeful foe in my path, and even the short respite he has allowed would never have been granted, but that he thought nothing could save me from my doom. Had he known that I possessed the king's signet, he would have given directions for my instant death, when first he broke into the sanctuary of this abbey."

"And the delay that has taken place," sighed Blanche Heriot, "serves only to prolong those miseries which, after all, we shall not be able to avert. The villain will triumph in the wrongs he has heaped upon us, and when you fall, dear Neville, who is there in the world that I shall care to live for."

"Still you look to the worst, while hope yet lives," exclaimed Neville Audeley. "Our messenger, it is true, has exceeded the time when I thought he would have returned ; but Herrick has a warm and generous heart. and he will be here anon, even though the news he brings may not be so favourable as I anticipated. Something has no doubt retarded him, but he knows the fatal moment, and will be here before it arrives."

"It must be soon, then," cried Blanche, with a shudder, "for each moment do I expect to hear the dreadful sound that announces the triumph of a deadly foe."

At that instant the abbot, attended by several of his monks, slowly entered the chapel, and the mournful look that sat upon each countenance betrayed the fears that they also began to apprehend.

"I have come, Neville Audeley," said the abbot, "to tell you that it wants but five minutes to the time when the curfew will toll forth its solemn notes. You are aware of my forced compact with Hugh Laneret, and much as I wish to save you, it will not be in my power to do so at the expiration of the appointed time."

"I am prepared for the worst," answered Neville, "though it must needs be confessed, I was not without hope till this moment. Hugh Laneret is, I suppose, already here to claim his victim?"

"He waits without the abbey walls," replied the abbot; "but the gates are to be thrown open to him when the bell sends forth its first cheerless sound."

"And will he dare violate the sanctuary afforded him by holy church?" asked Blanche, timidly.

"He is reckless, and will dare anything," answered the old man; "besides, it it has been frequently done since the distractions that have convulsed our unhappy country; and in the present instance we have no means to repel the violence, though Hugh Laneret may hereafter be called upon to answer for it."

"It is my fate to perish. I will fall without a murmur, or an effort to save myself from the hands of a blood-thirsty enemy," exclaimed Neville. "He perhaps may feel a triumph at the success of his schemes; but he shall at least see that I can endure death without flinching from it."

At this moment it was discovered that Blanche Heriot had quitted the chapel, and as her absence must have been caused by something extraordinary, instant inquiries were made, and from the report of a couple of monks, who just then approached, it was ascertained that she had been seen hurrying distractedly up the belfrey stairs, and a terrible suspicion took possession of every one that she meditated some desperate deed. Neville was the first to set the example of pursuit, and in an instant he was followed by all who were present.

Meanwhile Blanche, whose terror had been excited to the highest pitch, had mounted the belfrey stairs, and entered the gloomy chamber in which hung suspended the huge bell that was so soon to tone her lover's death-knell. Frantically she gazed upon it, as if some wild thought had entered her mind, and as her eyes were still turned in that direction, she beheld it slowly swing upon its axis,—each instant taking a longer and a longer sweep. Fired with desperation, she then sprang forward,—surmounted the framework that led up to it, and seizing upon the clapper, she was dragged backwards and forwards with fearful velocity. Still, however, she maintained her hold, and prevented the fatal sound she so much dreaded to hear; but at length faintness overpowered her, and unable to support herself any longer, she fell swooning to the floor.

At that instant the first dismal boom pealed forth, and as the dismal sound vibrated upon the ear, Neville Audeley rushed into the belfrey in search of her. At once guessing what had occurred, and the efforts she had made in his behalf, he raised her in his arms, but ere he could restore her to animation, Hugh Laneret, followed by a number of his troopers, made their appearance, and demanded his immediate surrender.

"On one condition I yield myself," answered Neville. "Suffer me but to remain till I am assured she lives, and I will then accompany you to the place where your vengeance is to be carried into effect."

"I will make no conditions," exclaimed Laneret, snatching the still fainting girl from his arms: "the moment of triumph has at length arrived, and your life, Neville Audeley, hangs upon my slightest word."

"You need not remind me of it," replied Neville; "for but too well I know the chance is yours, and that I have no mercy to expect. Do with me as you will, but in mercy spare her whose happiness you have wrecked for ever."

"She shall have as much mercy as she as ever shown to me," answered Hugh Laneret. "I have endured scorn and contempt when I offered love, and never did I yet forgive an injury or let it pass unpunished."

"Villain!" exclaimed Neville Audeley, "had I but arms, this last boast of yours would have been avenged."

"But as you are not trusted with such dangerous instruments," answered the other with a sneer, "I have not much to fear from your vain threats. You can rail at me now, Neville Audeley, because it is in my power to put an end to it when I please. These men that you see about us are sworn to obey my orders, and were I to wave my hand thus, they would so place themselves betwixt you and me as to leave very little fear of any harm coming from your empty boastings."

As he uttered these words three or four of his followers advanced and placed themselves in just such a position as he had described.

"You see," he continued, "what ready obedience they are prepared to pay me. These men fear, if they do not love me, and there is not one among them but knows that disobedience to my orders would be followed by the instant death of the daring traitor. I have trained them well to my service, and the same readiness that you saw them just now exhibit will they display when I give the word that consigns you to death."

"Let me hear no more of this," cried Neville; "if I am to die, let the sentence be quickly passed, but do not add insult to your revenge, by thus torturing me in the last few moments that I have to live."

"Nay, it gives sweetness to my vengeance," answered Hugh Laneret; "and I think if anything can give increased bitterness to the brief period you have to live, it must be the thought that your death gives to me the haughty girl who spurned the addresses of Hugh Laneret, for the lover who has proved himself unable to protect her when dangers were most threatening."

"Villain!" exclaimed Neville, "had I at this moment equal advantages with thee, thou wouldst not have courage to say so much."

"Comrades," said Hugh Laneret, addressing himself to the troopers, "we have heard the curfew bell toll forth, yet this traitor lives. Seize your prisoner, and bear him beyond the abbey walls, where he shall meet the doom I have condemned him to."

As the men were advancing to execute this command, a pistol shot was heard, and Hugh Laneret, uttering a groan of excruciating agony, sank mortally wounded to the ground. In another moment Herrick Evenden rushed forward, holding in one hand the weapon with which he had slain Hugh Laneret, and in the other the pardon which he had obtained for his friend. The wounded man, glaring horribly around, attempted to rise, but the effort overpowered him, and sinking back, he uttered a loud cry of anguish and instantly expired.

Being thus rescued from his perilous situation, Nevile Audeley quickly removed Blanche Heriot to her home, where, upon her recovery, she heard the joyous tidings of her lover's safety. To Herrick Evenden her gratitude to his eminent services was unbounded, and for the first time, for a long while past, she felt that the life of Neville Audeley was not endangered.

Within three months from that period she became the wife of him whose love for her had exposed him to so much persecution and peril, and as Kate Poynet was not disposed to forget her promise, she, on the same day, gave her hand to Tony Amblewit, who had proved himself worthy of the task that had been entrusted to him, when the safe return of Herrick Evenden depended upon his care and prudence. From that period the tradition was handed down from generation to generation, and even within the last few years there were not many persons in the neighbourhood who were unacquainted with the legend connected with THE CHERTSEY CURFEW.

PRINTED BY E. LLOYD, SALISBURY SQUARE, FLEET STREET, LONDON.

www.ingramcontent.com/pod-product-compliance
Lightning Source LLC
Chambersburg PA
CBHW082012170626
46817CB00009B/3075